# GRIT OF BERTH AND STONE

## BY LISA DUNN

**Grit of Berth and Stone**
By Lisa Dunn
Copyright © 2015 Lisa Dunn

Published by Anaiah Surge
An imprint of Anaiah Press, LLC.
7780 49th ST N. #129
Pinellas Park, FL 33781

First Anaiah Surge print edition March, 2015
Edited by Laura Maisano
Book Design by Eden Plantz
Cover Design by Katt Amaral

Anaiah Press | A Mighty Presence

To Amy, my Wise and Wonderful Sister, who told me, "Grit has to be Grit," and sometimes knew this story better than I did myself. I couldn't have written this book without your correction, insight, and encouragement.

# ACKNOWLEDGEMENTS

Endless gratitude to my husband, who told me I could be anything I wanted to be and supported me throughout the entire crazy process of writing GRIT; and to my children, my first live audience, my bluntest critics and surest fans, my Lego Thresh builders and little story weavers. I love you all more than words.

To my parents, who introduced me to the Author of Life and instilled in me a love of story. To Mark and Kim, for welcoming me into the family and always having a pot of coffee ready.

Heartfelt thanks to my early readers - Andrew, John, Amy, Mom, T.J., Trey, Laurie, the Ward family, Myssi - and to my South Carolina Writers Workshop critique group, for pointing out my mistakes and loving GRIT no less. To everyone at Anaiah Press who helped make this dream a reality, especially my editor, Laura Maisano, who pushed me to make my manuscript shine like a golden curl.

And to the Author of Life, whose story we cannot help but retell in every story we pen.

# ONE

Grit of Berth and Stone flexed her muscles taut. Her left forefinger moved over her bare right arm. Slowly zigzagging from shoulder to elbow, she touched each brand in the order in which they had been seared upon her arm. As she pressed her fingertip into her fifteenth brand, a strong arm wrapped around her waist, and a finger not her own dug into the empty space just above her elbow.

"Sizzle!" Coil's breath was warm on Grit's ear, and he reeked of damp earth.

Wrestling against his arm, she turned, and with her fingertip traced a line from his temple to his chin. "Watch it, Coil of Dara. I might cut you again, and this time, no amount of forest magic will erase your scar."

He laughed, a mirthless, distracted noise. Following his gaze, Grit looked toward the back of the meetinghouse. A wiry woman marched toward them, weaving through the crowd with ease.

"Fool child, I taught you better than to play with unclaimed boys. You're due for your branding." Dame Berth grabbed Grit's right arm and steered her away from Coil.

"Take your hand from my arm." Grit wrenched free of her dame's grip. "Your hold over me has ended."

Dame Berth studied Grit through dull gray eyes. "Since the moment I birthed you, I have been preparing you for this day. Whatever happens, child, do nothing rash. I didn't raise you for failure."

As the woman headed for the stage at the front of the room, Grit shouldered her way to tables of weapons and other

1

tools the elders of Thresh had set out to aid her in her test. She ran her finger along a broadsword's blood grove, ruffled an arrow's fletching, and paused with her hand over a roll of gauze. Glancing about the room, she strained to remember the strengths and weaknesses of those she'd sparred during her training. The choice would be simpler if she knew which of them Sage Brakken and the village council had chosen to hunt her, but it was useless. The council guarded its secrets well.

At the front of the room, twelve council members, including Dame Berth, sat in chairs arranged on either side of an expansive hearth. A blazing fire added discomfort to the warmth of the spring day. Sage Brakken rose from the first chair, crossed to the center of the low stage, and struck his staff upon the wooden planks.

"Sixteen brands for sixteen years, and sixteen days to shun one's fears." His booming voice cleared the room of chatter. "Grit of Berth and Stone, come forth!"

Grit strode between rows of crowded benches arranged before the low stage. Holding her back straight and her head high, she stepped onto the dais, never taking her gaze from Sage Brakken. Respect and proper conduct were laid aside during a Final Branding. The village of Thresh craved brazen defiance. She'd deliver that and more.

Stopping toe to toe with Sage Brakken, she looked into his hard, weathered face. "I'm Grit of Berth and Stone. Bring the dame and her little rod."

She glanced over her shoulder as a murmur of approval spread through the crowd. Behind Brakken, Berth and several of the council members nodded eagerly. The scornful smile faded from Dame Berth's face; she rose, walked to the hearth, took the metal rod from above the mantel, and thrust it into the bluest, hottest part of the fire.

"I don't take orders from an untested babe." The woman stood with one hand on her slender hip. "If you would prove your courage, you must come to me."

Grit did not hesitate, for to hesitate was to waver, and to waver was weakness. She advanced toward her dame and stopped just to the right of the spot Berth had indicated when she'd demanded Grit come to her. Grit spat on the spot.

Without a word, Dame Berth clasped Grit's wrist. Grit's scarred right arm extended toward her dame. The tip of the uplifted rod glowed red with cleaving heat as Berth raised it from behind her back.

Grit fixed her gaze on Berth's face and forced into her eyes the same intensity raging in those of the woman who had given her life. Berth's tight lips betrayed nothing but determination to triumph, but Grit swore victory to herself. *I will not go down, neither by this woman, nor by the iron in her hand.* She clenched her jaw, flexed her arm, and willed her body not to move.

Grit held fast as the rod sizzled against her first scar. She did not flinch, nor did she look away from Berth, even for an instant. The heat seared away the thick scar to eat into the tissue beneath. She held her breath, not wanting to inhale the stench of charred flesh.

*One. Two. Three.*

She spat over the rod, squarely hitting the wet spot left by her saliva moments earlier.

"One." She feigned a small yawn.

Berth lowered the rod and returned it to the flame. The villagers rose for a better view. Some in the back stood on benches. It would be a pity to miss even a moment of a Final Branding.

"So that's how you're going to play it, is it?" Berth's lips hardly moved.

"It is."

3

"Fool girl, this is the easy part."

The rod found Grit's second scar.

*One. Two. Three.*

Spit.

"Two." Grit squared her shoulders.

The third scar.

*One. Two. Three.*

Spit.

"Three."

After the fourth scar had been retraced, while Dame Berth reheated the rod, Grit scanned the quiet room. Near the back of the crowd, a mop of golden curls bobbed toward a side exit. Passing through the door, Coil glanced over his shoulder. He scowled at Grit.

*How like him to lose interest and leave.* Grit braced herself to accept the branding rod again.

The iron ate into her fifth scar. Jaw clenched, she counted to three, recollected Coil's departure, inhaled sharply, and threw in a fourth and a fifth count. She spat again.

"Five."

With each branding, she waited longer to spit and call the count. The longer she waited, the more excited the villagers grew. She could have called the count at one, like all of them had done, and walked away with honor. When she was through, their honor wouldn't be worth the ashes of their scars.

Grit's fingers tingled as Dame Berth squeezed her wrist tighter and centered the branding rod over the next scar. By now, she hardly felt the iron. She waited, impervious to the foul odor of burning flesh wafting from her oozing arm.

Coil returned as Dame Berth set the branding rod in the fire to reheat for the last time. Grit's steady gaze flickered long enough to notice his austere frown, but not long enough for anyone but Coil, who quickly looked away, to notice her faltering. A renewed determination surged through her body.

As Dame Berth touched the rod to Grit's arm for her sixteenth and final brand, Grit wrenched the branding rod from Dame Berth's hand. Grit stood in the center of the stage, her legs shoulder-width apart. Her vision blurred, but she didn't need her eyes to know where her sixteenth brand belonged. She had traced the spot a thousand times in preparation for this moment. She plunged the branding rod deep into the flesh above her elbow.

"One. Two. Three." Her pitch raised with every count. Her mind reeled with pain, but she resisted the scream that surged through her body. *To waver is weakness, to waver is . . .* Her gaze locked on Coil's blurry face. Now he did not look away. She spat out the bile that had risen from her gut and counted on, her voice deep and trembling. "Thirteen. Fourteen. Fifteen."

Scorching, agonizing, inhuman pain shot through her arm, raged up her neck, and pierced her brain. She held the branding rod firmly in her arm until she could bear no more. Only then, when her stomach's churning threatened to undo her, did Grit hurl the branding rod downward. It struck the floor, etching a depression in the wood. Grit spat on the branding rod, her saliva sizzling as it met the scorching metal. She turned to face the crowd, threw her head back, and shouted, "Sixteen!"

# TWO

The Final Branding was over. Grit's eyes, as she had intended, were completely dry. Not waiting to be excused, she marched from the stage, pushing her way through the crowd with her good arm extended. She continued into the sparring circle, where tables and benches had been set up for the day's festivities. On the far side of the fenced arena, Threshans lined up before several tables and served themselves from cooking pots, breadbaskets, plates of pastries, and various other dishes. They'd gorge themselves, even those who didn't bother to attend the Branding.

Most wore tan and green tunics with trousers, though some of the dames and damelings from the Inner Rings wore dresses of cream or dull earth tones. Useless attire, but at least they'd brought food to share. Grit glanced at her tunic, tucked into her belt. In the past, she'd remained in a sleeveless white shirt for a few days to give her brands time to heal. Without the shelter of Dame Berth's hut, she'd have to wrangle the tunic over her brands. She'd wait until she was out of the public eye to perform that feat of courage.

Grit held her throbbing arm close to her side, her left hand wrapped around her dagger's hilt, ready to strike any who jostled her. They'd all taunted her as she traveled from Dame Berth's mud and thatch hut on the Outer Ring to the wooden meetinghouse in the center of the village, but very few dared mock her now. No one was fool enough to touch her.

Sire Stone walked close by her left side. "Feed yourself, Grit. You have your test still."

"Even fools know that's where honor's won." On her right, Coil sneered at her mangled arm.

"If I didn't know better, Coil of Dara, I'd say you were concerned for my well-being. Even fools know that's where honor's lost."

"Leave her, both of you." Dame Berth stepped in front of Grit. "What do any of you know of honor? You . . ." She poked a finger at Sire Stone's muscular chest. "Do you intend never to sever your connection to your offspring? Why can't you restrain yourself to attending their branding ceremonies, like the other sires? Must you speak to them in the streets and visit them in my hut?"

Sire Stone's gaze dropped to his chest, where the long, gray key to Dame Berth's hut hung on a leather cord beside a smooth, white stone. "Perhaps you would like your key back. Perhaps you would rather have bound yourself to another man. Pierce, perhaps? Or are you, after all these years, still afraid the council will discover your secrets and send you to the Inner Ring?"

His bright blue eyes shone with cold intensity. Berth opened her mouth as if to speak, but quickly snapped it shut again.

A flicker of amusement flashed across Sire Stone's sharp features. "Leave it, little Berth. I doubt you regret our peculiar alliance any more than I do, and I don't regret it at all. I suppose other sires don't find their offspring as intriguing as I find ours. As for speaking with Grit or with any of the others, it is mine to decide how I treat my offspring. If you would disagree with me, let us take the matter before the council."

As he watched Berth, tiny lines formed at the corners of his eyes. The woman shook her head almost imperceptibly, her lips pursed in a manner suggestive of deep irritation.

Grit hugged her throbbing arm closer to her side, farther from Coil's stern gaze, and laughed to herself. None of this would go before the council. Sire Stone, as prominent on the council as Dame Berth, had made the woman mad on several occasions, but Dame Berth knew when to hold her tongue. Disputes over the upbringing of their offspring were never made public.

Dame Berth wasn't fool enough to draw attention to Sire Stone. Rumors lingered of Sire Stone's arrival into the village, his refusal to part with the white stone he always wore, and his acquisition of Berth's key. Grit had watched Dame Berth's muscles tense at the mention of Sire Stone wandering in the woods and mentoring sireless Coil. But, Dame Berth was shrewd. With an alliance of such long and exclusive standing, if any spoke ill of Sire Stone, they spoke ill of Dame Berth. She wouldn't take this to the council. As she had done every time Sire Stone challenged her on Grit's upbringing, Dame Berth yielded.

Sighing, she gestured toward the tables of food, already swarming with hungry Threshans. "Come, Grit."

The dame marched on with her nose a little higher in the air than usual. Coil stared unabashedly at Grit's arm. His lip curled in a sneer.

On an impulse, Grit placed her left hand on his shoulder, stood on tiptoes, and with his curls brushing her lips, whispered in his ear, "To Grit!"

She hurried to catch up with her dame, trying to put from her mind the feel of Coil's shoulder beneath her hand and his hair against her lips. He'd be smiling that gloating smile now, the one that always told her she wouldn't win as easily as she expected. Looking back would only feed his pride.

Dame Berth steered a dameling from their path. "You've officially left my protection, but I'll caution you once more. You and Coil have played your game long enough. I have no doubt most of your little battles go 'to Grit,' but if you continue, the battle will go to neither of you. It isn't prudent to ally yourself so closely with one sireling, especially an unclaimed like Coil. He's already a laughingstock."

"Ha!" The effort of the laugh sent a jolt of pain through Grit's arm. "Clearly you haven't been on the training fields in years."

"I'm not the fool you take me for. Coil of Dara may be nimble on his feet and fast with his sword, but he has yet to earn the respect of the council."

Grit frowned. "I've seen the council. I'm not sure I value their respect."

Dame Berth let the insult pass. "There is weakness in him, grave weakness, and unless he eradicates it, he'll never amount to anything. It's bad enough none of the sires have claimed him, and there are many who could. His disappearing into the forest, though, and coming back covered in berry juice . . . Well, Dara's mighty proud, considering she's an unclaimed herself, but I don't blame her for handing him over to Sire Stone."

The throbbing moved from Grit's arm to her head. "What's the point, Berth?"

Dame Berth stopped and faced Grit. "The point is there is something disturbing about Coil, and it won't serve you well to ally yourself with him any more than you already have."

"But Sire Stone has trained him . . ."

"Exactly." Berth swept her light-brown hair from her forehead. "Sire Stone has trained him, and we both know how delicate his reputation is. At least we can be sure he isn't that ridiculous boy's sire."

Berth looked back the way they had come. Grit followed the tired gaze of the only woman with whom Sire Stone had allied himself. There might be something in her warning against a close alliance with Sire Stone's protégé.

Coil stood where she'd left him, nodding his golden head as Sire Stone spoke. He had certainly attached himself too freely and too firmly to Sire Stone.

Dame Berth pressed a plate into Grit's hand. "Stone was right in this: You must nourish yourself. You have a test to pass, and you'll need all the strength you can get to outrun your hunters."

"You're on the council. Whoever my hunters may be, you know as well as I do they can't catch me." Grit frowned as Dame Berth heaped generous servings from each dish onto her plate.

"I warned you not to be a fool, Grit. If you continue to indulge such obstinacy as you demonstrated in your Final Branding, you will surely fail."

"More shame to the dame who raised me." Grit shrugged her good shoulder, took a salted potato from her plate, and crammed it into her mouth. "In sixteen years, you never gave me so much food. You're going soft, Berth."

A scrawny, black haired girl of seven squeezed between Dame Berth and Grit. A second girl, identical in every detail, stood behind the first, silently studying Grit through bright blue eyes as her twin spoke. "Seal saw Dame Dara washing her blanket this morning. I imagine by the time one takes it from the line, it might keep one warm on a cool night in the Northern Forest."

Grit swallowed the potato and smiled at her young siblings. "Well done, Seal, Oath."

Each twin grabbed handfuls of food from the table before darting away. Dame Berth set her plate down, leaned over, and removed her worn leather slipper.

"Cursed girl kicked sand into my shoe." She shook out her shoe, but her gaze remained fixed on Grit. "You know why I named you Grit, don't you?"

"You tell me every year." Grit glanced around, seeking an escape from a story she didn't care to hear again.

"Sand. Dirt. Grit. Call it what you will, it gets in one's shoe, rubs against one's foot, and would drive one to madness. That's what you are, child, maddening for all your irritating ways. In your first year, I thought I would lose my mind, so insufferable a babe you were."

Grit searched for a way through the crowd. "Perhaps you should have cast me onto Sire Stone's mercy. He's done an excellent job teaching me to spar these past four years. I'm quite sure he could have borne my squabbling."

Dame Berth slipped her narrow foot back into its shoe and stood upright. "Don't start thinking you overwhelmed me. As for handing you over to your sire, that would have been a shame worse than the Inner Ring."

"Still, perhaps you should have," Grit said.

Leaving Berth, Grit made her way through the bustling sparring circle and ducked into the meetinghouse to eat in solitude. She swallowed her pain along with her food and imagined each morsel traveling to a fingertip, a toe, an area in the middle of her back, in order to sustain that portion of her body over the sixteen days to come. She was a slender girl of average height, but when one measures a body bite by bite, one must eat a considerable amount to cover the entire thing.

As she bit into one of Dame Dara's fruit pies, she realized she had something more important than the distribution of bites on which to concentrate. She had not selected an aid. Nibbling the fruit pie, she crossed the empty room to peruse the tables of aids. There were all the weapons, bandages, foods, and tools she'd studied so closely before the branding. There was something else, too, that hadn't been there before. Her heart beat faster as she studied the small bowl of bright pink berries. Her arm burned as she reached to touch one of the berries with a finger. She laid her hand gently on the table instead, her fingertips curling around the hilt of a broadsword lying next to the berries. The choice would be easy, after all.

# THREE

Well-fed villagers trickled into the meetinghouse, and once more Grit stood before the council. Many Threshans had returned to huts, fields, and forests, but several remained to observe the Aids Ceremony. Sage Brakken said a few words, congratulating Grit on bearing her Final Branding well and admonishing her to choose her aid with prudence. Then Berth approached with a worn leather pack.

"The Dame's Aid. One day's provisions." She thrust the bag toward Grit.

"I'll use it well." Grit took the pack, awkwardly slinging it over her left shoulder with the same hand. Her right arm throbbed with every shifting of her body, but her face remained placid. Dame Berth stepped back to make room for Sire Stone. He cradled a small dagger in his calloused hands.

"The Sire's Aid." His deep voice was barely audible. He leaned close to Grit's ear and whispered, "When you are out of sight of the village, twist the hilt and apply the contents to your arm. It's your best chance of survival."

He laid the dagger in Grit's hand. She said nothing, only cocked her head as he clasped her hand. His hands paled against the olive tones of her skin.

She looked from Sire Stone to Dame Berth. Her three siblings were unmistakably sprung from Sire Stone. He couldn't have denied them, not with their straight black hair, sharp features, and piercing blue eyes, but she wasn't sure about herself. Once, on the shore of the Western Sea, she'd studied her reflection in the blade of Coil's sword. Dame Berth had the same large grey eyes, small upturned nose, and square jaw she'd seen in the polished steel. Even her light-brown hair, falling in wavy tangles around her shoulders, seemed a younger, less weathered version of Dame Berth's.

*I'm the spit and image of my dame. But what of Sire Stone?* She pulled her hand from his, her gaze following him as he returned to his place among the council members. *Nothing in me reflects him. He could've denied me unchallenged. Surely it was pride that kept me under Dame Berth's care, but why did Sire Stone claim me? Why did he spend these four years preparing me for warriorhood? Why did he not refuse my request for training as so many sires do their female offspring?*

"Have you selected an aid?" Sage Brakken's voice drew Grit from her reverie.

"I have."

She walked toward the tables and stopped in front of the broadsword and small bowl of berries. Sire Pierce nodded smugly. Wouldn't it please him if she chose the broadsword he'd wrested from an enemy's hand in his raiding days? That might be a greater humiliation to Dame Berth than the Inner Ring.

Grit picked up the bowl of berries and turned to face the council. "I choose these."

"Humph!"

Grit tightened her grip on the rim of the bowl. She refused to acknowledge the noise coming from the back of the otherwise silent crowd. She'd dealt with Coil enough for the day.

"B-b-berries?" Dame Berth shook her head and exhaled loudly.

"When you could carry the broadsword of a champion or any other number of deadly weapons or useful tools? The child is mad!" Sire Pierce looked upon Grit with his usual scorn.

She lifted the bowl to the level of her heart. "I choose these. If there is a problem with my decision . . ."

"There is no problem. She is of age. She has endured her branding. She makes her choice, and she lives with the consequences." Sire Stone addressed his remarks to the council, but cast a glance at Grit on the word "lives."

She searched the crowd for Coil. Had he told Sire Stone why her dagger left so few scars?

Sage Brakken turned to Grit, his bushy eyebrows drawn together in a stern expression. "Sire Stone's right. The girl goes with a day's portions, a tiny dagger, and a bowl of berries. Grit of Berth and Stone, you have the afternoon. We release the hunters at sundown. Your test ends at midday on the sixteenth day. If you manage to both survive the elements and elude your hunters, we'll bestow upon you all the rights and privileges of a free dameling. If you fail . . ." He made a noise somewhere between a cough and a laugh. "Well, we'll just see how you fare."

He stepped from the dais and exited the meetinghouse. The other eleven council members followed. Grit waited for the room to empty of spectators, but one Threshan remained, slouched in a chair beside the exit. As Grit approached, he stood, moved to the door, and positioned himself with his back against one side of the doorframe and his booted foot propped against the other side, nearly level with his chest.

Grit had no choice but to deal with a little more Coil. She snorted at his leg. He scowled at her mangled arm. She flexed her arm, and a deeper pain cut through the raging sting of her wounds.

"You might be the stupidest creature ever to breathe Chasmarian air." He shook his head and let out an irritated sigh. "If there's anything of value behind your pretty face, I caution you to stuff it with those berries as soon as you can."

"I intend to. Now would you move that scrawny leg out of my way? Your hair is pink, and I have places to go."

"So do I." Coil lowered his leg and sauntered out of the meetinghouse. His legs, far from scrawny, were lithe and muscular. They'd often carried his body from the center of Thresh to the sea faster than her legs could carry her. She hadn't lied about his hair, though. Coil's golden locks displayed a bright pink streak that had not been there before her Final Branding.

Only a fool would waste a head start lazing around the village. Grit waited long enough to see Coil amble down a side street just beyond Dame March's forge before popping a berry into her mouth. She stepped from the meetinghouse porch and walked purposefully across the dirt road. The smells of bread and fish wafted from the row of crowded market huts circling the wooden meetinghouse, but she passed without pause. The Inner Ring merchants were always on high alert on test days, eager to knock their betters out of the village before they'd even had a chance to meet their hunters. Her Dame's Aid and Coil's berries were all the food she could take from Thresh, unless she wanted to forfeit her honor.

She checked her peripheral view as she passed through the Middle Rings. Dames and damelings swept their doorsteps, silently guarding their tidy mud huts lest Grit spy anything she might sneak into her pack. A few years back, Varlet of Dara had stolen seven jackknifes on his way through. He fought his hunters off, but returned home to seven angry damelings. Middle Ringers were proud of their little blades. Grit wouldn't repeat his mistake.

"Grit!"

She turned at the sound of her name.

A lean boy slowed to a walk as he caught up to her. Dirt and cobwebs dulled his straight black hair. "Two sirelings seek honor through the capture or death of their prey."

"Why do you taunt me with the Hunter's Commission, Slate?" She picked another berry from her bowl and rolled it between her thumb and finger to feel the tiny bumps on its surface.

"Because I know who your hunters are."

"And?" She put the berry in her mouth, squished it with her tongue, and watched her younger sibling.

"And one of them is a well-grounded warrior." He looked very much like Sire Stone as he waited for Grit's reaction.

"Ha!" She nodded, satisfaction filling her heart as the berry's sweet juice slid down her throat. "That will be useful. And the other hunter?"

"The other hunter is strong, fierce, and more than able to compensate for his partner's weakness. He, more than anyone else in Thresh, stands a chance at defeating his prey. There was no dispute among the council members. Dame Berth will give him final instructions. Not," Slate smiled impishly at Grit, "that this particular sireling ever demonstrates much concern for the council's instruction."

Grit stopped and studied the boy's eager face. "How did you discover this?"

"It isn't that difficult to overhear even the most secret of council meetings, if one truly desires to do so." He pulled a cobweb from his hair and flicked it onto the street.

"You've been spying again. One of these days, you'll get yourself killed, intruding on conversations of which you have no part." Grit turned her oozing arm from a passing dame and spoke in a low voice. "I caution you to tell no one you've given me this information, Slate. It would nullify my test and shame us both. I won't return before your Twelfth Branding. Take

19

this, save it, and eat it directly after your branding. Don't let Berth see it. I don't think I need to caution you against Seal's and Oath's pilfering fingers."

She pressed a berry into Slate's hand. Frowning at his stained palm, she said, "Try not to crush that berry. They're hard to come by."

Grit made one stop before leaving Thresh. Seal and Oath had not lied. Dame Dara had indeed washed her blanket in the early hours of the morning. The blanket was nearly dry now. More importantly, it was unguarded. Seizing a priceless opportunity, Grit yanked the blanket off the line and crammed it into her pack, biting her lip against the burning in her arm as she made the necessary adjustments, and slung the pack over her shoulder again. The theft delayed her departure only a minute.

She looked neither left nor right as she left Dame Dara's yard and jogged through the last of the middle rings and on past the Outer Ring. There, on the very edge of Thresh, she saw nothing but the forest she hoped would hide and sustain her for the next sixteen days; she sprinted toward its cover. As she approached the first line of trees, she glanced back.

Coil leaned against his back fence, methodically popping berries into his mouth. She stumbled, and pain such as she had never known shot down her arm and across her chest. Recovering her footing, she pressed onward. With any luck, Coil of Dara had not seen her falter.

# FOUR

Inside the forest, where Coil's prying stare could not reach, Grit slowed. Her injured right arm cradled the bowl of berries against her stomach so none spilled. The bulky leather pack kept sliding from her left shoulder. As she raised her arm to reposition the pack, a small, white hen strutted onto the path. It stopped and clucked at Grit.

"Get back, feathered wretch." She bent and picked up a heavy stick. "I don't have time for your kind today."

The bird cocked its head.

"Go, I said!" She stomped her foot, sending a jolt of pain through her arm. The chicken looked at her with one beady orange eye.

*What is the awful beast doing? Why won't it go? Wouldn't it be something to lose my test to a chicken?* She'd never met anyone who'd been attacked by a chicken, let alone seen a chicken attack. She'd collected their eggs since she was a babe, even killed a few grown birds for dinner. They seemed harmless enough. They bobbed their heads, made funny sounds, and scampered around pecking at the ground. Sometimes they sat on the ground and fluffed up a tiny dirt storm, but they never did anything truly threatening. Still, the old dames had told enough stories, and so Grit jabbed her stick in the direction of the chicken. The bird fluttered its wings, but soon settled to watch her again.

"What do you want?" She poked at the chicken once more. Her arm throbbed. She dropped the stick. "Stay out of my way then, will you?"

Grit kept her gaze on the chicken as she devoured the remaining fruit. She swallowed the last berry and examined her arm. Her wounds no longer oozed, but the ache continued.

"Come on, stupid berries," Grit muttered, shaking her leg as if it would speed the process. "Get to work."

She rolled her eyes and threw her head back to look into the treetops. She waited, breathing deeply, for the pain in her arm to ease. The berries never healed her aches as quickly as she wanted them to do. Surely Coil could have spared a few more berries. This was taking too long. She tensed her muscles. The pain remained, diminished only slightly, but she was running out of time. She studied the chicken a moment, then, glancing beyond it, spied something white under a shrub.

Skirting the chicken, Grit made her way to the shrub and knelt in front of it. Her right hand remained in her lap, holding Coil's bowl, as her left fingers wrapped around the small object. The egg, still warm, fit perfectly in her small hand.

"Hello, dinner," she whispered. She wrapped a few large leaves around the egg, placed it in the wooden bowl, and tucked the egg in its makeshift case carefully into her pocket. The wood knocked against something hard. Grit pulled Sire Stone's tiny dagger from her pocket, slid it from its case, and examined its smooth white hilt and silver blade. Its blade was no longer than her finger. How could it be useful? Remembering her sire's instructions, she twisted the hilt and looked inside. A semi-transparent substance filled the hollow handle of the small knife. She dipped her finger into the ointment and sniffed it. It smelled of rain, earth, and something entirely foreign to her senses. The scent sharpened her mind. She touched the ointment to the first of her brands.

A pang of cold pierced her wounded arm like the Western Sea engulfing her body on the first swim of summer. Grit drew in a sharp breath, but let it out slowly as comfort washed over her. As healthy skin grew over raw flesh, it consumed the pain along with all traces of her injury. She dabbed the salve on the each of her burns, the cold initial sting less severe with each brand. By the time she'd covered the sixteenth brand, the second and third had healed. One by one, her wounds closed, revealing clean, smooth skin.

Her fingertip brushing her fresh skin, she traced two lines down her arm, the memory of her scars so clear she could almost see them still. But they were gone, and all she felt was the tender caress of skin on perfect skin. She tensed her muscles and pressed harder on her arm with all four fingers. No remnant of pain remained in the thin layer of firm muscle under her skin. She raised her arm and traced a large circle in the air. No doubt remained; her arm was restored to full strength and functionality. Even Coil's berries, marvels that they were, had never healed so quickly or so completely. Grit tilted her head and studied the tiny dagger in her hand. *What is this aid Sire Stone has given me?* She sealed the dagger to protect the extraordinary ointment. She might need it later.

The hen clucked again. Through the trees, she could just make out the village of Thresh. Even now, her hunters prepared to pursue her.

"You never saw me, bird." She returned the dagger to its case and wedged it safely beneath the bowl in her pocket. She studied the woods, turning in every direction but the one from which she'd come.

"South," she said. Her legs obeyed.

She ran for hours, leaping obstacles, but never slowing. Her only goal to place herself as far from Thresh as possible, she pushed her body harder than ever. As the orange glow of the setting sun filtered through the leaves above, Grit grunted and increased her speed. *Sage Brakken releases the hunters at sunset. They're coming for me now. I must keep going.*

When the forest grew completely dark and weariness threatened to overwhelm her, Grit stopped. Bending over with her hands on her knees, she took ten deep, slow breaths. *Rest or die. I cannot go on like this. Rest or die.*

Unused to being still, her legs twitched. Hunger pangs stung her sides. She fumbled in her pocket and retrieved the egg. *No fire to cook it. I haven't time, nor do I care to show my hunters where I am.* She cracked the egg and poured its slimy, uncooked contents into her mouth. She tilted her head back and swallowed hard, the raw yolk filling her throat as it slid toward her stomach. She cleared her mouth of the last of the egg's ooze and willed it to strengthen her for the strenuous night to come.

She reached into her pack, pushed aside Dame Dara's blanket, and pulled out a flask of water, a portion of her Dame's Aid. She sipped twice. Who knew when she'd be able to refill it? Numerous streams wound through the forest, but she had to outdistance her hunters. She dared not stop too often. She swished the cool water around her mouth before swallowing. Her thirst remained, but at least her mouth was not as dry as it had been. She tucked the flask into her pack and ran again.

She did not sleep that night. Surely the hunters had rested during the afternoon and pursued her with vigor. She'd need more than a few hours head start. She slowed her pace, but kept on.

She ran south, angling east or west periodically to throw the hunters off her trail should they discover it. She did not retrace her steps, as some do when fleeing through wild territory. Instead, she moved always away from the village and the hunters who pursued her. She stopped only when her body grew too faint to continue; when she did pause, it was never for long. She rationed the provisions Dame Berth had given her, taking only a few bites of bread or cheese and a few sips of water before continuing.

Her stomach craved a full meal. Her head spun from exhaustion. She tripped over her blistered feet, crashing into a tree. She clutched the trunk, breathing deeply. Prey had been caught on the second day. Caught and sentenced to the Inner Ring at best. Servitude to her hunter and death were options she didn't care to consider. She had to press on. The trembling in her legs would stop once she started running again, and it wouldn't be so hard to keep her eyes open.

The second night, Grit spied the entrance to a cave at the base of a hill. She climbed the hill and scanned the surrounding forest. Far to the north, smoke rose above the treetops. Her hunters couldn't be fools enough to light a fire, but the sight comforted her. If it was them, they were far enough away for her to rest soundly. She returned to the bottom of the hill and inspected the cave, only to find it offered no escape. Should the hunters track her to the cave's entrance, she'd be trapped. She found a fallen tree trunk nearby. In the dim evening light, she built a makeshift shelter against it, taking care to arrange branches, twigs, and leaves to look as though they'd fallen naturally into their chosen places. When she was satisfied with her handiwork, Grit wrapped herself in her blanket, wriggled into her shelter, and closed her eyes. As sleep overcame her, she saw a fleeting image of Dame Dara shivering in her simple bed.

The fool woman should have known better than to leave a nice blanket unattended. It was a wonder Coil grew up with any sense. She pulled the blanket to her chin. It scratched against her bare arm and stank of sour milk despite its recent washing, but it was finer than anything she'd slept with in Dame Berth's hut.

On the third night, Grit tucked herself into a narrow space between two towering gray rocks and pulled Dame Dara's blanket over her head. Having traveled far, hard, and late that day, she fell quickly into a deep sleep. She dreamt she was floating in the Western Sea, its waves rocking her body as Coil laughed nearby. When she awoke and removed the blanket from her face, the sun was high in the sky.

Emerging from the shadow of the rocks, Grit surveyed her surroundings. The trees had thinned. In the west, water shimmered in the brilliant light of late morning. A warm breeze brought the scent of saltwater.

*The Western Sea.* She strained her ears to hear the lapping of the distant waves, an echo of her dreams. Grit shook her head as she looked over the glistening waters. She pictured the coastline in her mind, trying to remember where it curved in and jutted out. She had a rough knowledge of Chasmaria's geography, enough to know her situation was grim.

All would be lost if they drove her into the water. No prey ever came back from the Western Sea.

She chewed a dry crust, sipped from her flask, and stuffed the blanket into her pack. Before leaving the rocks, Grit pulled out her dagger and etched a notch in the rim of the empty berry bowl. Three notches now marked the edge of the wooden dish. *Three notches for three nights. Only thirteen more to go.*

Leaving the Western Sea behind, Grit headed into the forest in a southeasterly direction. She maintained a steady pace through the thickening underbrush. The terrain sloped upward, and she pumped her legs harder. Early in the afternoon, she knelt by a stream to refill her flask.

She sensed him coming a split second before she heard the twig snap.

# FIVE

G rit crouched motionless and listened for the direction from which the hunter came. She stood, bent at the waist, eyes scanning her surroundings. The hunter's tan tunic and dark trousers blended almost perfectly with the forest around him, but almost was not enough to avoid Grit's detection.

He looked at his feet, probably cursing his own clumsiness. He was close, but with skill and speed, she might escape his notice. Her toes barely touching the ground, she tiptoed into the denser growth behind her. She'd almost reached thicker cover when his head jerked up. She froze in her tracks, willing her body to disappear.

It was too late. The hunter smiled, one side of his mouth turning up sharper than the other. He shouted something over his shoulder and sprinted toward Grit, splashing across the shallow stream.

Diving into the brush, Grit broke into a run. She did not zigzag, as she had in the days when she and Coil, mere babes, had neglected the filling of their baskets to sharpen each other's skills in games of Prey and Hunter. This was not a game. If she did not immediately put considerable distance between herself and the hunter, things would most definitely not go in her favor.

She barreled through the forest, tearing off leaves and breaking low branches here and there, in hope that the hunter would stop at a damaged tree and decide to search its higher branches. Prey had often been caught clinging to tree trunks, betrayed by branches they'd snapped on the way to their hiding places.

Grit sped on, dodging trees and hurdling fallen logs. Her feet were quick and sure, her legs strong and steady; her heart and lungs kept pace. But Grit had limits, and the hunter was pushing her to them. Over the pumping of her blood and the pounding of her feet, she heard leaves crack and twigs snap behind her in rapid succession. She had no ground left to lose.

Tall trees, thick with leaves, stretched above Grit's head, the sky blocked out by their verdant foliage. She picked the giant with the densest growth and braced her feet as gently as possible against the trunk to avoid scuffing the bark. Listening for her hunter's approaching footfalls, she scurried quietly up the tree, through soft, closely packed leaves into the higher reaches. When the hunter's pace slackened, Grit stopped, flattened her body against the trunk, and awaited her fate.

"Ho!" the hunter called over his shoulder. A menacing chuckle rose from the base of Grit's tree. The hunter scanned the lower branches, paying close attention to the trunk.

Grit could not see his face, but she recognized his laugh of impending triumph. Slate had not misinformed her. Turf of Elna and Bord was one of Sage Brakken's chosen hunters. He was indeed, as Slate had said, a very "well-grounded" warrior. In any other situation—for example, when she was not in a tree waiting to see if she would live or die—she would have laughed at Slate's description. Turf's "grounding" was the best-known secret on the warrior training fields. Grit and Coil had decided to let Turf rise a little higher in the council's esteem before leaking his secret. It would be more fun, after all, to watch him fall from a lofty position.

But now it was Grit who had to worry about falling. She clung tightly to the trunk, squeezing her eyes shut and willing Turf to leave.

He stayed. Worse than that, his fellow hunter arrived and began to scrutinize the tree with him. The two hunters stepped back and looked up, arms crossed over their chests.

"Do your thing, why don't you?" Turf spoke as if climbing a tree was below his dignity, a task to be passed down to the lesser hunter who stood next to him. But fear hid beneath the words. She could hear it in his voice.

The second hunter sprang deftly into the tree, his boots making only soft sounds against the trunk. A moment later, the leaves below her feet rustled. Then all quieted, and she dared look down. A patch of pink and gold hair showed through the leaves. Her worst suspicions confirmed, Grit swore to herself. She hadn't climbed high enough.

Coil was close. If he gained one more branch, he'd be close enough to reach up, grab her foot, and dash her to the ground. She'd likely strike a few branches on the way down and be dead before the forest floor cracked every bone in her body. Her only salvation lay in the possibility that he might spare her life and claim her as his slave. Neither death nor slavery suited Grit.

She closed her eyes, held her breath, rested her forehead against the tree trunk, and willed her toes, her feet, her legs, all the way up to the last filthy hair on her unkempt head to disappear.

She did not disappear, but neither did Coil advance.

"I don't see her, and the branches have thinned. I can't climb any higher," he said.

Grit opened her eyes and puzzled over the branch on which she stood. The whispery sounds of Coil's retreat ended with a soft thud.

"I'm sure she's up there." Turf crossed his arms over his round chest and nodded toward the tree as Coil rejoined him.

Coil passed his hand over the tree's rough trunk. "Oh, I have no doubt she went up. The question is whether she's waiting above our heads or miles away, laughing at having outrun us. Shall we wait here, or would you like to pursue our prey?"

Neither hunter spoke for a moment.

Turf shifted his weight. "We could track her through the treetops. You can do that, can't you? You're supposed to be able to climb and twist your way through any obstacle, Berry Boy."

Coil shook his head. He examined the tree's higher branches. "It wouldn't work. She is lighter than I and can gain limbs I would snap like twigs. In this tree, say, she could—and obviously did—climb to levels I can barely see. There's no way I could track her from tree to tree."

"I thought Brakken picked you for this very situation."

Coil shrugged. "So he did. But even Sage Brakken must know our prey is swift, fearless, and more adept at treetop travel than we—than I am. I'm sure he knows nothing of your level of expertise."

Coil's arrow hit its target. Turf grunted, but did not reply. The two sirelings studied Grit's tree, considering what to do about the problem of prey beyond their reach. At last, Turf broke the silence.

"It's useless to stay here. You're probably right. The stupid girl is more than likely miles away by now, mocking our sloth. We'll have to split up, cover more land that way. Maybe we'll pick up her trail when she comes down. She'll have to put her feet on the ground sooner or later. I'll go east."

Having made his decision, Turf headed east without a backward glance.

Coil studied Grit's tree a moment longer. Shaking his head at the clumps of leaves, he mumbled, "To Grit."

He sauntered due west, and Grit's muscles relaxed as the tangled curls disappeared from view. When her hunters were a safe distance away, she eased herself down one branch. She stopped, her mind whirling with Coil's words. *Whether she's above our heads or miles away . . . more adept at treetop travel . . .* He'd shown her how to do it and pushed her higher and higher into the treetops, but was she better at it than Coil? Could treetop travel be her salvation?

She inched her way toward the end of her branch. At the very moment when the willowy branch began to bend under her slight weight, Grit sprang to the nearest tree. A soft laugh escaped as she steadied herself. She could do this. Like playing a childhood game, she could leave Coil and Turf behind. She could pass her test and become Thresh's greatest warrior.

She traveled south for hours, pouncing from tree to tree, always above the branch at which Coil's greater mass would force him to stop. Where the trees were spaced too far apart, she descended, selected a tree slightly out of her southern course, and climbed again.

When dusk fell, Grit slid down a tall oak. She stood in the darkening forest, tiredness overwhelming her body. Everything ached, and as she thought of the hunters she had avoided, she wished one of them had given her a larger bowl of berries. Her stomach tightened and her mouth watered at the thought of an entire pack full of juicy, nourishing fruit. She reached for her pack, but stopped with one hand on her shoulder. The rough fabric of her tunic pricked her raw palm. Her pack was missing. She must have left it beside the creek. Her flask of fresh water probably lay right next to it. No food. No water. No blanket. Only a wooden bowl and two daggers, one of them too small to hurt a mouse.

Too tired to curse, mourn, or plan, Grit curled beneath a large shrub, raked a few handfuls of leaves over her lean frame, and slept.

****

She woke beside a swiftly flowing brook. The treetops had taken her into unfamiliar territory. Coil and Turf seemed a world away. She drew her dagger and considered her situation. She wasn't entirely without resources. It was late spring; the worst of the frosty nights had passed. With shrubs to shelter her and makeshift leaf blankets to provide a thin layer of extra warmth and concealment, she might survive the remaining nights. She'd shivered often enough on the floor of Dame Berth's hut. As for food, she'd been foraging since she could walk, and Berth had trained her to survive on small, hard-earned portions. When she returned to Thresh, she'd have a week to eat and sleep all she wanted, and she could build a hut of her own with a fire to keep her warm all year long. She had plenty of time for hearty food and comfort.

For now, though, she had the fortune to have fallen asleep under a grizzleberry bush. Unlike Coil's sweet berries, these berries tasted bitter, but they were edible and plump with thirst-quenching, lip-puckering juice. Before she traveled on, she filled her stomach, her bowl, and her pockets with the tart, purple fruit.

Over the next four days, she alternated running, walking, and hiding. Treetop travel was strenuous, not to mention risky. She'd only to resort to it in an emergency. The pressure to flee was not as intense as it had been in the beginning, nor did she have the stamina to sustain her earlier pace. She ate grizzleberries, mushrooms, and other edible plants and drank from each cool spring she crossed. She slept only when she tired of moving. If not for pursuing hunters, she might have luxuriated in her solitude.

Instead, she tensed at every sound and scanned her surroundings constantly. Sleep came in fits, never fully satisfying her worn body. She longed to return to Thresh, collapse on her mat, and sleep until both mind and body awakened. Perhaps Dame Berth would purchase a meal from the Inner Ring. For all their weakness, the Inner Ringers could bake a fine loaf of bread and fry a fish so tender it fell apart on one's plate. It was unlikely, of course, but Dame Berth had served such a meal on Grit's Twelfth Branding, so it wasn't impossible. She could sleep in peace, too, if Seal and Oath would stay out of the hut.

Upon etching the eighth groove in her bowl, Grit set her sights to the northwest. By marking rivers, elevation, and other landmarks, she gained a vague notion of where in Chasmaria she had strayed and which direction to take on her return to Thresh. On the sixteenth day, the road into the village would become neutral ground. The hunters couldn't touch her there. She mentally outlined a rough course to the Koradin-Thresh Highway, hoping to reach it early on the sixteenth day without first meeting Coil or Turf.

When the sun rose on the final day of her test, Grit was miles from Thresh, but mere yards from the highway. From her hiding place, she peered up and down the road. Swift as lightning, she darted to the wide path, leaping the final step. She had heard of women, in other worlds and at other times, who dipped their weary feet into basins of warm, fragrant water to soothe away their aches. *They know nothing of the bliss of safe earth beneath weary feet. I've as good as passed my test.*

In the early afternoon, Grit first made out the outline of the village. Before long, she could see the gap in the Outer Ring indicating where the hard-packed road led into the heart of Thresh. Some distance ahead of her, a stooped figure struggled to push a wheelbarrow onto the road. The wheel stuck in a spot of sand. When the woman pushed, the wheel dug in deeper. When she pulled, the barrow tipped.

Grit came upon the old woman and stopped. She wasn't old; she was ancient. Her back twisted in an awkward curve, and wispy white hair framed a face from which skin hung in countless limp wrinkles. Her eyes appeared clouded and watery. Her hands . . . Grit stared at her hands as they tried to steady the tipping wheelbarrow. She was so frail, so fragile, it was a wonder her hands didn't crack under the strain of her efforts.

On an impulse, Grit stepped toward her. "Woman, you're a fool to be so far from the Inner Ring. Let me help you." She reached for a handle of the wheelbarrow. As her toe sank into the sand, the old woman straightened to her full height. She towered above Grit's upturned face.

Grit jumped back and watched in wide-eyed horror. The old woman's face contorted with a host of evils far beyond Grit's ken. The hag's eyes, cloudy a moment before, now burned with unmitigated hatred.

"Fool!" The dreadful creature wrapped a steely hand around each of Grit's slender arms, lifted her into the air, and threw her headfirst into the empty wheelbarrow. A demented, unearthly laugh emanated from a toothless mouth as Grit crashed into silent darkness.

# SIX

"Fool!" Dame Berth's voice pierced the darkness. Grit opened her eyes, but the light was too much. She squeezed them shut. Easing one eye open, she tried to focus on the leather slipper in front of her face. Her vision blurred as a small shape fell from above. A puddle of spit settled into a deep, freshly cut groove in the floor. Had the woman spit at her? Her head spun as she rolled from her side onto her stomach. She pressed her forehead against the floor to shield her eyes from the light and stop the incessant throbbing. The spit wet her temple. Voices above set her brain whirling.

"Almost in the village . . ."

*Does he need to yell?* She fought back the urge to vomit.

"Regardless . . . defeated . . . Turf . . ."

*Turf, Turf, Turf . . .*

"A grave mistake . . . even a babe knows . . ."

*A babe knows what? What is this? Where am I? There was a woman . . .* Grit strained to remember, but she saw only blackness, and all she heard was a high-pitched screech.

She opened her eyes. Harsh reality had to be better than whatever that nightmare held.

"She was on the Koradin-Thresh Highway."

*I was on the highway. The highway is safe. I passed.* Grit opened her eyes wide, and this time they remained open and focused. She ran a mental inventory of her body. Her head, though throbbing with pain, seemed to be in one piece. Her shoulders dug into the hard wood floor. Her arms, twisted behind her back, refused to move. They were bound together at the wrists. She skipped over her legs quickly, frantic to

35

determine whether her ankles bore a matching restraint. They did. Grit fought the urge to resist her bonds.

*Stay calm. Don't move. Wait. Wait. Wait . . . Listen.*

"An infant's folly, I repeat."

Grit closed her eyes and hoped Dame Berth wouldn't spit at her again.

"Still, she did survive. That's something to consider."

No one answered Sire Stone. Grit sensed them watching her, waiting for her to either refute or vindicate their judgments. *I must rally what little strength I have.* She inhaled deeply and, willing away the pain in her head and the weariness all over, twisted her body and sprang into a crouching position.

"Bring water." She rose, with as much grace as one can have with one's wrists and ankles tied together, and shook her tangled hair out of her face. "I've returned from my test, and I thirst."

Dame Berth laughed. "Ho, the mighty infant cries for refreshment!"

"Sit, child." Sire Stone swept a chair underneath Grit's rear end as she lost her balance. She toppled backward and landed in the chair with a thud.

The twelve members of the council stood in a circle around her on the low stage of Thresh's meetinghouse. Beyond them, two others sat in chairs to the left of the stage, one erect and eager, the other slouched and disinterested.

Grit scowled at Sage Brakken. "Why am I bound?"

"You are bound to prevent your attempting another act of extraordinary stupidity," he said.

"An infant's folly. The first lesson we teach our bubbleheaded offspring is never to approach a stranger without a ready weapon. You failed your test, Grit, where an infant would have succeeded." Dame Berth spat at Grit's feet and turned to pace the edge of the low stage.

"Failed?" Grit stomped and struggled against her bonded limbs to rise. "Failed? What rubbish is this? I survived my sixteen days! I sustained my body and preserved my mind. I eluded my hunters when they could have dashed me to my death. I outran and outwitted those you deemed most capable of defeating me. I am alive! I have passed my test, and you cannot say otherwise!"

"Grit." Sire Stone pushed her back into her seat with a firm hand on her shoulder.

"You were wheeled into the village unconscious." Sire Pierce stooped to stare into Grit's eyes. "You were wheeled into the village by one of the hunters you claim to have outrun and outwitted. Tell me, foolish girl, how you can claim to have passed your test?"

"I'd like to hear this myself." Turf of Elna and Bord rose from his chair and sauntered into the circle of council members. He stopped beside Dame Berth. "I'd like to hear how my dainty, empty-headed, little prey thinks she defeated me."

An ugly smile spread across Turf's asymmetrical face as he drew closer to Grit. Slowly and gently, he twisted a lock of her hair, twigs and all, around his forefinger. She glared at him, her top lip curling in the beginning of a snarl. He yanked. Hard.

Grit spat in his face. "I climbed a tree, coward! Shall we tell the council about that?" Only Sire Stone's restricting hand pressing harder and harder upon her shoulder kept her from hysteria.

"Shall we tell them how you made . . ." Grit checked herself just short of uttering Coil's name and forced herself not to look at the disinterested sireling who remained seated beyond the council. "How you made a fool of yourself, cowering on the ground while your fellow hunter searched the treetops? Shall we tell them about that, you sniveling louse?"

"Mind yourself, Grit. Turf is not under scrutiny here," Sire Stone said in a low voice.

Grit heeded her sire's warning. To lose control of her emotions was to secure her demise. She might defend herself and so regain firm footing in the council's opinion, but it would require measured words; quick, careful maneuvering; and perhaps a well-placed dagger. She fixed her gaze on Turf's jugular and scooted into the center of the straight-backed chair.

Sire Stone's hand relaxed and slipped from her shoulder. Turf looked at her uneasily and not at all kindly, but he said nothing more. She glowered at him as he slunk to Dame Berth's side. *Coward of cowards.*

Slumped in his chair, Coil examined his fingernails with no hint of interest in the discussion. How many times had they mocked Turf? How often had they anticipated shaming him before the council? But now, when Grit threatened to expose the coward, Coil found the dirt beneath his nails more intriguing than Turf's shame or his sparring partner's survival. Why had he spared her in the tree if only to let her go down before the council?

Grit glared at him. He raised his eyes to hers briefly before becoming engrossed once more in cleaning his fingernails. She had vague memories of him, at the age of twelve, standing stock still and dead silent on the offspring training field while Sire Stone circled him, watching for the least movement, the slightest indication of alertness. She'd heard rumors that her sire had required the impulsive boy under his training to give detailed, accurate, chronological accounts of each day's events.

*I wonder how much Coil of Dara has observed with no one noticing. None of the council members look at him, much less ask his opinion of my case. He's as insignificant to them as the dust beneath my boots. But perhaps that's his intent . . .*

"Can we reach a verdict? What do we do with the child now that she's failed her test?" Sage Brakken asked.

Sire Stone frowned. "I'm not convinced she has failed. Her capture occurred after midday, and she was on the Koradin-Thresh Highway. My child, Oath, has testified Grit kept one foot on the road until the hag lifted her into the air."

"Are we to trust the word of a thief? The entire village knows what that child is. Her word is unreliable at best, deceptive at worst." Pierce smirked at Dame Berth.

"Whether we accept her word or not, there's still the matter of whether her hunter acquired her by just means. Hunters aren't permitted outside assistance." Sire Stone leveled his gaze at Turf.

"Put her in the sparring circle. Let her fight warriors until she proves her worth or falls to her death," Sire Flex said.

"Imprisonment might suit her better," Sire Pierce said. "Lock her up with only the refuse of the village for food and drink."

Council members tossed about ideas for Grit's future, each suggestion less agreeable than the previous. The contest went on for several minutes while Grit sat quietly, studying the council members' faces. Only Berth and Sire Stone contributed nothing. The dame nodded or grunted at each plan of action, but committed to none. Turf stood beside her, arms folded. He, too, was quiet, though he whispered now and then into Dame Berth's ear. Sire Stone stood to the side, watching each speaker in turn. Coil appeared to be taking a nap.

"Historically, captured prey has become the possession of the victorious hunter." Sire Swot, a head shorter than Dame Berth, wrung his hands together.

"Ah, Swot, now I remember why we keep you on the council." Sage Brakken pointed a crooked finger at the unobtrusive man. "Every now and then, your unnatural fascination with history proves minimally useful. So you tell us she is her hunter's rightful possession?"

Dame Berth asked, "Who'd want such a shamed fool? I wouldn't give her the honor of licking my floor."

No one answered Berth. All eyes were trained to her left, and so she, too, turned to Turf. He glared at Grit with disgust, his lip curled into a sneer.

"I say we strap her to the top of one of those trees she likes to hide in and leave her there as an example to the babes of what happens to stupid children who lose sight of their goals and stop to help strangers."

Grit leaned forward, licked her cracked lips, and smiled at Turf. "Only if you do me the honor of tying me there yourself."

Grit sat back, immensely pleased with herself. None of the anxiety she suppressed seeped into her voice. Her smile widened, and she feigned a pleading tone. "Would you do that, Turf of Elna and Bord? Would you tie me to the highest branch? Or perhaps the better question is 'could you?'"

Turf nodded in Coil's direction. "Berry Boy would be more suited to the task, seeing how the two of you have spent so much time chasing each other around the treetops and all."

"Enough of this foolishness." Dame Berth stole a glance at Sire Stone. "In the absence of an uncontested victor, my final word as her dame is to insist on her banishment. If her sire concurs, there can be no more discussion."

Sire Stone held Berth's gaze a full minute, then nodded slowly. "It is acceptable to me."

"Then banishment it shall be." Sage Brakken leaned back in his chair. "Are there any objections?"

Sires Hawk and Palter squirmed, but neither objected.

"As a matter of procedure, does the second hunter have anything to contribute?" Sage Brakken asked. The council, Turf, and Grit turned toward Coil, whose head jerked up as if he'd just been startled from a light doze.

"Only this." Coil rose to his full height, but remained in front of his chair. "I request the record reflect I had parted ways with Turf of Elna and Bord days before the so-called capture occurred. I suspect the council will discover that individual to have made a cowardly and illegal alliance. I desire to sever all connection with him lest I be included in his inevitable shame."

"You realize by doing this, Coil of Dara, you surrender the honor that falls to you as Turf's co-hunter?" Sire Pierce asked.

"I don't believe his current honor will survive long. Let the record reflect all of this," Coil said.

A murmur of complacent consent arose as the council agreed to Coil's demand. Sire Swot scratched an official record on parchment.

"Well, there it is," Sage Brakken mumbled. "Coil of Dara forfeits today's honor to prevent tomorrow's shame, and Grit of Berth and Stone leaves the village. It's past midday now. She must be gone by this time tomorrow. I hunger. I'm going to find a meal."

Grit shook her head at Brakken. "That's right. Gorge yourself on the fat of Thresh. Whose pots shall you dip into today?" They were bold words, but she didn't care. What could Brakken do to her now?

He turned in the doorway, his gray eyes stern. "You are no longer of Thresh, little girl. Where I satisfy my appetite is no concern of yours."

He passed through the door with several council members in his trail.

"Shame to the rest of you, as well!" Grit didn't care if all of Thresh heard her accusations. "Stay and let me tell you about

Thresh's council of fools. Swot, your offspring's crippled dame walks with greater honor than you. Pierce, you vile man, let the damelings be. Can't you see they despise you? Stone, Stone, Stone . . . Surely it's a shameful man who sends his own offspring into exile."

Sire Stone stopped, but did not face her. "Be still, Grit, before you shame yourself."

"It's too late for that." Turf's dark eyes shone with satisfaction as Sire Stone continued out of the meetinghouse.

"Try not to climb too high in Brakken's esteem, Turf. He might eat you." Too disgusted to look at his ugly face, Grit stared out the open door.

At this hour, the curving dirt road brimmed with busy villagers. A few passers-by peered through the door and moved on. She gazed over their heads, waiting for the meetinghouse to empty. A curly, golden head blocked her view for a moment as Coil left the meetinghouse and ambled into the street. Only Turf and Dame Berth remained.

Grit rolled her shoulders. "Will someone untie me now, or am I to travel through Chasmaria bound hand and foot for the rest of my life?"

"It's tempting," Turf said.

Dame Berth elbowed him. "Untie her."

Grit stared out the open door. Turf twisted the rope around her wrists. The rough cords sawed into her flesh. He pulled them tight, tighter than necessary. The ropes slackened and fell away. A moment later, rope burned across her ankles. She felt the edge of his blade against her leg; she wouldn't kick him. Let him treat her harshly. He wouldn't get another chance, and she wouldn't let him see her pain. His blade cut through her bonds, but she remained still.

She did not rise until Turf and Berth had departed, nor did she look at her wounded wrists and ankles. When she stood, she walked straight out the door and into the gentle bustle of the street. Two proud steps later, she stopped. She had no idea how to spend the next twenty-four hours, let alone the rest of her life.

# SEVEN

G rit raised a hand to shield her eyes from the midday sun. Villagers hustled past the meetinghouse and down the long road that led out of Thresh. Young children darted through the crowd, heading to the sea or into the woods to fill their empty baskets with fish, mushrooms, and wild fruit. Older children conducted themselves with a sort of bravado, wielding swords, daggers, bows, and spears. In another year or so, the strongest and most fortunate of them would join their sires on the offspring training field. With any luck, they wouldn't spar each other for four years only to fail their tests because some of them can't honor the hunter's code.

She stepped into the street, narrowly missing a youth hurrying to the training fields. The quick-handed boy danced around a sour dame, relieving the distracted woman of her pockets' contents. Several pairs of boys squared off for spur-of-the-moment wrestling matches. One bold girl leapt onto a sturdy boy's back, threw her arms around his neck, and attempted to strangle him until he knocked her head against the wall of a nearby hut. She fell to the ground, laughing. Grit had seen the pair sparring on the training field. If Brakken pitted them against each other, would either let the other escape into the forest?

The dames watched, sometimes whispering to one another and sometimes barking instructions to their offspring. A few men walked the streets, but most were already in the training fields, sharpening their skills or awaiting their pupils. Grit stood in the middle of the street, soaking in her last taste of Threshan life.

Her head ached. She reached up to feel a crusty lump on the back of her head. *The wretched hag had a wheelbarrow. Where'd she come from? Where'd she go? All I remember is her mouth and that laugh . . .* It was like waking in the dead of night to the silence of forgotten dreams. Enlightened only by the sparse details she had learned through the council, she tried to piece together the events leading to this moment.

It was after midday on the sixteenth day. She hadn't left the highway's protection. She'd kept a foot on it; Sire Stone said Oath saw that much. So, she'd met the requirements of her test. Turf had no right to take her as captured prey. But he didn't take her, and she hadn't been captured. The hag had deceived her. Sire Stone said nineteen days had passed. Had it been three days since she saw the old woman? She was an idiot to have offered to help her in the first place. Why had she done that? Dame Berth was right; it was an infantile error. But who was that old hag, and how did Turf fit into all of this? Most pressing of all, what was Grit supposed to do now?

Only one thing was clear: Thinking hurt. Desperate for sleep, Grit traveled the familiar route to the Outer Ring. In a mental fog, she stood before Dame Berth's hut. Its sturdy mud walls supported a thatched roof. For all the woman's paltry meals, at least her roof never leaked. Grit paid little attention as Dame Dara passed her on the pathway to Dame Berth's door.

"Thieving scoundrel." Dame Dara hissed at Grit, never breaking her strident pace. The large bundle the dame carried under her arm bumped Grit, but she was too tired to care.

Dame Berth stood in the open doorway of her hut. "What do you want?"

Grit's eyes widened in disbelief. "What do I want? I've spent the last sixteen days fighting for my life and the last sixteen nights sleeping—if I slept at all—on earth and rock, ever on the alert for hunters, human or animal. Tomorrow I face more of the same. You ask what I want? I want a few hours of rest on the comfort of my own mat, fool woman!"

Berth glowered at her eldest offspring. "You have no mat in this hut."

Grit rolled her eyes and sighed in exasperation. "My mat. Just give me my mat. I'll take it somewhere else to sleep if you won't let me enter your rotten hut."

"The only mats in this superior hut belong to my youngest offspring. My eldest carried his mat to his sire's hut two weeks ago, right after his Twelfth Branding. I had an extra mat, but I just sold it to Dame Dara. Apparently, she expects to produce yet another urchin." Dame Berth crossed her arms.

Grit whirled around, but Dame Dara was nowhere in sight. Turning back to Berth, she narrowed her eyes. "You sold my mat to Dame Dara?"

"Oh, was it yours?" Dame Berth laughed. "I thought it belonged to an intolerable infant whose dame should have thrown her onto her sire's mercy at her first breath."

As Berth slammed the door, Grit realized with a sinking feeling that her dame had disowned her. Fifteen years and nineteen days past Grit's First Branding, Dame Berth left her offspring to the mercy of her sire. It meant nothing to Grit. She wasn't a babe who would perish if her sire rejected her as well. Yet *Grit of Stone* sounded so bare, so empty. It was bad enough to lose both her honor and her home. Berth might have left her name alone.

*Grit of Stone, Grit of Stone.* She tried to accustom herself to her new reality.

**** 

The wide expanse of grass on the south side of Thresh teemed with warriors and youth. Arrows whizzed through air, metal clashed against metal, and wood thudded against wood. The deep bellows of men, and of boys pretending to be men, rumbled over the fields, punctuated by the shrieks of raging girls and a few exceptionally fierce women. Sires and seasoned warriors walked among the combatants, harassing them into better form. The smell of sweat and blood hovered in the air above the fields.

Grit plodded westward along the edge of the warrior field, where older warriors practiced and sirelings and damelings vied for apprenticeships with the most renowned warriors. She fixed her gaze on two sirelings sparring skillfully in the corner of the warrior field. As she approached, the taller of the two held up a hand. His opponent lowered his sword and turned around.

"Ho, Grit!" The first sireling shook his shaggy brown hair out of his eyes. "I heard you're leaving, so I've stolen your partner."

Grit looked from the sireling to his sparring partner. "How unfortunate for you, Talon. I'm afraid Coil might kill you. It seems almost shameful to destroy the only solid thing Sire Swot ever produced, but there it is."

Talon blushed under his tanned skin, but did not respond to Grit's insult to his sire.

"He's in no danger. If anything should happen to Talon, I'd need to find a new sparring partner. With my luck, Turf of Elna and Bord would apply, and I'd have to shame my sword with his foul blood." Coil held his sword up and admired the thick blade. Touching its tip to Grit's chest, he said, "I wish you weren't going. My sword and I will be exceedingly bored in days to come."

Grit directed Coil's blade away from her heart. "You could always expose Turf's shame. Better yet, you could track down an old woman who can't handle her wheelbarrow and kill her. She's as much responsible for all of this as Turf."

Coil planted the tip of his sword in the earth and looked Grit in the eye. "I could and I will expose Turf as a coward, Grit, but I'm not sure Sire Stone would approve of the second part of your plan."

Grit snorted. "Sire Stone has never been wheeled unconscious into his village by a dishonorable hunter, though, has he? Believe me, the experience changes one's outlook."

Coil tapped his fingers on the hilt of his sword as he studied Grit with a stern expression. When he spoke, his voice came low and unflinching.

"I will bring down that wretched hag and any who stand in the way of my doing so. Talon has borne witness to many sparring matches. Now, he will bear witness to an alliance."

His eyes shone with wild energy. Grit's heart quickened.

Coil turned to the sireling at his side. "Talon of March and Swot, you've heard my vows to shame and destroy Grit's enemies. If I do not keep my word to Grit of Berth and Stone, she may pierce my heart with her dagger."

"What does Grit of Berth and Stone bring to this arrangement?" Talon asked.

What could she bring? What could she give Coil if he brought down Turf and the hag? She'd give her very blood to see the pair destroyed.

"Nothing." Coil scanned the warrior field, as if looking for an individual among the crowd. "It will be my pleasure to keep this vow. I've long anticipated Turf's fall, and my esteemed sword has acquired a taste for hag's blood."

"You will soak the earth with that woman's blood and number Turf among the lowest of Thresh's lowest?" Grit's fingers danced over her dagger's hilt as she studied Coil's face for any sign of faltering.

"I will give my very blood to bring them down, if that is what you wish."

"It is."

Talon frowned. "It's uncommon to vow aid without condition. In fact, it simply isn't done. Perhaps you might reconsider the terms of this alliance, Coil, as well as the possible outcomes."

"These are the only terms I offer." Coil ran an admiring hand along the central ridge of his sword. He spat in his hand and held it out to Grit.

With a solemn nod, Grit spat in her palm and gripped Coil's hand. "I accept all terms offered by Coil of Dara."

Talon shook his head. "I don't like it at all, but as I have borne witness to your sporting skirmishes, I now bear witness to your peculiar alliance. Coil of Dara will pour out his blood while Grit of Berth and Stone does nothing."

"You can stop using that name. I have no dame," Grit said.

Both Talon and Coil raised their eyebrows. Coil sheathed his sword.

"Berth disowned me." Grit dug her toe into the soft earth. Surely admitting it would get easier in time. "It's no big matter, so don't look so alarmed. I'm not the first to leave Thresh in shame. I wager I won't be the last."

Talon took a sharp breath, turned his head to one side, and studied Grit with his lips pursed.

Grit said, "What is it, Talon? Have I said something shocking? Stop looking at me like that."

"It's nothing. Just something I read last night, a story of sorts. It spoke of a time when the outcast would be freed from shame. There were other parts, darkness and blood and pain . . ."

"You should spend less time with your sire. You sound as befuddled as Swot. It hardly suits you. I'm tired and must speak with Sire Stone, in the chance he hasn't decided to disown me as well. Good luck with the hag, Coil. I want her blood to drench the earth."

Leaving the sirelings, Grit walked the perimeter of the offspring field, where sires trained twelve- to sixteen-year-old offspring in the arts of combat. In the middle of the field, her sire stood with his arms crossed in front of a black-haired boy of twelve who struggled with a sword too heavy for his young arms.

"Hmm. I think a lighter sword, Slate, or perhaps a dagger might suit you better." Sire Stone took the broadsword from his hands.

Over the boy's head, Sire Stone's gaze met Grit's. "Go, boy. Fetch a lighter weapon from the armory. Swing it around before you bring it back to make sure it balances well in your hand. This," he hefted the sword, "is ridiculously large for you. You must not think you are greater than you are when selecting a weapon, or you will fall by your own hand."

"But I will grow into it," Slate said.

"Not today, you won't. Now go."

Slate took the broadsword from his sire's outstretched hand. Fumbling with the heavy weapon and finally dragging it along the ground, he left for the armory without noticing Grit standing with her head bowed several feet behind him.

"Grit," Sire Stone said when Slate had gone. "Grit, meet my eye and speak to me."

She looked into her sire's bright, blue eyes.

"I would very much like to sleep, Sire Stone, but I am no longer afforded the privilege of a resting place."

"Berth has rejected you, then, has she?" Sire Stone clenched his square jaw.

"And sold my mat to Dame Dara."

"Well, that's just like Berth." He shook his head. "Never mind. Whatever the council says, I'm not entirely convinced my offspring failed her test. You'll stay in my hut. Here's the key. Go now and sleep. You look horrendous."

Grit trudged to Sire Stone's hut. With one hand on the timber doorframe, she slid the key into the lock and turned it until she heard a soft click. Pushing the heavy wooden door open, she entered the dim hut. A bed and one mat were the only sleeping accommodations. She couldn't take the bed. Offspring never did, and she didn't want to risk losing more of her name by offending Sire Stone. Slate's mat was as thin as she remembered it, but the blanket rolled inside was thicker than the one he'd used when he lived with Dame Berth. She rolled the mat out, pulled her sibling's blanket over her sore head, and slept.

# EIGHT

That evening, after eating well and conversing sparsely with Sire Stone and Slate, Grit wandered to the Western Sea. She stood on the rocky shore, contemplating the last nineteen days and planning her future. A gentle crunch of pebbles indicated the approach of another person.

"Have you come to mock me or kill me?" Grit asked. "It seems hunters these days don't exactly follow the rules."

"It doesn't concern you why I came. I just came," Coil answered.

Wave after wave stretched over the pebbled shore only to retreat to the sea. Grit tried to lose herself in the scents and sounds of the salty water, but Coil smelled of rosemary, and every breath he breathed stirred unformed questions from the darkest corners of her mind.

"Did you see me in the tree?" She couldn't look at him, for fear of finding answers she didn't dare to know.

Coil laughed bitterly. "Humph! I saw you, smelled you, could have reached out and dashed your little body to the ground."

"Then why didn't you?" Her tone was flat and detached, but her mind raced to word each question properly. "Why, when I was so firmly within your power, did you retreat? Had I told the council what I suspected, that you saw me and let me go, they would have spent the afternoon debating whether to banish you or label you Ineligible. Given their current blood thirst, you might have fared even worse. A hunter, silly Coil, never places himself within his prey's power. Why didn't you destroy me?'

53

Grit faced Coil, daring him to answer. She couldn't overlook his weakness in the tree, the folly by which he'd forfeited the honor of capturing his prey. In all their childish sparring, he never once relented until her dagger had hit its mark. She had to know why he let her escape.

Coil hesitated before answering, taking a deep breath and letting it out slowly. "It's quite simple. I hate him more than I hate you."

He sounded strange, as if he spoke of things deeper than the sea upon which he gazed. "I would rather have let you escape than share with Turf of Elna and Bord the honor of capturing the most capable prey in Threshan history, not that he hasn't claimed all the honor for himself anyhow."

He'd taken a risk, but for what? For pride? For some distorted sense of honor? It didn't seem to have helped either of them.

"You could have claimed me as your slave."

"I don't need my heels bit by a tethered dog. You know as well as I do that's what you'd have become." Coil faced her, an impenetrable expression on his face. "Have you decided what to do with your freedom?"

All harshness evaporated from her voice. "Yes. I'll follow the coast to the Southern Realm. It is warm now and will remain so for several months, but the winter chill will come eventually. I want half a chance of surviving it. I found a cave during my test. It's not far, but it's far enough from here. I'll camp there until I've regained my strength, and then continue south. Sire Stone agrees to the soundness of my plan. I haven't decided anything beyond reaching the Southern Realm. If it suits me, I may stay there. If it doesn't, I'll find some other place that does."

For the first time in years, either Coil held his tongue or he had no cruel comment to throw at her. They stood side by side, surveying the western horizon.

"While we are asking difficult questions, why didn't you betray me to the council?" Coil asked.

"I don't remember, but I must have had sound reason. Perhaps I didn't wish to destroy the only possibility of Thresh ever boasting a warrior worth fighting." She kicked at a pebble and gave Coil a sidelong glance. "That is, if you get over your little aversion to killing girls in trees."

Coil clenched his jaw. "So that's it? You simply wanted Thresh to have a warrior worthy of your blade?"

"What do you want me to say? This is foolishness, speaking of things that should never have happened. I've had a treacherous day, and my head throbs unbearably when I try to remember anything beyond the route to Sire Stone's hut. I don't want to think about my test, what you did or I did, or what either of us wants. None of it matters, Coil. I'm leaving."

As she turned to go, Grit's shoulder bumped Coil's. He grabbed her wrist.

"It doesn't have to be like this. You could stay."

His fingers were warm around her wrist. She stared at his hand. What was he doing? Did he really believe she could defy the council? He was a fool of the highest sort to behave like her leaving mattered. She wanted to pull her arm away, but it seemed a kind of weakness to draw back from him. She stood fixed on the spot, her arm relaxed in Coil's firm grip.

She looked into his agitated eyes. "Have you forgotten so soon? The great Sage Brakken has spoken."

"So defy him. Demand to fight the champion. You can beat Varlet. You're faster, and I know my sibling's weaknesses. Conquer him, and the council will have no choice but to let you stay. You can do this, Grit. You can make them let you stay."

She could not take her gaze from his. She had never seen him like this, so desperate for a foolish cause. "Perhaps I do not wish to stay."

He spoke so softly now she could just make out his words. "Then perhaps there are those in Thresh who would go with you."

"Anyone who'd go with me is a fool. We both know that. Let me go."

She yanked her arm away, but his grip had already loosened. They stood still, the only sound the sad lapping of the Western Sea.

"You may challenge the champion yourself. It will give you and your esteemed sword something to do when I am gone," Grit said.

Grit left him staring at the waves as they rippled over the pebbly shore, his thoughts as much a mystery to her as the depths of the ocean. Her head ached, but more painful was the realization of how little she understood. Her pace quickened with the agitation of her spirit.

She didn't believe he'd let her go to keep Turf from honor. Why hadn't she exposed Coil before the council? It might have won her some honor and secured her a place in Thresh. She had no reason to protect Coil. He was just a sparring partner, meant for nothing more than to sharpen one another's combat skills. Her duty to him didn't extend to her test, and certainly not to a trial before the council. She should have unveiled his cowardice. He had a chance at great honor and scurried away like a terrified mouse. That wasn't the Coil whose cheek she'd labored to slash a month before. If they knew he had protected her from Turf . . . And now he had urged her to fight to remain in Thresh and suggested he would accompany her into banishment. She'd never known him to be so weak.

*Why didn't I tell the council? Why does he urge me to fight? Does he mean he would go with me? Could I yet save myself from banishment? No, I don't wish to do that, but why . . . Why doesn't my head stop hurting?*

Such thoughts swirled through Grit's weary head as she walked up the path to Sire Stone's door. They continued as she crossed the threshold without acknowledging her sire, who opened the door. Her mind did not settle until she wilted onto the makeshift mat Sire Stone had made for her out of spare blankets. Her eyes closed as soon as she laid her head on her arm, and she slept soundly until dawn.

A night of deep and dreamless sleep served to alleviate Grit's distress. Her headache had diminished, and she could think clearly again. As a precaution, she steered her mind away from all memories of her test and the council, save those details of her forest ordeal that might aid her as she ventured forth. Rising from her mat, Grit willed herself not to think of golden curls and magenta berries.

As she ate the breakfast Sire Stone set before her, she planned her departure. She wouldn't wait until midday. She possessed nothing but the clothing she wore, plus the wooden bowl in her pocket and two daggers, her own and her Sire's Aid. She was ready to go.

"I'll leave when I'm through eating," she said to Sire Stone.

"So soon?" Sire Stone asked. "You have the entire morning to— "

"To do what? I've already packed what's mine." Grit patted her pocket.

Sire Stone swallowed his last mouthful of eggs. "If your mind is made up, I won't argue. Besides, I don't know what argument I could make. I don't see the sense in idling about, eit' er."

57

He rose from the table and crossed the room. He bent and folded the spare blankets on which Grit had slept, placing them in a neat stack against the wall. He held the last one in his arms.

Sire Stone held the blanket out to Grit. "Take it. I've heard rumors that Dame Dara, though she recently acquired an extra mat, is experiencing a dire shortage of blankets. I sincerely doubt she'll have any hanging on the line this morning."

"I doubt it also, Sire." Grit met her sire's eye with ease. She took the blanket. Its soft, thick warmth put to shame the rags under which she'd shivered in Dame Berth's hut. "Surely you don't mean for me to keep this."

"I'm sure you will use it well," Sire Stone said. Then, as if he did not wish to hurry time, he said "I suppose you will go now?"

"I have no reason to stay." It was true, but still her feet felt too heavy to move.

"Make haste to warmer regions then. I trust you will find more in banishment than you expect. It does not have to be a death sentence, Grit. Though it is the end of all you have known, it is also a beginning." His blue eyes glistened with tears, but he smiled as if he believed what he said.

Grit did not know how to answer these strange words. Hugging the blanket to her chest, she nodded. "I will abuse neither your aid nor your name."

She said no more, but nodded again to her sire as she left the hut. How strange to think she would never again see his face. Passing between his hut and Coil's, she headed out of Thresh. As she left behind the fence separating the Outer Ring from the training fields, Grit's posture grew increasingly straight and each step increasingly sure. Perhaps Sire Stone was right. If this was a beginning, she determined to make it a strong one.

# NINE

The sun rose steadily over the empty warrior field. Sparse tufts of grass sprinkled the well-trodden dirt.

"Grit!" A child's voice broke the morning silence.

A black-haired girl ran swiftly from the Outer Ring, clutching a bundle to her chest. Agile as a deer, she jumped with ease over tall clumps of grass at the edge of the warrior field.

"Oath," Grit said as her sibling came near. "What is that bag? Where's Seal?"

A mischievous giggle slipped form Oath's pink lips. "She's with Dame Berth, receiving another speaking lesson. Her silence irritates the dame to distraction this morning."

"Berth might as well attempt to beat a tree to speech as try to train Seal to talk," Grit said.

Seal's lack of speech had long infuriated the dame. When she delivered Oath into the world, Berth had sworn at the scrawny, mute babe. Minutes later, Seal had entered the world, screaming to be heard several huts away. When Berth held up the truculent infant to glare proudly into her newborn eyes, Seal had promptly and permanently shut up. She'd sealed her lips together and refused to open them except to nurse. The spiteful girl still refused to speak. Her thoughts, when shared, came to their hearers via Oath, who had learned to cry and to talk in the normal course of infant development. Oath alone knew Seal's mind, and the two often carried on silent conversations unheard by even the keenest of ears.

Grit eyed the leather bag in Oath's arms. "What about that? Where did you get it?"

"Oh! This is yours."

"How is it mine?" Grit accepted the bag from Oath's outstretched hand. Light for its size, it felt sturdy in her hands. She traced the intricate scrolling design of tangled vines carved into the bag's flap, and then opened the pack to peek inside. A small pink berry rolled into her hand. She dropped the flap and attended to Oath. She'd explore the bag's contents later.

"Coil told me to give it to you," Oath said.

"He didn't think you might keep it for yourself?"

Oath's bright blue eyes widened with pride. "He threatened to cut off my hands if he ever saw it in anyone's possession but yours—and to sew my lips together with twine if I ever told anyone he'd given you this."

"I bet he would do it, too. Did he say anything else?"

"Only one thing. He said . . ." Oath paused, as if to make certain she remembered the words correctly. "'To Grit.'"

\*\*\*\*

Once Grit reached the cover of the woods, she crouched and opened Coil's bag. She pushed berries aside, eating a few as they rolled out of the bag. It was full to the brim with berries—juicy, sweet, healing berries.

A smile flickered at the corner of Grit's mouth as she remembered Coil walking through the village, the entire left side of his face pink with berry juice. His hair, too, had been smeared with pink, and she had not neglected to mock him for it. She had slashed him well earlier that day, but thanks to Coil's steady diet of berries and his liberal smearing of berry juice over the wound, her dagger's mark healed completely by the week's end. She wasn't sure how the berries worked, only that they did. Coil's wounds never failed to heal quickly and given time, completely, ever since he'd discovered the berries in some secret corner of the forest.

60

Through the trees, Grit could see the village. She could still go back to betray Coil to the council or to let him come with her. He might prove useful in the forest. But no, it was utter foolishness to think like that.

After indulging in a few more berries, she closed the bag and set off in search of the cave she'd rejected on the second night of her test. It was not difficult. She didn't retrace her erratic path of nearly three weeks prior, but walked due south, marking familiar sights to keep herself on the correct trail. She might go an hour without recognizing anything, only to notice a rock shaped like a miniature hut or an elm bending just so. In two days, Grit found the cave. She ate a few handfuls of berries before she entered the cave, unrolled the blanket Sire Stone had given her, and went to sleep.

For two weeks, Grit's mind and body recuperated from the rigors of her test and the reality of her exile. She was on her own. Dame Berth's roof would no longer cover her head. There would be no Seal or Oath to forage for their meals. No more Sire Stone to train her. No Coil to spar or to race to the Western Sea. She slept more than she had in her life, stretching out on a mat of leaves as soon as the sun set and often rising when a new day's sun shone high in the sky. During her wakeful hours, she ate berries and whatever else she could forage or kill. Sometimes she caught a fish in a nearby stream; twice she pounced upon rabbits and treated herself to a hearty meal. With no hunters to fear, she built a fire. It wasn't cold at this time of year, but a fire could cook small game and keep wild animals away. Tending it kept her mind busy when she wasn't sleeping.

One bright, moonlit night, dreams of a golden-haired sireling disturbed Grit's slumber. He was chasing her to the sea She dove into the water, but it was warm, not cold.

She woke in a sweat. Throwing aside her blanket, she walked into the clear air outside the cave. She sat on a log before the fire, stoking the flames until they rose and crackled in the quiet night. As she watched the dancing flames, Grit forced her mind to empty of all her past experiences. She willed her memories into the middle of the fire and imagined the flames consuming them, one by one, until every last memory of Thresh wafted away in the fire's smoke. There went Turf and his taunting sneer, Dame Dara with her unjustified disdain, Sage Brakken, Sires Pierce and Swot. Sire Stone struggled to remain in her memory, circling her with an approving eye during her last training session. Slate, Seal, Oath, Talon . . . All of them into the fire and gone. Grit clenched her teeth and drew her dagger.

There was Dame Berth, easing her dagger from its sheath and placing it in Grit's hands after her Twelfth Branding. *"Use it honorably. This weapon wasn't meant for spineless babes."*

Grit twirled the dagger between her fingers and aimed for the fire. Her arm swung to rid herself of Dame Berth, but at the last moment, her hand wrapped tightly around the dagger. *It's my dagger, not hers. I won't throw away what's rightfully mine.* She sheathed her dagger and willed Dame Berth into the fire.

Yet there were some memories that refused her attempts to cast them into the flames, and no amount of screaming, "To Grit!" would compel them into the fire. Coil would not abdicate his place in her memory, and all Grit's efforts to dethrone him served only to reinforce his position.

Coil waited in the meetinghouse, among the throng gathered for her Sixth Branding. He scowled over Dame Berth's fence, telling Grit she'd planted the potatoes all wrong. He laughed on the training field, raising a sword too large for his thirteen-year-old frame and daring her to nick him with the dagger she'd just inherited. He lingered in every corner of

Thresh, challenging her to race him to the Western Sea. And he was in the Western Sea, his jubilant face turned toward the sun, his arms stretched out, his body unguarded.

"To Grit! To Grit! To Grit!" Her throat burned from the refrain, but still Coil was in her tree, his hands inches from her feet, declaring his prey had escaped.

In a rage, Grit threw her stick against a tree, dumped the contents of her pack, Coil's pack, and ran to the creek that passed near her cave. Her knuckles scraped against the rocky creek bed as she pulled the pack through the water.

"To Grit, to Grit, to Grit . . ." she muttered as she doused her fire.

Her fingers bleeding, she crammed her blanket into the still dripping bag and stomped into the moonlit night, leaving behind her home of two weeks.

Grit screamed to the glowing moon. "I am done with Thresh! Done, done, done!"

# TEN

After leaving the cave and the still smoldering fire, Grit hiked with increased urgency toward the Southern Realm. She needed to reach warmer regions in time to build a durable shelter, perhaps even a crude hut, before the summer's end. At times, her resolute feet traced the undulating coast of the Western Sea. Where the coast curved outward, she traveled through the forest until she reached the sea where it curved inward once again toward the east. Always, she maintained a steady pace, her eyes scanning her surroundings while her mind plotted her next steps. As she had done during her test, Grit stopped only to eat or sleep when hunger or fatigue threatened to overtake her body.

At midday on the twenty-first day, Grit came upon a promontory. A narrow strip of land jutted into the sea, rising high above the water. Grit weighed her options and decided to go over the small peninsula. Climbing at an angle, she headed for the lowest point, where the slope appeared least severe. After several falls and a few scrapes against the rocky earth, she reached the top.

She stood a moment, aching hands resting on her hips. Trees covered the promontory, the late afternoon light filtering through their leaves. A gentle breeze swelled from the sea to brush against Grit's sweaty face, and soft grass stretched from the edge of the trees to cushion her blistered feet. Grit took a deep breath and inhaled that warm, evocative fragrance unique to the sea.

*But there is something else, too. Something in this air smells not of earth and sea, but of food and of . . . of . . . of something almost familiar, if only I could place it.*

She entered the forest slowly, all senses on alert. The sweet fragrance filled her nostrils, accentuating the emptiness of her stomach even as the colors around her seemed to brighten. The air blew warm and gentle across her skin, tickling the hairs on her arms. As she drew nearer to the source of the fragrance, her mouth watered, and her insides ached. Breathing in the irresistible air, she half believed she might gain sustenance from the fragrance alone.

This food, for surely it was food, was like nothing she'd ever smelled before, fuller and more satisfying than anything she'd known in Thresh, with a hint of that one familiar thing she couldn't quite remember. She pressed on, determined to discover the source of the fragrance and satisfy her hunger through trade or treachery. As she possessed little, and none of it of any value, she wrapped her hand around her dagger's hilt and made her way through the trees.

The delicate aroma grew to enfold Grit, so that she could not turn without catching its sweetness, and she noted another odd sensation. A bubbly chatter, similar to the sounds the chickens made, but higher and lighter and full of something she couldn't describe, beckoned to her. She inched forward, following both fragrance and sound. Entering a small clearing in the woods, she stopped, blinking at the sight before her.

A man who appeared to be somewhere in his late twenties rose from a magnificent chair at the head of a table spread with every savory dish Grit could imagine, and many delicacies she couldn't begin to describe. He opened his arms to welcome her.

"Grit, at last you arrive! I've been waiting for you."

Above the aroma of the food, Grit detected the fragrance she had tracked to this clearing emanating from the man. His light brown hair hung around dark eyes that studied Grit with a peculiar interest, half daring and half begging her to approach. When he spoke, a cloud of small, brightly colored birds settled each on the back of one of the many chairs spread on either side of the table. They left the seat opposite the stranger empty and seemed to look in turns from the man to Grit. Unsettled by the little creatures, as well as by the multitude of imposing birds of prey perched around the clearing, Grit looked from the birds to the man.

"Please, none of the birds will harm you. Take your chair and dine. You must be famished," he said.

Grit slid her dagger from its sheath. "Who are you?"

"I'm Kinsmon," he said as if it explained everything. He indicated the birdless chair across from him. "Please, take your seat."

"How do you know my name?" Her fingers danced on the hilt of her dagger as her eyes scanned the table. A knife, a heavy goblet, a fork . . . any of these might serve as a weapon if her dagger proved insufficient.

His lips turned up in a slight smile. "Grit of Berth and Stone, named after the grain of sand that infested your poor dame's shoe, you have much to unlearn. Long before your dame named you in spite, I named you in love."

For an instant, the man appeared much older, perhaps as old as Sage Brakken. Grit blinked, and he again resembled a young sire.

He said, "We may discuss that later, though. First, will you feast with me?"

Emptiness gnawed at her stomach. She glanced at the small loaf of bread at the end of the table nearest her. She could finish it off in ten bites if she could get her hands on it. "How do I know it isn't poison? How do I know your food will not burn away my insides and utterly destroy me?"

"Your question is no surprise. You are not the first to ask this question, nor will you be the last." Kinsmon's carefree tone contrasted sharply with Grit's fierce gravity.

He grew serious, leaning forward with his hands on the table and studying Grit through dark, fathomless eyes. He shook his head slowly. "My food is not poison, Grit of Berth and Stone, but it will consume you, burning away and utterly destroying all you think you are. That's generally the first consequence of my feast, but it is not the last."

He continued in a kinder tone. "The most remarkable result of consuming what I offer is for you to discover yourself, if you have the courage to do so. I will tell you no more at present, except that the ultimate consequence of dining with me defies your current, sorely limited comprehension of what is beneficial. My food is good, Grit, the most nourishing you will ever ingest. Will you sit now?"

"What if I took just one bite? To test it?"

Grit sheathed her dagger, but kept her hand over the hilt. Something about Kinsmon's manner relaxed her, though her senses remained on alert. She swallowed the saliva that had pooled in her mouth.

"You could take one bite. Others before you have attempted to make this bargain with me. Most who request just one taste remain to feast fully. Those who walk away after one bite, I must caution you, meet with one of two dismal futures. Either they savor my food, never quite forgetting its flavor, and yearn to taste it once more . . ."

"Or?" Grit leaned forward to hear Kinsmon's voice as it quieted, her gaze fixed on his wistful face.

"Or their fearful mouths spit out my food and they grow so bitter, angry, and hateful, they destroy everything in their paths," Kinsmon said.

"But," Grit said with slow, quiet confidence, "is that not a life of honor, to destroy that which would deter one from one's goal?"

Kinsmon shook his head and sighed. "Oh, Grit of Berth and Stone, who has woefully much to unlearn, there's no honor in destruction. In time, you'll come to understand this truth. Today, however, I ask you only to sit and feast with me. Will you do so now or must you parry longer? Have you the courage to dine with me?"

In the pink light of coming evening, Grit's gaze circled the clearing and settled on the table. It was a feast beyond compare, yet it came with a warning. The flame of challenge burned in Kinsmon's brown eyes, sending a message Grit recognized instinctively and embraced in the very core of her being. Behind the challenge, however, she detected a foreign twinkle.

"Am I bound to you if I eat, or will I be free to go when the meal is over?" she asked.

"Hmm." Kinsmon sat back in his chair and crossed his arms. "Yes and yes. But you are stalling, Grit. We could discuss every possible outcome of your decision until morning, but when you get around to deciding whether to accept or decline my offer, it comes down to one question: Have you the courage to believe I will help you and not harm you?"

Kinsmon rested his chin in his hand and studied Grit as she searched his face. No duplicity showed in his determined expression, only a willingness to wait as long as he must for her to decide. He refused to tell her everything she wanted to know, but no malice accompanied his reticence. She'd be a fool to place herself at the mercy of a stranger again; the hag taught her that much. But Grit couldn't resist Kinsmon's table. It was more than weariness, more than hunger. Kinsmon issued a challenge, and she would not be found wanting courage.

LISA DUNN

"I have such courage and more." Her hand dropped from her dagger to her side. Then, because she did not want him to think he persuaded her of anything, she said, "Anyway, I'm famished."

"Then sit, dear girl, and feast." Kinsmon's entire countenance shone with a strange brilliance.

To her amazement, the watching birds took flight all at once. Circling Kinsmon, they next flew to the chair he had offered her. Moving like twenty-four feathery hands, the brightly-colored birds lit on the chair's back and arms and together slid the chair away from the table.

Grit lowered herself into the chair without taking her gaze from the rainbow of feathers. She swatted at one that flew near her head. "What are these creatures? I've never seen anything like them."

Kinsmon's eyebrows raised slightly. "You have not seen many things, growing up in Thresh as you have. Besides vultures and chickens, you have in that region, if I am not mistaken, few birds other than ravens, crows, and the occasional sparrow. Am I correct so far?"

Grit nodded and shifted in her seat. How did he know she was from Thresh?

"Why do you think that is, Grit? Why, when birds are so many and varied, do so few frequent your village? Think, girl. What do you do if, say, a sparrow flutters across your path?"

"Shoo it away, naturally."

"Why? What has the sparrow done? What do you expect it to do?"

Grit stared at him, remembering Dame Berth's explicit instructions on the appropriate treatment of birds, *"You must at all expense keep them at a distance."* Nothing in her experience explained Dame Berth's urgency to keep the birds at bay. She cocked her head at Kinsmon.

70

"I don't know. All the dames tell of chickens pecking children, ravens and crows stealing bread, and vultures bringing death, but I don't remember them ever doing more damage than making away with a crumb or two. Frankly, I don't think they are as bad as all that."

Kinsmon half smiled. "You are on your way to understanding why you've never seen anything like these creatures. You begin to see how irrational apprehension has chased beauty from your village. From birth, fear has held you. It has imprisoned you and still imprisons many in Thresh, Chasmaria, and beyond. Until now, fear has been your governor. I intend to acquaint you with a fairer master. But I forget myself . . . Let us eat."

He motioned to the birds, which fluttered about filling his and Grit's plates with delicious morsels of food. Grit marveled at both the nimble servers and the repast they delivered. Plump fruits, crisp vegetables, soft bread. Fish with a creamy sauce drizzled from a silver ladle held in the beak of a golden bird. Inhaling the table's mingled aromas, she watched the gravy fall. A spectral memory, not fully dispersed by the cave's fire, revived.

Grit remembered the small hen, watching as she dipped her finger into the hollow hilt of the dagger Sire Stone had given her. She saw her finger, moving ever so slowly toward her nostrils. She smelled the sweetness of the dagger's salve as if it were present with her still.

With a start, Grit looked across the table. Kinsmon was smiling, his attention fixed upon her upper right arm. How could it be? That sweet, exotic fragrance she had followed to this place was that of the ointment in her Sire's Aid. *What is this man?*

"Go ahead, Grit," Kinsmon said. "Enjoy."

He cut a piece of fish with his fork, speared it, and lifted it to his mouth. Grit followed his example, letting the fish fall apart in her mouth before chewing and swallowing. They dined in silence, Kinsmon devouring the meal with relish as Grit savored each cautiously taken bite. From time to time, she stole a glance at Kinsmon. Was it possible he wouldn't harm her?

Midway through the meal, a fierce looking bird flew into the clearing and perched on Kinsmon's chair. Grit dropped her fork and picked up her knife.

With a grave expression, Kinsmon watched the eagle fly to rest on a high branch. Two more raptors, a falcon and a hawk, joined the roost within minutes.

"You keep a dreadful number of birds." Grit set her knife beside her plate.

"They are only dreadful to the fearful."

"Humph!" Grit bit the end of the loaf she'd spied earlier. "One needn't be afraid to think that's too many birds for one clearing. Why do you need so many, anyway?"

"Birds, like people, have many gifts if you take the time to nurture them." Kinsmon poured a magenta liquid from a silver pitcher into two matching goblets. When he finished, a pair of turquoise birds lifted one goblet by its handles and carried it to Grit, setting the goblet onto the table before flying to join their peers in the trees.

Kinsmon gestured toward the pitcher. "My special brew. I think you'll find it quite to your liking."

As he raised his goblet to his lips, Grit peeked into hers. The still surface of the liquid reflected nothing in the fading light. She wrapped a hand around each of the curved handles and lifted the goblet, swirling its contents. She glanced at her host, who considered her over the rim of his cup. Resolutely, Grit touched the goblet to her bottom lip and tipped the thick liquid into her mouth. It rushed over her tongue, flowed against her cheeks, and tingled down her throat as she swallowed. Its exquisite flavor called forth smothered memories of a pinkish-blond sireling. Grit slammed her goblet down and spat on the table.

"What is this beverage?" Her spit formed a dark pink circle on the white tablecloth.

"Do not be afraid to think of home, Grit."

"Home?" Grit said with a snort. "I have left Thresh behind. From now on, home is wherever I find myself."

Kinsmon sipped from his goblet. "Foolish talk does not suit you. Let another claim his home is wherever he finds Grit of Berth and Stone. As for you, your home shall be where I send you."

"Where you send me?" Grit shoved her plate away, knocking over her goblet. Juice spilled from the cup, engulfing the circle of spit. Grit rose to her feet and glared at Kinsmon. "You said I would be free to go. When you said I would be bound to you, I didn't realize you meant to make me your slave."

"Heavens, no, dear girl! You are not my slave, but my heart and hands. You're irregular and clumsy now, I grant, but trust me, you'll grow into yourself. Please, do calm down. I mean you no harm, Grit, only goodness. Here, I have something for you."

Kinsmon rose from his chair and walked around the table to stand before Grit. He leaned back to sit on the edge of the table and pulled something out of his pocket. He held the item in his hand, gazing at it in silence before lifting a thin thread of gold from his palm. On the delicate chain hung a small white sphere, shimmering in the light of the candles the birds had lit midway through the meal. Grit gaped at the orb.

"I . . . It's . . . I . . ."

73

"The word you seek is 'beautiful.'" Kismon let out a quiet laugh and dangled the iridescent sphere close enough for Grit to caress it between her thumb and fingers.

"This is for you, Grit of Berth and Stone. I told you I named you in love. I do not lie. This is a pearl. In the seas at the southernmost tip of the Southern Realm live oysters, similar to the clams found near Thresh. When a small fleck of sand insinuates itself into the oyster's shell, the oyster secretes a substance to surround the sand and so alleviate the discomfort inflicted upon it by the tiny grit. It continues to secrete this substance, eventually forming the thing of beauty at which you now marvel."

He leaned forward to secure the gold chain around Grit's neck. She gazed at the pearl, rolling it in her fingers, as Kinsmon went on. "You, dear Grit, are like that tiny grain of sand. You are a spur in the flesh of Chasmaria, but I promise, great beauty will emerge from your trials. All Chasmaria will be made lovely. As you hold the pearl in this moment, so tenderly and surely, so hold this promise always."

Kinsmon's voice had dropped to a melancholy whisper. He stood and placed a gentle hand on Grit's right arm. "If you will stay, the birds have prepared a tent for you. Rest well. When you rise tomorrow, if you choose to travel with me, I will shelter you in the Southern Realm."

# ELEVEN

G rit stood in the center of the tent Kinsmon had prepared for her, taking in every detail of her surroundings by soft candlelight. The square, white tent was clean; too clean. Grit lifted her foot off the white canvas stretched tight over the ground. She'd scuffed it. What did Kinsmon expect, sending a muddy traveler into his pristine tent?

A chair stood in one corner, and a small table beside a cot held a pitcher of water, a cup, a bowl, and a silver-handled mirror. Grit sat on the edge of the cot. Its softness surprised her, and she laid herself down, taking care to leave her boots hanging over the cot's edge. Lying with her face pressed against the smooth, fresh sheet, she feared she might spoil the fine linen. She stood and paced. *I don't belong in the tent of a wealthy stranger. He'll likely murder me as I sleep.* She felt for her dagger at her hip, withdrew it from its sheath, and spun it around with deft fingers. *I'll kill him first, if it comes to that.*

The light of the candle reflected off the silver mirror on the table. Grit leaned forward and blew the candle out with a huff. In the darkness, she removed her pack, opened it, and slid the silver mirror into the middle of Sire Stone's blanket.

She had no personal need of a mirror, but if she found a buyer, she might sell it for a large sum. She perched on the edge of the chair and waited in the darkness for the hour when she was certain Kinsmon, in his tent across the clearing, would have succumbed to sleep.

At last, Grit rose and slung her pack over her shoulder. Drawing back the tent flap, she peered into the moonlit clearing. All was still and quiet. She stuck one leg out of the tent and then the other, keeping her gaze fixed on Kinsmon's tent. She backed into the cover of the trees surrounding the clearing. Above, an owl hooted. Grit nearly dropped her pack. *Fool birds.*

She scanned the area, squinting for a better view of Kinsmon's tent. Noticing neither motion nor noise from the campsite, she turned and scurried through the woods, her soft step barely audible even to her well-trained ears. As she emerged from the forest on the southern side of the promontory, a narrow strip of grass stretched between the tree line and the steep slope to the Western Sea.

A warm breeze, rich with salt, blew across the peninsula. Below, the waves crashed against the shore. High above, tiny points of brilliant silver pierced the infinite darkness.

"Have you ever tried to count them?"

Grit jumped, startled by Kinsmon's voice. She clutched her dagger as she spun to face him.

He sat in the shadows, reclining with his back against the trunk of an old oak. She stared at him, waiting to discern his features more clearly.

"Well, have you?"

Grit slid her dagger into its sheath. "Have I what?"

"Ever tried to count the stars." His voice swelled with the cadence of the waves, washing over her and soothing her aching soul.

"Why would I do that?"

"To find out if you can."

She looked into the endless darkness, her gaze darting from one star to the next. "Utter foolishness. Of course I can't. No one can."

"I can." Kinsmon sat forward and hugged his knees. "I named them, too, you know. Long ago, I named each star and every constellation. That group there . . ." He pointed. "No, to your left, Grit. That group is called The Hunter."

Seven stars shone more brightly than the rest. Grit shifted her pack, dug her toe into the soft earth, and turned her gaze to the sea. She no longer cared for stargazing.

"Yes, I named your hunter, too." There was a hardness in his voice now. Grit drew in her breath and waited for the pain in her chest to pass. "Don't think I don't know all about Coil of Dara."

Grit faced Kinsmon, thankful for the darkness that hid the heat rising in her cheeks. "What do you know of Coil of Dara? And how dare you speak his name to me?"

"I know he was not named for his incessant movement, but for the strength he possesses in his stillness, for the power that grows in his soul when placed under pressures that would cause others to bend, to crack, to break."

He waited, but Grit did not respond. She did not wish to acknowledge her memories of Coil of Dara.

"I speak his name because you need to hear it. Coil of Dara made a vow to you."

"It means nothing." Grit clenched her jaw to keep from speaking more. Who did Kinsmon think he was, to speak as if he knew so much? She looked over the Western Sea and focused her eyes and mind on the moonlight reflected on the waves.

Kinsmon stood beside her now, just a few feet away. She could hear his slow breaths, smell his peculiarly sweet fragrance. She stepped away, not wanting to be ensnared by his kindness. He felt like something close, like home at day's end or the comfort of a familiar smell, but he was new and foreign, too. He was a stranger, and she would not put herself at his mercy.

"The darkness is great, Grit of Berth and Stone, but there will always be points of light. Though clouds may veil the stars so you cannot perceive their light, still they shine as brilliantly as ever. But go. Flee to the south, far from Coil and Thresh and all who have disappointed you. When you reach Port Colony, go to Fellows Inn on Market Street and ask for Harth. Tell her Kinsmon sends you. She will fill your stomach and give you a bed for the night."

Grit refused the urge to look at him. "Why should I follow your directions? Why do you suppose I'm heading to Port Colony? I'll go . . . I'll go . . ." She pictured Sire Swot's map of Chasmaria and settled on the country's southernmost tip.

"Why should you follow my directions?" Kinsmon's soft laugh was like music in the dark, conjuring images in Grit's mind of glorious things yet unseen. "In this situation, dear Grit, you should follow my directions because to do otherwise would be a useless waste of a good mirror."

He squeezed her shoulder and, without another word or a backward glance, retreated into the forest.

Grit remained on the promontory's edge a full ten minutes, first taking steps toward the forest, and then moving to the very precipice. There, she turned and stared into the trees until all traces of Kinsmon had vanished. She hiked her pack further up on her back and began the slow climb down the promontory's southern edge. A quarter of the way down, her dagger's sheath caught on a protruding rock. Grit cursed softly.

"I should have killed him," she muttered. "Killed him and filled my pack with food."

Her heart, however, did not wholly agree.

# TWELVE

Grit traveled southward from the promontory, following the curve of the shore. By early afternoon, sweat dripped down her back. She shed her linen tunic, revealing a black undershirt. As she tucked her tunic into her pack, she gazed upon her bare, unscarred arm. Sixteen brands, all gone. She glanced about the empty beach, discomfort creeping into her heart. *What have I to show for sixteen years of life?* A gentle wind blew across the beach, cooling her sweat-dampened skin. She turned from the sea and the memories carried on its breeze.

"Humph!" She hoisted her pack onto her back. "If anyone doubts my strength, it'll be their folly, not mine."

She put her flask to her lips and tipped it to the sky, but only a drop of water fell onto her parched tongue. Somewhere ahead—it couldn't be too far—was a river. She marched forward, set on finding the river as quickly as possible.

Within an hour, she spied the river in the distance and angled her course into the woods to meet it further from the sea. When she reached the river, she knelt on its bank with cupped hands, lifted a handful of cool water to her mouth, and drank.

"Ugh!" Again and again she spat, trying to rid her mouth of the stinging salt. She kicked her pack, propelling it toward the river. Just before it fell into the swirling water, she scooped it up and tumbled onto the soft grass, hugging the pack to her chest.

"This is foolishness, all of it." She moved her cheeks in and out in a vain effort to produce enough saliva to ease the salt sting and quench her thirst. "Utter foolishness. I'm going to find water."

She rose and tromped eastward, stopping every half mile or so to test the water, careful only to taste a drop at a time. An hour inland, the river ran fresh. After gulping from her cupped hands, Grit filled her flask.

She fastened the cap and surveyed the forest. Two figures approached from the east. Grit shoved her flask into her pack and darted from the riverbank. The figures hastened toward her, one several paces ahead of the other. It would be just like Brakken to send hunters after her, even in her exile.

She looked into the needled foliage of the tree against which she stood. It would have to do. She wrapped her hands around the lowest branch and lifted herself into the tree. She climbed quickly, shutting from her mind the memory of her last time in a tree. *Coil is not here to chase me. Or to spare me.*

"Wait, Zag!"

The first figure, a dark-haired boy not much older than Slate, stopped beneath Grit's tree. He whirled on the child who had called his name.

"We haven't time for dallying, Peril. The village burns, boy. Quicken your pace."

Grit sniffed the air. A trace of smoke mixed with the scent of pine.

"But I'm hungry. I lost my basket when the army came."

"Quit whining. I'm hungry, too." Zag turned and marched westward.

As Peril passed beneath the tree, Grit shifted her pack. A small bundle of scraps she'd stolen from Kinsmon's table remained of her provisions. One hand released the tree and clutched the strap of her pack. The boys would survive. If they didn't, more shame to the dame who bore them. Grit had no duty to them.

"I don't want to leave." The younger boy dropped his hands to his sides and glanced back the way they'd come.

"Keep moving. I don't want to die."

Blond head bowed, the younger boy followed his companion away from Grit's tree. As they disappeared from sight, she climbed higher.

Smoke rose in the east, darkening the late afternoon sky. A mounted army circled the smoldering village, trampling or swinging broadswords at any villagers who tried to escape. Inside the village, men, women, and children tossed buckets of water on flaming huts, their anxious cries muffled by distance. Between the forest and the village, a helmeted man observed the scene astride a giant white horse. A petite woman on a nervous pony watched at his side. She arched her back and turned in her saddle. Her gaze swept the treetops and fixed on Grit's tree.

As the branch upon which Grit stood swayed with the wind, she hugged the trunk tighter. Was this how Turf, coward of cowards, felt in a tree?

Though too distant to distinguish more than the vague lines of the woman's face, Grit stood transfixed, her awareness of the branch beneath her feet giving way to an overpowering sense of the woman's presence. Grit closed her eyes and clung to the trunk, the edges of the pine bark cutting into her palms and scraping against her cheek. *You cannot see me, woman. You cannot see me.* She opened her eyes. The woman's attention had turned to the village. Grit remained in the tree, mind alert and limbs trembling.

As darkness fell, the village quieted. The man spurred his snow-white horse to a trot and rode through the shattered village gate, and the woman followed on her pony. The army ceased its circling and fell in behind the pair. Amidst a shower of pine bark, Grit shimmied down the trunk. She rubbed her palms on her thighs. Splintered bark pressed into her skin.

The moon shone brightly as she stood on the edge of the riverbank. From this low vantage point, Grit could not see the village, nor, she hoped, could the woman see her. She heaved her pack across the river. It landed with a thump on the far back. Triumph surged through Grit's spirit, and she lowered herself into the river. The water soothed her aching body. She opened her mouth to relieve her thirst, then dove beneath the surface and kicked off from the sloping riverbed.

*South again.* She resisted the river's westward pull. Her arms cut through the water, propelling her toward the distant bank.

****

It had been Talon's idea to pull out the maps. Sire Swot had shown them the chasm-cut mountains rising in the northwest, arcing almost to the eastern border of Chasmaria before turning and sweeping back down to the southwest. Swot knew nothing of the Southern Realm, but he knew of Port Colony. The city sat on the coast of the Western Sea midway between the Southern Realm and Thresh. It was a busy city, filled with traders and swindlers, and the people of Thresh had no need of it.

Grit was no longer of Thresh. Her body poorly rested and her last morsels of food consumed for breakfast, she traipsed southwest through the forest. So what if Kinsmon was right about her going to to Port Colony? She'd find the city, benefit from its bounty, and be gone. Near midday, she reached the Western Sea and continued along its shore. Late afternoon, she spied the outline of a massive city that seemed to crawl from the water into the rolling, inland hills.

With renewed vigor, Grit jogged south, arriving in the city near the dinner hour. The sights, sounds, and smells of Port

Colony overwhelmed her as she walked through the crowded streets of Middle Chasmaria's largest city. Booths heaped with fruits, vegetables, meats, cloths, and house wares lined the streets. Dirty vendors guarded anything one might wish to possess, awaiting only the proper payment to release the goods. They cried out to passersby, hoping to make customers of strangers. The fragrance of savory foods mixed with the odors of waste running in the gutters and stench wafting from unclean bodies. It was like the Inner Ring's market huts, amplified a thousand fold and soaked in the dregs of a hundred villages' waste heaps.

As she passed a stall loaded with fruit, Grit placed her hand over a shiny, red apple. Her hand fit perfectly around the fruit. She ran her tongue over her front teeth. They'd fit perfectly into the apple's side. Her mouth watered in anticipation. She glanced to either side. The vendor, a plump man wearing a shimmering violet shirt, was bargaining with a customer.

Grit stood a moment longer, her hand resting on the apple. Then she slid both hands into her pockets and strolled away with drooping shoulders.

"Thief!"

Following the cue of all around her, Grit turned to look back the way she had come. The fruit seller shrieked, "Thief!" over and over again. His fat, shaking finger pointed straight at her.

She drew her hands from her pockets and held them at shoulder level. "Why do you scream at me, old man? I have nothing that belongs to you."

"Grab her!" He shouted to someone on Grit's left.

A muscular man advanced. Grit ran, crouched over to duck between the people blocking her escape. Thick hands encircled her waist, hoisted her off her feet, and twisted her body midair.

Her stomach lurched as she fell onto his broad shoulder. The guard wrapped a rock-hard arm around her body, pinning her arms to her sides.

"Let me go!" Grit kicked at the man's thighs. When her screams and her feet failed to secure her release, she sank her teeth into his sweaty back.

"Oh, but you're a lively one!" The man laughed and tightened his grip around her body.

Grit turned her head and spat on his stubbly cheek. He set her down in front of the fruit vendor's stall. He remained behind her, his arm hooked around her neck to prevent her from bolting.

"What'd she snatch?"

"Check her pockets, Vell," the vendor said.

Grit scowled as from behind, her captor reached his free hand into one pocket and then the other. He fumbled as the leather band around his wrist caught on the hilt of her dagger.

"Touch my dagger again, even by accident, and I won't hesitate to plant it in your heart," she said, her voice low and menacing.

The big man's breath was hot on her ear, but he was careful to avoid her dagger as he took his hand from her pocket. "You're in no position to bargain, girl."

In his right hand, Vell held the apple Grit had stolen. The gathered crowd glared at Grit. They would not come to her aid, but Kinsmon's silver mirror might.

Grit did her best to nod with Vell's arm still around her neck. "That swindler should pay closer attention to his customers. Had he not been so busy trying to cheat that other fool . . ." She jerked her head toward the customer with whom the vendor had been arguing. " . . .He would have received full payment and more for his rotten fruit. I'll pay still, if you'd be so kind as to grant me access to my pack."

Vell released her from his chokehold, but stood ready to pounce if she made any sudden move. He needn't worry. She wasn't fool enough to bolt, not now anyway. She kept her eyes on him. *Gain his confidence. Eventually, he'll relax his vigilance.* She shrugged her pack off her back.

"There's no question of my ability to pay." Holding her pack against her chest, propped on a raised leg, she rifled through its contents. "I can and will pay far more than the value of the entire stall."

She pushed aside Sire Stone's blanket, grabbed the silver handle of Kinsmon's mirror, pulled it out of the bag, and held it out to the vendor.

"Here. Payment in full and more. Let it be a lesson to you not to show such disregard for your paying customers. You're most welcome."

He snatched the mirror from Grit's hand. Clutching it to his breast, he smiled a cruel, unfeeling smile. "Payment for stolen property accepted. Payment for the crime of thievery, to be determined. Take her, Vell."

# THIRTEEN

With Vell's strong arms locked tightly around her thighs, Grit could offer little resistance. He carried her over his shoulder down Port Colony's main thoroughfare, laughing off her protests, kicks, and bites. At the end of a row of shops and taverns, he climbed the steps to a small building. Once inside, he set her on her feet, grabbed her wrists, and secured them with chains to a metal bar running the length of a high counter.

"Don't bother struggling. It won't work," he said.

Grit wriggled her wrists within their bonds and stilled herself. Vell was right. He had secured the shackles so tightly as to eliminate any hope of escape. Her mind raced as she scanned the room. Two doors, one through which they had entered and another behind the counter. One window to her left, high in the wall. Two more on either side of the front door. A bench underneath the window on the right. And behind the counter . . . Grit stood on tiptoe to see over the counter. Parchments cluttered a desk.

Vell bowed his dirty blond head and rifled through the parchments until he had uncovered a bound leather volume. He opened it and looked at Grit, his hazel eyes critical. "Your name and place of origin?"

Grit tapped her fingers on the metal bar to which her wrists were chained. *A fool if he thinks I'll tell him anything.*

"Let me guess." Vell propped his chin in his hand. "You come from the northern regions of the Mid-Chasmarian forests. You're too dark and your features are too soft to be of Northern Mountain blood. You don't have the windblown look of the Eastern Plains, and the Southern Realm . . . Well, you definitely aren't from those parts. Just the sight of you would frighten half the folk there. It's a good thing the chasm cuts them off from the rest of the country, or they wouldn't have lasted as long as they have."

He continued to study Grit's face, undisturbed by her glare.

"So, where is it? What village spawned the little devil who stands before me?"

"Koradin." Grit spat on the floor, so distasteful was the name of that village.

Vell leaned over the counter and placed his hand over her right hand. He gently pushed her sleeve up to expose her forearm.

"Liar." His grip tightened around her elbow as he leaned closer, eyes gleaming. "The ink of Koradin has never marked your arm. Unless you are the weakest of the weak, you are no child of Koradin."

Grit struggled against his grasp. "Fine. Thresh."

Vell pushed her sleeve up to her shoulder. He let out a slow sigh and placed both hands on the counter, one on either side of Grit's shackled wrists. "Where are your brands?"

Grit could conceive no lie to compensate for the unbelievable truth. "They disappeared."

"Just like that?"

Grit nodded.

Vell crossed his arms over his broad chest. "Now we have a problem. I might have let you out within a day or two. There's not much we don't overlook here in Port Colony. Thieving strangers is near the top of the list. Even so, with that mirror in Loam's hands, a day or two might have covered your crime. But now you are lying to me, and that I will not tolerate. Wait, what's this?"

He reached out and pulled at her necklace with his thumb and forefinger. The pearl, which had been hidden inside Grit's shirt, now dangled near her chin.

"I didn't steal it," Grit said.

Vell let the pearl drop. "Where'd you get that mirror?"

"I didn't steal that, either, if that's what you're worried about." The truth pricked at Grit's conscience. She shook her head. "At least, I didn't steal it from anyone in Port Colony."

"Will you tell me your name?"

Grit did not like the way he looked at her, as if he knew something she did not. "No."

Vell bent over the bound leather volume, pen in hand. "Unnamed thief, possible spy." He looked up to see Grit's response to his accusation.

She met his gaze without blinking.

"To be held for an indeterminable time." He blew on the ink, then pushed the record book aside. "Until I know more of you—your name and your origin, to start with —you remain in my custody. These are days when one cannot be too cautious. I like your spirit, but as I have said, I do not tolerate liars. Recompense set at fifty thousand sterlings."

"Fifty thousand sterlings?" Grit's chains clanked against the metal bar. "You couldn't collect such an amount if you scoured all of Thresh. Surely you don't consider me so dangerous."

"You have stolen without remorse, paid your victim with what is most definitely stolen property, threatened to end my life with your dagger, and refuse to state your name and place of origin. Forgive me if I don't want you roaming the streets of Port Colony." He came around the counter and stood behind Grit. "Forgive me, also, if I do not trust you to give an accurate account of the items in this pack of yours."

"Take your foul hands off my pack!" Grit struggled against her bonds to jerk Coil's bag from Vell's grasp.

"Hold still or I'll cut it from your back."

"If you damage my pack, you'll owe *me* fifty thousand sterlings." A strap dug into her shoulder. She closed her eyes. *Don't let him break it.* "You've no idea of its worth."

"One shabby blanket, a wooden bowl, and . . ." Vell's voice altered as he reached deep into the leather pack. "What's this? Another dagger, too small to be of much use."

He set the contents of the pack on the counter, out of Grit's reach. Leaning back with his elbows on the counter, he studied her face. "Is there anyone to whom you might apply to pay your recompense?"

"No one."

"Then you leave me no choice."

He moved to stand behind her again. Before she knew what he was up to, he reached around and withdrew her dagger from its sheathe. She kicked at him, but he had already moved beyond her reach.

"I told you I'd kill you if you touched my dagger again." She kicked vainly at her captor, her body twisted as far as her chains would permit.

"Will you calm yourself, or must I help you?"

"I'll take no help from you, you thieving, hideous beast! Give me my dagger or I swear, I'll plant it so deep in your chest you won't know if I stabbed you from the front or the back!"

Quietly, Vell reached into his pocket, withdrew a thin silver tube, and put it to his lips. Grit spied the miniature arrow just before it stung her neck. Her vision blurred.

"Rump-fed maggot." Grit's mouth foamed with something vile. The shackles cut into her arms as she fell to her knees.

****

90

Grit woke with a throbbing sensation in her neck. Her hip ached where bone had made contact with hard floor. Her hand tingled, too, as if she had slept too long upon her arm. When she lifted her head, the dizziness nearly made her vomit.

She looked around slowly, careful to avoid the bright light several feet in front of her. The ground was stone, with metal bars rising out of it at intervals just a few feet from her head. She swallowed the rising bile and forced her gaze to follow the line of one of the bars all the way to the ceiling. The light moved so that it shone in her eyes.

"Grit of Berth and Stone." A female spoke from behind the hideous light.

"Who are you, and how do you know my name?" Grit covered her eyes with her arm. "And would you get rid of that infernal light?"

The light dimmed, but did not disappear. "My name is Whisp, and it is my business to know things. Rise if you are able."

Grit pushed herself onto her elbow and reached for her weapon.

"Where's my dagger?" Even as she asked, she remembered kicking at the person who had stolen her weapon. A memory formed in her mind of a burly blond man with a silver tube to his lips. "He stole it. Stole it and poisoned me. Where is he? Vell. I'll kill him."

Whisp said, "If you keep talking like that, we'll have to keep you here. Your recompense has been paid. Rise. I'll take you somewhere more comfortable."

"Why should I trust you?" Grit placed both hands on the floor and pushed herself onto her hands and knees.

"Would you rather stay here?"

"No, but I don't care to be indebted to a stranger, either." Her arms shaking, she lowered herself onto her forearms, laid her head on the floor, and waited for the room to stop spinning. She squeezed her eyes shut against the sounds of metal clanging and scraping.

"Put your arm around my neck." Whisp crouched beside Grit, her straight, blond hair brushing against Grit's cheek.

"I want my dagger," Grit said as Whisp guided her arm over her shoulder.

"You'll get your dagger soon enough." Wrapping her arms around Grit's waist, Whisp pulled her to her feet with surprising swiftness. Her arm felt like iron across the small of Grit's back.

Though slender, the girl exuded power. "Come, now. One foot in front of the other."

Face to face, Grit estimated Whisp to be close to twenty years of age. Not quite a girl, though her complexion was clear as a babe's. Her features were ordinary, yet her expression so intense and her hair so blond as to make her look exceptional. *She smells of sour vomit.* Grit swallowed, and her throat burned as acidic phlegm descended. *Oh.*

She turned her head and stumbled out of her prison, leaning on Whisp. They made their way up a flight of stairs, each step sending Grit's head into a whirl, and entered the room where Grit had last seen Vell. He was there now, standing by the front window, his back to them.

"Vile beast." Her words sounded distant, hollow, and unconvincing.

He turned and held out her pack. "It's all there. Your blanket, bowl, and both daggers. Everything but the mirror you were so foolish to give away."

With her free hand, Whisp took the pack from Vell. "Burn her record, along with any others we don't want seen, before your shift ends. Our spies predict an inspection, and I highly doubt you'll be able to hand the council fifty thousand sterlings, to say nothing of a few of Strike's most wanted."

Vell nodded brusquely and opened the door for them. Grit leaned over to spit on his boot. Her arm slipped from Whisp's shoulder, and she fell into Vell. His strong hands grabbed her under her arms and lifted her up.

"Save your venom, little devil." He eased her back to Whisp's side. "Are you sure we can trust her?"

Whisp positioned her arm firmly around Grit's ribcage. "You saw the necklace, Vell. She is as much on Kinsmon's side as you and I."

"Perhaps." Vell eyed Grit. "But I'd wager fifty thousand sterlings she'd plant her dagger in my heart if she had the strength."

"Shouldn't have touched it," Grit mumbled. She wondered, though, if Vell might lose that wager. Had his eyes flickered with concern when he'd shifted her weight from his hands to Whisp? They couldn't have. But now he smiled as if he understood her spite and liked her no less, and she did not hate him for it.

Outside, the sunlight stung Grit's eyes. The bustling life of Port Colony blurred into one swelling sea of swirling colors and nondescript shapes. She clung to Whisp, willing her feet and legs to move to the dameling's rhythm lest the waves sweep her into unconsciousness.

"You to help," Grit said. "Didn't ask."

"I know." Whisp steered Grit around a cluster of people. "And I won't ask you to repay me. Just walk."

She led Grit through the crowd, across the street, and up four steps to a wooden walkway in front of a line of shops.

"Turn here. Fellows Inn."

It took a few moments for Grit's eyes to adjust to the dim light of the inn's interior.

A busty woman with graying hair left off wiping a table to greet them. Her plain dress seemed at odds with the vibrant attire of the inn's patrons. "Ah, Whisp!" She threw her towel over her shoulder. "How is she?"

"Not so good. I'm afraid. Vell was prepared for a much larger enemy. She's been out for two days, Harth."

"Hairy maggot that I'll kill." Grit tried to speak, but the words came out jumbled.

"Take her upstairs," the woman said. "I'll send Scarlett shortly."

Whisp led Grit across the room. Grit clung to every detail her fuzzy mind could hold. Men and women, dressed in every bright color, crowded at tables, drinking from heavy glass mugs. Partially eaten loaves of bread and bowls of beef stew littered the tabletops. Hushed whispers and loud shouts volleyed around the dining area. An occasional holler escaped from the kitchen. The smell of roasting beef and vegetables assaulted Grit. She couldn't tell if she wished to empty her stomach or fill it. She sighed as Whisp stopped at the foot of the staircase in the back corner of the room.

Grit reached for the railing, but still held onto Whisp as they climbed the dark, narrow stairs and proceeded down a dimly lit hallway. Wherever Whisp was taking her, it had to be better than Vell's prison. Even if it wasn't, she was in no condition to resist.

She squeezed her eyes shut. "Lie down?"

"Soon," Whisp said, her hand on a doorknob near the end of the hall.

She pushed the door open, and they entered a small room furnished with a bed, a straight-backed wooden chair, and a square table with a washbasin. Whisp helped Grit sit on the bed. Then, as Grit lowered her head onto the pillow, she bent to lift Grit's feet onto the bed.

"Your pack is here, on the floor. Scarlett will be up soon to check on you. Sleep if you can."

Grit put her hand to her hip.

"My dagger," she muttered.

A moment later, she felt the familiar hilt under her fingers and the soft, foreign touch of Whisp's fingertips against her forehead.

"Please don't use it on Vell. I'd hate to lose a fortune I don't possess," Whisp said.

# FOURTEEN

Grit did not know how long she had been sleeping when the door opened and a red-haired dameling entered, carrying a steaming water pitcher. Grit propped herself up on one elbow, her dagger ready.

"Where's Whisp?"

The dameling looked over her shoulder as she closed the door. Her voice was high and soft. "She's downstairs. A band of warriors from the Eastern Plains just arrived. I won't hurt you. Please, will you put that knife away?"

Grit loosened her grip on her dagger and lowered her hand. She did not sheath her weapon, but tapped the flat of the blade on the side of her leg as she studied the dameling. She was taller than Grit and slightly thicker. Had she been in the habit of sparring, as she obviously was not, she might have been a formidable opponent. Instead of firmly toned arms, her short, puffed sleeves revealed a thin layer of softness beneath smooth, unmarked skin. They'd put her on one of Thresh's innermost rings, among the pitiable women whose strength of body and will childbirth would surely erode.

Yet the dameling seemed unmindful of the dishonor she should bear. She smiled broadly, an inextinguishable light in her green eyes. Her thick, wavy, red hair hung loose to the middle of her back. Around her neck, she wore an elaborate necklace unlike any Grit had ever seen. Three stones like carved ice hung from the center of the silver chain, with smaller red and blue gems hanging in matching pairs on either side. What sort of girl was she?

"You must be Grit," she said. "I'm Scarlett. I understand you've been treated most harshly. I do apologize for Vell. He is overly zealous at times, but he's still learning. He means well, anyway."

She poured the steaming water into the basin, dipped a cloth in it and waited a moment, passing the cloth from hand to hand. At last, she held the cloth out to Grit.

"What?" Grit stared at the cloth.

"Your face is covered with filth."

Grit shrugged. "It often is."

"Would you like me to wash it for you?"

"No." Grit sheathed her dagger, snatched the cloth from Scarlett's hands, and dabbed her face with it. There was no way she'd let this girl touch her. "Is that sufficient?"

Scarlett's brows drew together as she studied Grit's face. "For now. Do you feel well enough to eat?"

"Of course I do. Where's the food? I was told this Harth would give me a meal." Grit threw her legs over the side of the bed. She felt weak still, but hoped a meal would steady her trembling muscles.

"Slow down." Scarlett placed a hand on Grit's shoulder, but removed it when Grit drew back. "Do not attempt to rise yet. Save that for tomorrow. Tonight, you have the luxury of dining in bed."

She smiled warmly, as if she did not know Grit had never slept in a bed, let alone eaten in one. It wasn't as strange as she'd thought it would be, sleeping in a bed with a frame and mattress like Dame Berth's rather than on a mat on the floor. She could get used to it. The girl, however . . . Grit squirmed under Scarlett's pitying gaze. What did she want?

"Do not look at me like that. I am not to be pitied," Grit said.

"You are very much to be pitied." Scarlett pulled the chair away from the wall and sat several feet from Grit.

She folded her hands in her lap. "You are unaware both of your strengths and of your weaknesses. You have yet to learn that it takes more courage to stay than to flee. I tell you this now because, though you pretend you could run downstairs for dinner, you would not make it two steps before falling flat on your face."

"When I am well—"

"When you are well, you may send me from your room or leave yourself. If it suits you, you may scream all sorts of obscenities at me. I only ask that you not harm me physically." Scarlett nodded toward Grit's dagger. "Pain doesn't suit me at all, and it would only reinforce Vell's unflattering opinion of your temper."

Grit snorted. "Vell knows nothing of my temper."

Scarlett leaned back in her chair. "Do you like stories, Grit? I could tell you of Port Colony's infamous cousins. I don't suppose their tale is widely told where you come from."

"I don't suppose it is." Perhaps all Scarlett wanted was a victim upon whom to unleash her tongue. With any luck, the story would be short.

Scarlett sighed. "I'm not at all surprised. Many villages have completely forgotten the tales of their origins. But long ago, this land was not ruled by savagery and greed, as it is now. Dames cradled their offspring tenderly, children had no fear of hunger, and sires sheltered all. Into that beautiful age, the cousins Thresh and Koradin were born."

Grit started at the name of her village, but quickly recalled Sire Stone's lessons in feigned disinterest. She rolled onto her back and stared at the ceiling.

Scarlett chattered on easily. "On opposite sides of the tiny village that would become Port Colony, the boys were born to the sisters Spring and River. The babes' first cries echoed through the village as one, filling its residents with joy.

"Thresh and Koradin grew up side by side, the closest of allies. Then *she* came into the village, a beautiful young woman, who captured their affections and planted havoc in their impressionable hearts. They quarreled over her, a dreadful creature who harbored no affection for either of them. The dispute became so violent, the council of Port Colony banished Thresh and Koradin. Such feuds can poison an entire village."

Grit propped herself up on her elbow and looked full into Scarlett's earnest face, anxious to hear the story's end. She'd never considered Thresh and Koradin could ever have been anything but enemies.

"The council hoped the banishment would give the cousins opportunity to forget their feud, but it didn't turn out as they'd intended. Bitter, angry, and resentful, Thresh and Koradin parted ways at the base of a promontory on the Western Sea. Koradin headed east. Thresh struck out to the north. The cousins founded that region's most prominent villages, the seaside village of Thresh and the fortified village of Koradin."

"But what about the young woman? What happened to her?"

"Havoc?" A troubled expression crossed Scarlett's delicate features. "Havoc thrived on chaos and left no corner of Chasmaria untouched by misery and confusion."

"Why do you tell me this story?" It made no sense. What was she to do with a history lesson of a place she'd sworn to forget?

Flustered, Scarlett shook her head and straightened her skirt. "I don't know. I thought . . . I thought . . . ." Her green eyes, wet with tears, met Grit's steady gaze. "I thought you should know that the world wasn't always so unkind. I believe it will not always be so cruel."

Scarlett wrapped a loose thread around her finger, her gaze darting from Grit, to the ceiling, to her darkening fingertip.

Grit leaned back on her pillow. "You forget I am not to be pitied. The dameling had it right. Best to leave Koradin and Thresh to themselves. Wipe your eyes and bring my dinner."

****

"Do you miss anyone?" Scarlett asked as Grit dropped her spoon into her bowl.

"I don't understand your question," Grit said through her last mouthful of stew.

Scarlett set down her spoon. "I mean, do you ache to see anyone from your home? Are you troubled by your absence from your dame, your sire, your siblings, or any others with whom you often spent time?"

"Oh." Grit swallowed. "No, I don't miss anyone."

Sorrow flooded Scarlett's eyes as she leaned forward in her chair and took Grit's empty bowl.

Grit let out a deep breath and fiddled with her fingertips in a manner familiar, but not her own. She'd said something shameful, but had no idea how to correct her error. What did Scarlett want her to say? She didn't miss Dame Berth's rod or the rumors about Sire Stone. She'd had to save her sibling's thieving, meddling skins too many times to count. And Coil, who taunted her at every chance . . . She turned her attention back to Scarlett.

"I miss my dame when I am at Castle Concord." Scarlett twirled the spoons around in the top of the two stacked bowls. "We used to live together at the castle, but when her sire died, he willed this inn to my dame. She left the castle to ensure Kinsmon's scouts would always find a safe harbor here. I miss her sorely when we are apart, which is one reason I visit whenever I'm able. Port Colony has grown less safe in recent

101

years, and I fear it will grow increasingly dangerous for Kinsmon's scouts and friends."

"Where . . . What is Castle Concord?"

"Castle Concord is Kinsmon's base in the Southern Realm. It's a wonderful place, white and lovely, and situated in the heart of a lush valley. You must come see me there when you are well."

Grit shifted herself in the bed. "Do you have a sire?" She hoped Scarlett would not pursue the subject of visiting Castle Concord.

"I did." A note of deep sadness entered the dameling's gentle voice. "I miss him, too, though I hardly recall his face. My dame tells me I look just like him. I wish I could see him and decide for myself."

"You're of age, aren't you? Why do you not go to him?"

"He died when I was young. He'd never been well. It was his illness, in fact, that cost him his test. When the village council banished him, he traveled to Port Colony and collapsed in the doorway of the inn. There my dame found him. She was just a dameling then, but she nurtured him back to health, and they spent four happy years together. The fifth year of their time together, his illness returned to consume him. Not long after his death, my dame's sire sent us to Castle Concord. He felt it best I grow up somewhere gentler than an inn in Port Colony."

Scarlett smiled, but sadness remained in her green eyes. "What about your sire, Grit? Was he a kind man? Do you miss him?"

Grit focused more intently on her hands. She rubbed her fingertips together, as if to cleanse them of indelible dye. With a quiet shock, she recognized her fingers mimicking the motions Coil of Dara used to rub away the pink stains of his berries. She

GRIT OF BERTH AND STONE

clapped her hands together and concentrated on holding them still in her lap.

"I miss no one."

"Hmm." Scarlett cocked her head. She stood beside Grit's bed, hesitant to leave. "You might not miss anyone now, but I'm sure you will someday. I miss Dagger something awful when he goes away."

"Who's Dagger?" The name intrigued Grit.

"Dagger is my friend."

Grit looked blankly at the dameling, not understanding her words.

"You don't know what that means, do you? It means simply that I have known Dagger several years, share many good memories with him, and enjoy his company. When my dame and I came to Castle Concord, I was four, and he, seven. That was," Scarlett calculated quickly, "twelve years ago. I'm eager to see him again, though no one knows when he might arrive. That is how it always is with Dagger."

Grit barely listened to Scarlett. Head bowed, eyes intent, she slid her left thumbnail under each of the fingernails on her right hand, dislodging tiny bits of dirt and dead skin, as if she might, by copying his actions, dislodge Coil of Dara from her memory.

Scarlett placed a soft hand over Grit's. "Stop. Your hands are clean."

Grit clenched her hands in fists to restrain their movement and looked at the dameling. "Why have you stayed with me all this time?"

"For many reasons. First, because Vell is still a little terrified you will plant your dagger in his side. Second, because Whisp is concerned you might somehow harm yourself. Third . . ." Scarlett hesitated.

"Third?"

"Third," Scarlett said with quiet finality. "Third, I have come to wish I might count you among my friends."

"Why would you want to do that?"

Scarlett squared her shoulders. "Because in all the time I have been here, though you have been less than gracious, you have neither screamed for me to leave nor attempted to leave yourself. I suspect you like me more than you care to admit, even to yourself."

Scarlett turned and left the room before Grit had time to respond. She threw herself against her pillow and cursed her slowness of mind. She glared at the door through which the dameling had left. What would it mean to count Scarlett as a friend?

# FIFTEEN

rit woke with a start. She snatched her dagger from under the blanket and scanned the corners of her moonlit room. Laying still in her bed, she listened. Muffled sounds came through the floorboards, as if someone were moving furniture in the room below. What was going on down there? Who rearranged a room in the dead of night? She strained her ears and heard voices. This was more than an innkeeper preparing for the morrow's crowd. A distinguished guest? A clandestine meeting? What could warrant such activity at this hour?

Grit swung her feet over the edge and waited to see if her head would tolerate being upright. Vell's poison no longer clouded her mind. She stood, her legs stable as ever.

With light steps, she crossed the room. She eased the door open a crack and peered into the dark hallway before squeezing between the door and its frame. With a hand on the wall, she tiptoed to the head of the stairs and descended into the main dining hall. The muffled sounds became louder and clearer. She turned toward a door behind the stairwell.

Standing beside the doorway, Grit pressed her body against the wall. She didn't wish to be discovered, not with her heart racing like this. How Slate managed to eavesdrop on the council's secret meetings, she'd never understand.

Inside the room, which appeared to be a smaller dining hall, several people sat around a table that ran the length of the room. Among the strangers were Vell and Whisp, as well as two men and a woman she saw in the main dining hall when Whisp had first brought her to the inn.

At the head of the table sat a young warrior, his elbows on the table, his face covered by his pale, long-fingered hands. Deep in thought, he seemed oblivious to the soft chatter of the others settling into their seats. Though none of the room's occupants appeared armed, Grit felt for her dagger. If it was foolishness to approach a stranger without a ready weapon, it was stupidity to linger unarmed outside a room full of them.

On the other side of the wall, a sharp cry arose. Grit slid her hand around the doorjamb and peered into the room. A woman with long, untamed curls sat in a chair in the corner, her head bowed over a squirming infant. As the babe settled to nurse, the dame turned her gaunt face to the ceiling.

"You. Come in." The voice of the young warrior at the table's head startled Grit.

She turned her head toward him, her hand still gripping the doorjamb. Piercing blue eyes under a shock of straight jet-black hair met her gaze. His pale, angular face was the face of Sire Stone, twenty or so years younger.

Grit gasped and drew her dagger. "Who are you?"

He rose from his chair and crossed the room to meet Grit. Even his gait was similar to Sire Stone's. She pushed herself away from the wall and stood squarely in the doorway. She'd fight him if need be.

On the other side of the table, Vell pulled the silver tube from his pocket and twirled it between his fingers. "Perhaps she should be under guard."

"Put it away, Vell." The sireling continued toward Grit. "See her necklace. Kinsmon trusts her."

Vell narrowed his hazel eyes. "You don't know her like I do. There's a little devil in her."

"She is one of us." The sireling's tone was sharp. He looked from Grit to Vell, and his expression softened. "As are you, Vell. From this moment, you are to defend this girl, though it cost you your job, your status, your very life. Do you understand me?"

"I don't need his protection." Grit glared at Vell. She'd been a fool to think he approved of her. Here he was, calling her a devil in front of all of them.

The sireling whirled to face Grit. "I didn't ask if you needed his protection. It is yours, whether you want it or not." He turned back to Vell. "Do you understand me, man?"

After a wary glance at Grit, Vell nodded and sank into his chair. His pipe clanked as he set it on the wooden table. The dark-haired sireling turned back to Grit, who remained in the doorway. *Tightly wound*, that's what Berth would have called this sireling, and that's where his similarity to Sire Stone ended.

He stepped forward and extended his right hand. "Grit of Berth and Stone, I presume. I'm Dagger. I arrived just a short while ago, but Whisp has informed me of your situation. It is my pleasure to meet you."

So now he was attempting pleasantries. Grit stared at his extended hand, her lip curled into a scowl. "I'll make no alliance with a stranger."

"Ah, you have indeed been plucked from a Chasmarian village!" A soft, almost scornful laugh escaped with Dagger's words. "I don't offer my hand as an alliance, but as a pledge of trust. I'll not harm you, nor will any in this room." He shot a meaningful look at Vell.

Grit couldn't tell whether it was his resemblance to Sire Stone or the challenge in his eyes that made Dagger seem familiar and emboldened her to take his hand. Though she itched to pull away from him, Grit willed herself to stand firm. Dagger's pale hands were soft and smooth against her darker, more calloused skin. She measured his character by the firm steadiness of his grip and the unwavering studiousness of his clear blue eyes as they met hers. He was over-confident, but she liked his boldness. He wasn't afraid to mock her, yet when he called her Grit of Berth and Stone, it sounded as natural, as right and honorable as when Kinsmon said it. It sounded as if she were still herself.

He tightened his grip. "You may be just plucked from some humble village, but you are among friends. Join us."

He released her hand and gestured toward an empty chair. It might be a trap, but she had to know the nature of this odd gathering. She pulled the chair from the table and sat, comforted by the open door just a few feet away. A quick escape never hurt.

A young warrior she hadn't seen before watched as she settled into her chair. He shook his sandy brown hair out of his eyes and frowned. "Why don't you sit at the table?"

Grit crossed her arms over her chest and shook her head. One hand drooped so that her fingertips rested on her dagger. The warrior shrugged and turned back to the table.

As Dagger resumed his seat, Harth entered, carrying a wooden tray loaded with various cheeses and several sliced loaves of bread. Scarlett followed with a silver pitcher in each hand. Harth distributed food, and Scarlett poured magenta liquid into glass mugs.

A murmur of thanks rose from around the table, and they ate. Though Grit had eaten only hours earlier, she savored each bite. By now, she'd swallowed enough of Harth's food to fear no ill effects from it. If they wanted her to die by poison, they'd have let Vell have his way. Grit glared across the room at him. He picked his silver pipe off the table and slid it into his pocket.

Though she ate freely, Grit drank cautiously, resisting memories of Coil with every sip of Kinsmon's special brew. It was enough to see his golden pink curls in her dreams. She didn't need to be reminded of them during her waking hours.

She focused on the discussion at the table, which seemed little more than a recounting of past events at Castle Concord until Dagger set his hands on the table and turned to the broad-shouldered man seated on his left. "Tell me, Oak, what have you discovered in your travels?"

Oak, a massive man with a thick, graying beard, set down his empty mug and spoke in a voice as strong as his appearance. "There is great unrest in the Northern Mountains. Many of the sirelings have abandoned their villages. It's rumored they've allied themselves with a native, long-absent warrior of Summit Colony. No one's named this warrior, but I have my suspicions."

For a moment, Dagger seemed drained of energy. Regaining his composure, he answered, "Your suspicions are correct. Strike of the Northern Mountains has been reported in that region in recent months, with many cruel and foolish sirelings in his service."

"It is the same in the Eastern Plains," said the warrior who had spoken to Grit. He bit off a chunk of bread and continued. "In the beginning, we assumed our youth had failed their tests, but when so many never returned, we began to suspect some sort of interference. It had to be more than mere weakness on the part of the offspring. They'd all been diligently trained."

Dagger nodded, a grim expression on his face. "Accustom yourselves to such news. We will hear of many more youth, as well as men and women, sacrificing themselves to Strike's twisted ambitions. Fools, all of them, but it is sure to happen."

The babe wailed. The conversation at the table paused, but was taken back up by the woman Grit had seen in the inn earlier. She strained to hear the woman's report, but the fussy infant distracted her.

"Shh," Scarlett whispered over the babe's head. She placed a hand on the young dame's shoulder. The dame shifted in her seat, as if she didn't approve of Scarlett's touch, and patted the screaming babe's back more vigorously. The child burped, then threw his face against his dame's shoulder. When he raised his head, a wet spot marked her gray dress.

Grit gave up on following the conversation at the table and studied the dame closer. She was slightly built, but with a rare strength in her diminutive form, a strength that had been pushed far beyond its limits. High cheekbones accentuated her gaunt face, and dark circles underlined eyes that seemed to take in every detail of her surroundings.

She turned her gaze on Grit, and Grit sat motionless, allowing the dame to take stock of her as the babe continued to squirm in her arms. *It is only fair to allow her to scrutinize me as closely as I have her.*

Scarlett followed the dame's gaze. "Perhaps . . . Perhaps Grit might soothe the child."

Grit shook her head. She'd only held her younger siblings out of necessity. It had never crossed her mind to touch an infant not thrust into her arms by her busy dame. *She's mad if she thinks I'll touch a stranger's offspring.* The dame wrapped her arm protectively around the babe's arched back.

"Grit," Scarlett said in a constrained voice, "it is a small thing to hold this babe, but by doing so, you may give Laurel a moment's rest. Laurel, look at Grit. She is as afraid of holding that babe as you are of letting him go. You needn't worry she'll steal him."

"I'm not afraid of a babe." Grit realized too late what her words committed her to do.

## SIXTEEN

Grit felt awkward holding her hands out to receive Laurel's babe. Reluctantly, Laurel shifted the infant from her shoulder into Grit's arms. Deathly afraid both of touching him and of dropping him, Grit wrapped her arms tight around his body, with one hand extended up his back to prevent him from hurling himself from her arms. Laurel's critical eye did nothing to ease her discomfort. Grit turned her attention back to the table in an effort to discourage the dame's attention, and the child settled with his head against her shoulder.

Harth shifted in her seat. Dagger sat forward, a hand on either side of his empty plate. "What is it, Harth?"

"Only this, and I'm not sure it's worth mentioning, but I thought maybe you should know. Last week, I overheard a pair of travelers in the dining hall. I didn't mean to listen to their conversation, of course, but one told the other of a Threshan girl who'd completed her test, only to be overcome by a hag, who sold the girl to one of her hunters."

Grit's muscles tensed. The babe raised his head and lowered it again onto her shoulder.

"I'm not sure what became of the girl. But it has me wondering if Havoc might be at work again," Harth said.

"Havoc never stopped working." Dagger, eyes bright with subdued anger, looked at Vell. "If you want a devil, look to Havoc. She's maintained a steady level of fear and misery throughout Chasmaria for generations. Now Havoc's found a new game to play and a willing pawn. Only a fool would believe Strike of the Northern Mountains is the great mastermind he pretends to be."

The dark-haired man seated next to Vell leaned forward in his chair, resting his elbows on his thighs. "But why do the people align themselves with Strike? Do they not observe his cruelty? Do they expect him to be kinder to them than he is to his own flesh and blood? "

Dagger ran a finger along the edge of the table. "You forget your origins, Vision. Remember how little alliances once meant to you, and how much you would have given to have power such as Strike's. Following Strike seems unthinkable to you who have seen goodness and truth. Those who follow Strike do so in blindness."

"What of the Golden Demon they speak of in the Northern Forest?" Oak scratched the side of his bearded face. "I don't believe he follows in blindness."

Dagger was silent a moment, his gaze fixed on Oak. When he spoke, he did so in a guarded tone. "Do not use that name. Thus far, he is a whisper among the battle cries of crueler men. You assume much when you say he follows Strike, and even more when you call him a demon."

"Is there any doubt?" Oak asked. "He enters villages as Strike's forces leave, his one objective to destroy the weak and the helpless left by bolder warriors. It's foolishness to deny the extent of his brutality."

"It's foolishness to suppose you know his motives." Dagger spoke so softly Grit barely caught his words.

Whisp shook her white-blond head. "I'm not sure you fully understand, Dagger. In one small village, he left no corner of the Inner Ring intact. He tore apart homes, slaying any who stood in his way. What madness could prompt a man to inflict such cruelty, if not the madness of a demon?"

Dagger took a deep breath before answering. "What drives this man, I cannot say, but I will not tolerate his being called a demon, nor will I permit any to erroneously link him to Strike.

He may follow in Strike's footsteps, but we have no evidence of an alliance between the pair. In my judgment, the Golden Warrior is a separate entity, and will likely destroy himself before too long. Is it true he operates with an accomplice?"

Whisp nodded. "The Silent Shadow, and he is just that. He doesn't lift a finger against the people, only observes the Golden Demon's work."

"Warrior, Whisp. Golden *Warrior*. Do we know nothing more of him?" Dagger's blue eyes scanned the faces of his companions.

Vell waved a hand in Grit's direction. "Ask her. She claims to be from those parts. What do you know of this Golden Warrior?"

"I know nothing of your Golden Warrior or Demon or whatever you wish to call him." Grit shifted Laurel's infant to her other arm and rubbed his back with her right hand. "And you are the one who claims I come from the Northern Forest. If you recall, I said nothing of my origin."

Vell pointed at Grit with a crooked smile on his face. "I tell you, Dagger, she's a devil."

"You are not enemies." Dagger's voice was low, almost cautionary, as he looked from Grit to Vell. "And there are no devils in this room."

"Dagger, you have been near Koradin. What is the status of that village?" Whisp asked.

Dagger ran his fingers through his hair and sighed, glancing once more at both Grit and Vell before addressing Whisp's question. "Unless I am mistaken, Strike is headed toward Koradin and will take more than its youth. Koradin provides a strong fortress and a secure dungeon. Its situation must be enviable to our enemy. Sage Frost is not the warrior he once was. Koradin cannot resist Strike's offensive, which is sure to come soon."

113

Scarlett's hand went to her neck. Whisp, too, clutched something dangling from a gold chain around her neck. Vision, Oak, and Vell grasped their leather wrist bands. Harth twisted a pearl ring around her finger. Glancing at her own pearl, Grit wondered if Kinsmon had given these strangers promises as well.

*All of Chasmaria will be made lovely, that's what Kinsmon said.* Grit barely understood what lovely meant, but she sensed it was the opposite of all of this. The opposite of fear and cruelty and a group of people meeting at midnight and speaking of demons.

"What are we to do, then?" Vell asked, his fist on the table.

Grit pursed her lips and patted the babe firmly on his back. She could tolerate Whisp, Scarlett, Dagger, even Laurel and her drooling babe. She might grow to tolerate Vell, provided he keep that pipe of his in his pocket. But she could never consider herself a part of "we."

"We watch and wait. A time is coming when the friends of Kinsmon will rise to overthrow Strike and Havoc and all the evil with which they infest our country. There will be no more cruelty or greed or foolish, arrogant pride. From royal thrones, the prophecies tell us, vast love will unfold." Dagger looked around the table and past the young warrior from the Eastern Plains to Grit, slouching in her chair against the wall. His gaze rested on Laurel's babe. "Chasmaria will be beautiful again. Together, when the time is right, we will usher in her beauty."

Grit yawned, pushed herself out of her chair, and passed the babe to his dame. Free of her burden, she sauntered across the room. She stopped at the doorway and turned to find Dagger watching her, a question in his eyes.

She answered without hesitation. "This is all very fine talk, but I don't care to kill myself fighting for something that won't happen. And, you're wrong about Strike. He's nowhere near

Koradin. I saw him four days ago, just the other side of the Tabes River. I imagine the woman with him was your Havoc. They put on quite a show of flames before entering the village."

"Do you jest?" Dagger asked.

Grit snorted. She'd had enough of Dagger's pompous speech. "Why would I jest? Ask the two boys, if you can find them."

Dagger stood, his chair scraping the floor. He leaned forward with his hands on the table. "What two boys? Tell me you are not so great a fool as to leave two children to fend for their meager selves. Where did they go?"

"They aren't *my* babes. What interest have I in their affairs?"

"Every interest in the world!" Dagger bowed his head and took a deep breath. "You wear that pearl around your neck, Grit of Berth and Stone. It means something, whether you acknowledge it or not. It means many things, in fact, and one of those things is that those boys—indeed every human being you encounter—is someone in whose affairs you have an interest."

Grit held her pearl between her thumb and forefinger, but kept her gaze fixed on Dagger. "You must have mistaken me for someone else. I'll be traveling on in the morning, and I must get some sleep. Try to keep the noise down."

Once outside the room, she drew a deep breath and leaned over, her hands on her knees. It was almost too much, these strangers plotting an impossible new Chasmaria. Her pearl dangled near her chin, accusing her of treachery. *What was I to do? Feed Peril? Offer Zag protection? Who's to say we wouldn't have killed one another? Far better to walk alone than risk betrayal.*

She glanced at the open doorway, shook her head, and strode to the stairs, trying to eradicate the boys' names, faces, and voices from her memory. She had no interest in their affairs, no interest in any of their affairs. Let Dagger, Scarlett, and the rest do what they would. Grit might die an outcast in the Southern Realm, but she wouldn't die in a hopeless war against an unchangeable world.

Halfway up the stairs, a strong hand wrapped around her right arm, arresting her ascent. As she whirled to face her assailant, he grabbed her other arm. Grit struggled to free herself.

"Who's the devil now, Vell? Let me go."

"Shut up. Don't draw attention to yourself. Just tell me, what are your plans?"

Grit laughed softly. "Do you really think I'll tell you where I'm going?"

He loosened his grip, but did not release her. "No, but will you tell me anyway?"

"You must be mad."

Vell bowed his head. "I might be. Then again, you might be, too. Just swear to me you will keep your eyes open as you travel. Do not entrust yourself to any who do not bear the promise of Kinsmon. And for the sake of all Chasmaria, do not betray the secrets you have heard tonight."

Grit cocked her head. "So, you don't want to kill me?"

"It depends upon the moment, but overall, no. Why don't we make a deal? I won't raise my pipe to poison you again, and you'll do all I've asked."

"A vow? You want to make an alliance?"

Vell nodded, his weathered face hopeful.

"But who will witness?" Grit asked.

"Do you trust any in that room enough to call as a witness?" Vell nodded over his shoulder. "I didn't think so. This is between you and me, Grit of Berth and Stone. I swear I won't kill you, whether by my pipe or any other means. Now you swear you'll keep your eyes open, entrust yourself wisely, and speak nothing of anything you've heard tonight."

He released her arms and held out his hand. After a moment, Grit placed her hand in his. It was a small thing to swear, after all, and would persuade him to leave her alone.

"I swear it."

It was only when she had closed her door and Vell's voice rose above the others in the room below that Grit realized how very little she had sworn to.

Vell had sworn not to kill her, but all she'd done was swear to protect herself and not betray a party in whose affairs she had no interest. She'd never made such a worthless vow.

Considering she'd depart Port Colony in the morning and would likely never see Vell again, it seemed a pointless vow on both sides. Yet as she stretched out on her bed, Grit strained to hear once more the voice of the ally she did not care to have.

# SEVENTEEN

The sea filled Grit's dreams, but this time it was not the Western Sea, but the Southern Sea. Its gentle waves upheld Grit as she floated in the salty water. Half awake, she curled her body and burrowed her head under the pillow to steal a few minutes more sleep. There was too much noise in the room next to hers. Dagger or some of the warriors who'd arrived the night before must be getting ready to leave again. The time had come for her to leave, too. The dream of the Southern Sea left an ache in her gut. She'd wasted too much time in Port Colony.

The dining hall bustled with activity when Grit descended. She wound her way through the crowded room, pack slung over her shoulder, taking care to avoid anyone who had attended the previous night's conference.

"Oomph!" Turning from a table she'd been serving, Harth bumped into Grit. "Pardon me. I didn't see you there."

"It's nothing." Grit bowed her head and tried to move around the plump woman.

"Oh, it's you," Harth said. "Where are you going in such a hurry? And with your pack, too?"

"I'm leaving." It was none of the woman's business where she was going.

"Surely you can spare a few minutes for some breakfast. Let me pack you a lunch, as well. Wherever you're headed, you'll need something to sustain you along the way."

Grit wished to object, but the opportunity for food was too tempting to refuse. She'd spent enough of her life hungry. Plus, if she ran into Peril and Zag . . . *But foolishness. Dagger is mad if he thinks I owe those two boys anything.*

Grit frowned at the innkeeper. "Fine, but make it quick."

Harth disappeared into the kitchen, and Grit found an empty stool at the counter. As she drummed her fingers on the countertop, the young man on her left turned to face her.

"My name is Arrow." It was the shaggy-haired warrior from the Eastern Plains. "I would've introduced myself last night, but you left so suddenly."

"A wise person rests well before a long journey." Grit had heard this somewhere, probably from Sire Swot.

"Will you be traveling with us to Castle Concord, then?"

"No."

"Why not?" He pushed his sleeves up and crossed his arms, elbows resting on the countertop. For an instant, before his scarred hand covered them, Grit glimpsed four circular marks just above his elbow. She reached out to touch his arm, but pulled her hand back.

"You're branded," she said.

Arrow glanced at his arm and shrugged. "Half the people in the Eastern Plains are. The rest are tattooed. All depends upon your village."

"I had brands." Grit caressed her right arm gently, a knot forming in her stomach as she thought of what was not beneath her sleeve. It wouldn't matter at the Southern Sea. No one would care that her honor had been erased.

"Had?" Arrow's voice harbored no surprise, no malice, only calm interest.

"Yes, had. Sixteen of the finest brands ever seen." Grit smiled sadly and pressed her forefinger into her sleeve, marking where her brands had been. "The last one, the best one, I did myself. Stole the rod from my dame and buried it in my arm."

"You branded yourself?" An odd, disbelieving expression clouded Arrow's intelligent brown eyes.

As Grit nodded, Harth returned with two plates heaped with eggs, bread, cheese, and fruit. She set one before Grit and the other before Arrow, who grabbed his bread before Harth had removed her hand from the plate's edge.

"That seems a stupid thing to do, branding yourself." Crumbs fell from Arrow's mouth. "The first thing Whisp told me when we met is that to heal calls for greater strength than to wound. That's one reason I'm here, I and my humble band of warriors."

He waved a hand toward a group of young men and women seated at two large tables pushed together. "We aren't many, but we would give all we have and all we are to bring health, safety, and peace to our home."

Grit swallowed. "Well, I have no home." She pushed her sleeve up to reveal clean, unmarked skin. "No more brands, no more home."

Arrow leaned closer to examine her arm. "Where did they go?"

"Disappeared."

He set down his bread and faced her. "Then why will you not come to Castle Concord? Kinsmon gives a home to all who enter."

Grit chose her words and spoke them slowly, as if explaining death to a child. "Because I have no home, not in the Northern Forest, not in Port Colony, not at this Castle Concord. I will travel south to the very edge of Chasmaria and still find no home."

"What will you do then, when you reach the very edge of Chasmaria?"

Grit squirmed on her stool, her breakfast no longer appetizing. Nothing less than the Southern Sea could satisfy this ache. How long must she wait to look upon its waves, to taste its salty air? Why must Arrow ply her with questions?

What she would do upon arriving at her destination was nothing to him. Perhaps she would build a hut. Perhaps she would swim into the Southern Sea and never again set foot on Chasmarian soil. Whatever she would do, she was not willing to confess to Arrow her lack of planning.

She picked up her fork and pointed the tines at him. "Perhaps I will eat my breakfast in peace."

"I hope you may." He seemed to mean something more than she could comprehend.

Grit leaned over her plate and Arrow returned to his meal. Harth placed a cloth sack on the counter. "Did I hear you're aiming for the Southern Sea?" she asked.

Grit grunted and nodded. She looked from the sack to the dame.

Harth patted the sack. "This should last you several days. Follow the street out there south out of Port Colony, then take East Fork Road. That'll take you to Sages Bridge, which you should be able to cross with no trouble at all. Take South Fork, along the shoreline, and the chasm will keep you from the Southern Realm. The waters are rough where the river lets into the Western Sea, and you'd never make it across."

Grit placed a hand on the sack. Her fingertips just touched Harth's.

"Thank you," she said before she knew what was coming out of her mouth.

She let her fingers remain against Harth's a moment longer. Lifting the sack from the counter, she nodded again to the dame, and then to Arrow, who watched quietly as she backed away.

Harth called to her over the noise of the dining hall. "You are always welcome here, Grit."

Arrow raised a hand in farewell, his mouth full of food.

Outside, Grit tied the sack of food to one of the straps of her leather pack. She looked up and down the street, then descended the steps into the morning crowd and headed south. At the end of the street, on the outskirts of Port Colony, she stopped. The road split into two, one route leading south through open fields along the Western Sea and the other leading east into the Mid-Chasmarian Forest. As Grit turned to look back at the city she had left, the sack of food swung against her hip. Harth's instructions echoed in her mind as she considered the paths before her.

*Take South Fork, and the chasm will keep you from the Southern Realm. The waters are rough where the river lets into the Western Sea, and you'd never make it across.*

Grit set her jaw and headed south. After several steps, she stopped, closed her eyes, and took slow breaths. What if the dame had told the truth? Coil's roundabout tactics had won him many a sparring match against more direct opponents. A map might show South Fork Road to be more direct, but only experience could tell the depth, width, or wildness of the river that coursed along the bottom of the Southern Chasm.

She bit her lip and glanced at her boots. Her fingers fiddled madly with her dagger.

*Look at me . . . Following the counsel of a fool dame.*

She turned and retraced her steps to the signpost, her fingers calmer with every step. She lifted her hand from her dagger, adjusted the pack on her shoulders, and set her course down the eastern road.

*East Fork Road to Sages Bridge, and a dagger for the dame if she's steered me wrong.*

# EIGHTEEN

**E**ast Fork Road followed a southeasterly course. By midday, Grit had traveled deep into the Mid-Chasmarian Forest. She stopped, opened Harth's sack, and selected a small loaf of dark bread and some dried meat for her lunch. She ate quickly, finishing the last of the bread as she walked.

By evening, when she stopped for dinner, Grit's legs ached from the exertion of climbing increasingly steep hills. Ahead, mountain peaks loomed over distant treetops. Grit lowered herself to the ground, her back against a wide tree trunk. She reached into the sack and pulled out a pastry. She bit into the flaky crust. Sticky apple filling dripped from her lower lip. As she licked it, she thought of Dame Dara and of the fruit pie she'd savored after her Final Branding. An image rose in her memory of a bowl of berries beside a broadsword. She took another large bite of the pastry. Her hand was on the broadsword. Another bite, and she had claimed the berries.

She closed her eyes against the memory of her Aids Ceremony and tilted her head back. When she opened them a minute later, the last of the sun's rays shone through the branches above her head. From the thick, rough trunk, limbs extended in every direction. From each limb, smaller branches and twigs reached out to touch one another until they formed a tangle of wood and leaf. She closed her eyes again, and she was in the tree, clinging to the trunk and willing herself not to move, her breath caught in her chest.

She looked down. A hand, fingertips stained a dark pink, wrapped around the branch, almost touching her boot. A second hand gripped the branch, trapping her feet between the two encroaching hands. As she stared into the foliage below, the wind rustled the leaves, revealing the round, smiling face of Coil of Dara.

"You will not catch me," Grit said, her voice steady, unfeeling.

Tightening her hold on the trunk, she raised one foot and brought it down with all her might on Coil's hand. His face contorted with pain, and his hands slipped from the branch. Bile rose in Grit's throat as his blue eyes disappeared into his skull, leaving gaping black holes. From his mouth, black smoke billowed. His lithe, muscular body flopped this way and that, battered by branches as he plummeted to the forest floor.

Grit awoke just in time to escape the horror of Coil's bones cracking against the ground. Leaning over, she cleared her mouth of the awful taste the dream had left. Still heaving, she unclenched her fists, but the fingers of her left hand stuck together. Raising her hand to her face, she smelled a faint fragrance of apple. In the dark of the night that had descended while Grit had slept, she wiped the remnants of Dame Harth's pastry from her hand onto the grass at her side.

"Coil," she whispered, half afraid to speak his name even when no one listened. "Coil. Coil. Coil."

She fell onto her side, her head against the soft earth, and waited for morning. Sleep would not come. She did not wish it to come. But her body, mind, and soul could not continue without rest, and so she waited numbly for the morning sun to light her path.

When morning came at last, Grit rolled into a sitting position, ate a quick breakfast, and continued on. The terrain rose steeply, and by late afternoon, the trees had thinned. As she came upon a small cluster of conifers, she slowed her pace and untied her sack of food. She sat in the shade, relieved for the shelter from the sun. She peered into the open sack and wrapped her hand around a slab of dried meat. Someone was watching her. She drew her hand from the sack and reached for her dagger. Only when the hilt was firmly in her grasp did she look up.

A man and a woman, each dressed in an odd assortment of fabrics and colors, stood on either side of her.

"What's in the sack?" the woman asked. Short, choppy hair stuck out from her head.

"Nothing." Grit slid the pack over her shoulder, drew her dagger, and eased herself onto her haunches.

The man's smile held no warmth. "Then you won't mind giving it to us."

"I would mind that very much, actually." Grit's gaze darted from one to the other of the would-be thieves.

"Look at the necklace." The woman giggled, one hand over her mouth and the other pointing at Grit's neck. "I want it."

Grit propelled herself to her feet, but the man tackled her before she had taken a second step. His body collided into hers, and they fell together onto the soft earth. She tried to roll away. His legs pinned her to the ground. Something in her leather pack dug into the small of her back.

"Get off me!"

Grit thrust her dagger toward his thigh. He grabbed her arm, wrested the dagger from her grip, and held it to her neck.

"Alls we want's the necklace."

Grit turned her face away, sickened by his rancid breath.

"And the sack." The woman bounced on her toes. "We want the sack, too. Don't we want the sack?"

"And the sack," the man said.

Out of the corner of her eye, Grit spied a rock. She struggled to free her arm. "And if I refuse? What then?"

He laughed, expelling an invisible cloud of stench over Grit's face. She struggled not to turn away again.

"What then?" Grit asked, taking pains not to inhale.

He leaned in closer, so that his nose almost touched hers. The tip of her dagger pressed into her neck dissuaded Grit from slamming her forehead into the man's nose.

"Then we take it from you."

Sitting back, he yanked Grit's pearl away from her body and slid her dagger under the chain. He held it there a moment, the chain pulled so tight it dug into the back of Grit's neck. In one quick motion, he jerked the dagger up and back. The golden chain hummed down the length of the blade.

A strange look came over his face. As Grit lifted her head from the ground, the pain at the back of her neck eased. Her pearl remained between his grimy fingers, linked to the golden chain that had not been severed by her dagger.

Again, the man sliced in vain at the necklace. After another failed attempt, he threw the dagger over his shoulder and tried manually to break the chain.

Grit struggled beneath his weight, clawing at his hands as he tried to unclasp the necklace.

His fleshy fingers fumbled with the clasp, and he dropped the necklace onto Grit's chest. He turned to the woman, who watched from several feet away with her bony fingers in her mouth. "How bad do you want it?"

Twisting and sliding, Grit managed to unseat the man in his distraction. She scrambled to her feet, kicking at him as he tried to grab her. She spied her dagger lying in the middle of the road and ran to retrieve it.

The woman pointed with both hands. "My necklace! Get my necklace!"

The man, now on his feet, darted toward Grit. With the two bandits between herself and the trees, Grit sprinted away, hoping she could outrun the man. She pumped her legs, her muscles stinging against the steep incline. At last the terrain leveled.

He was getting closer. What could she do? Where could she hide? The flat, rocky terrain offered little protection. She ran a few more yards and stopped abruptly, almost losing her balance. She steadied herself and let out a soft laugh. "The Southern Chasm."

Ahead of her, the earth opened, as if an enormous dagger had inflicted a deep gash upon Chasmaria's face. Planks of dark wood suspended from strong, yellow rope spanned the chasm.

"And that must be Sages Bridge."

She glanced over her shoulder. Her pursuer approached. Grit fixed her attention on the southern side of the chasm. The mountain rose in a steep wall with dark spaces suggestive of caves. If she could make it across, she might find refuge and escape among those caves.

She rushed onto the bridge without slowing. The bridge swung widely. She placed a hand on the rope railing and continued across, shifting her weight to counterbalance the swing of the bridge. She set foot on the southern side of the chasm, then turned to gauge the man's progress.

He stood on the other side of the chasm, a horrified expression on his dirty face.

"Keep your necklace. We don't want it, after all." He shook his head and stepped back from the bridge. "What are you, a fool or a demon?"

Grit laughed, a loud rolling sound that came from her gut and echoed over the chasm. "Whatever I am, I've bested you!"

He walked backward, as if afraid to lose sight of Grit. Finally, he turned and jogged back the way they came. When she was certain he was gone, Grit stepped to the edge of the chasm and peered over the side. Jagged rock dotted with scraggly shrubs dropped to the canyon floor. Far below, a river raged through the chasm, flowing toward the Western Sea. Grit lifted her gaze to the bridge and furrowed her brow.

The bridge swayed gently and seemed to change in appearance. One moment, the ropes were yellow and new. The next, they were brown and frayed. The planks shifted to expose gaping holes and broken boards. She touched the railing with her fingertips, and the bridge appeared as she had first seen it, strong and whole. Was she some sort of fool or demon, to cross such a bridge?

What was this place? Her head spinning, Grit clutched the pearl that had driven her so quickly into the Southern Realm. It could have killed her, crossing that bridge. What if she'd fallen? The pearl and the allure of the Southern Sea were clouding her mind. What was this southward pull, and why did she care if a lunatic took her necklace? She was a fool not to have seen the dangers of the bridge.

She put her fingers to the necklace's clasp, but stopped. The thought of tossing the pearl into the chasm sent an empty chill through her entire being. She backed away from the bridge all the way to the steep rock, and tucked herself into a narrow cave. There Grit sat, her back against the wall, staring at the bridge with Coil's pack in her lap and her hand wrapped around her pearl until darkness veiled her sight and sleep released her from her vigil.

## NINETEEN

Sleep did not prove restful. In her dreams, it was not the man from whom Grit ran, but the idiot woman who had coveted her necklace. Her crossed eyes widened at the sight of Grit's pearl, reaching for it with jagged claws, her toothless mouth grinning. Without warning, the foul, gaping mouth uttered a familiar shriek. The woman's figure morphed into that of the hag with the wheelbarrow. Though Grit wielded her dagger with vehemence, the creature evaded her blade, clenched Grit's arms, and sent her hurtling over the edge of the chasm.

Grit woke with a start, sweat dampening her brow. She rose and stood in the cave's entrance. The morning sun cast a soft, pink glow over the chasm. Grit scanned her surroundings, finally settling her gaze on the bridge, with its rotted rope and missing planks. She was alone, safe on the southern side of the chasm. After stretching her sore muscles, she turned and stooped to pick up her pack. It was then she noticed a dim light shining at the back of the cave. Placing a hand on the cool stone wall, Grit proceeded with careful steps deeper into the dank cave. She focused on the light as the way grew darker. The point of light grew larger with each step, until she could make out an opening in the rock.

Exiting the tunnel, her spirit soared in the full light of morning. She took a deep breath, thankful for clear, pure air. A narrow road curved into a valley below. Boulders lined the road in front of her, but further down, tall, lush trees replaced the gray stones. The road cut through verdant pastures and brilliant gardens to pass before a grand palace. The low, white castle was rectangular in shape, deeper than it was wide, with red-topped turrets accenting each corner. Windows and balconies decorated its walls, and a white latticework fence enclosed the flat rooftop. A large courtyard stretched through its middle. People milled about the grounds, some alone, some in pairs or small groups.

On the southern side of the castle, warriors sparred under the supervision of a man who strode among the ranks, stopping now and then to correct improper form or to pat a triumphant combatant on the shoulder.

"Castle Concord," Grit whispered, recalling Scarlett's description of Kinsmon's home in the Southern Realm.

She smiled as she caressed the hilt of her dagger. She'd raised her weapon to defend herself from the man on the other side of the chasm, but it had been too long since she had last sparred for sport.

She could descend into the beauty and comfort of this place. She could walk among the gardens or take up her dagger and spar a worthy opponent. Surely, someone here fought as well as Coil. She might settle for one who could match Talon's skill. She could rest overnight, and then continue on her way.

A horn sounded. The warriors stood at attention, facing the man at the head of the ranks. Grit could not hear his words, nor did she care to subject herself to his, or anyone else's, command.

"Utter foolishness to think of joining them. This is no more my home than Thresh."

She shook her head at the castle and walked on. She could no more unpack her bag at Kinsmon's castle than resist the Southern Sea. There, she would finally be able to rest—not just for a night, but for a lifetime.

A small footpath broke from the road a few feet ahead of her. She followed its curve in the opposite direction from the castle. Soon, she found herself traveling a well-worn lane with wild hedges on either side. She picked edible leaves and berries along the way to take the edge off her hunger. She should have fought harder to keep Harth's sack of food from the man and woman the day before.

Just after midday, a cart pulled out from a side road, blocking Grit's way. An old man sat in the seat, holding the reins of a shaggy pony.

Grit stepped back, hand on her dagger.

"Where're you headed, my girl?" the old man asked.

"Nowhere." With her free hand, Grit tucked her pearl into her shirt.

The man leaned forward in his seat and placed his elbows on his knees. A sparkling, red stone dangled from a silver chain around his neck. He rubbed the stone across his lips, as if that, combined with squinting at the sun, would help him think more clearly.

"Well, now, that doesn't make much sense at all, does it? Clearly you're headed somewhere, though you may not yet know where. If you'd said 'nowhere in particular,' I might have believed you, but now . . . Now I'm not sure what to make of your answer."

"The Southern Sea, then," Grit said. "Would you mind not blocking the road?"

His eyes sparkled. "Did Kinsmon give you that pearl you tried to hide?"

Grit narrowed her eyes and drew her dagger. "Don't bother trying to steal it. Someone already tried and failed. You won't fare any better than he."

The man threw back his head and laughed. He looked at Grit, still shaking with laughter.

"Dear girl, put away your dagger. I've got my own necklace." His body stilled and his weathered face grew serious. "I'm no fool. I've lived long enough to learn no one can steal a promise, not with all the effort in the world. Oh, you could give your necklace away. In fact, you ought to if you find someone who has need of the promise it holds. Give it freely in that case, and you'll lose nothing in the giving. The both of you will gain exactly what each needs.

"Now, then, I'm heading south myself, and I've a cart full of vegetables, as well as some bread the old woman baked early this morning. Hop up. Help yourself to a full belly and rested legs."

Grit looked from the old man to the back of the cart to her dusty boots.

"You can get off whenever you want," he said.

Grit eyed the red stone and recalled her vow to Vell. *He bears the promise of Kinsmon. Perhaps I can entrust myself to him. Besides, a cart is faster than walking.*

"I'll sit in the back." She sheathed her dagger, climbed into the back of the cart, and situated herself between baskets of carrots and potatoes. The old man reached into a sack behind him and tossed her a loaf of bread.

"Don't worry. I won't ask you to reveal any secrets. Won't even ask you your name. That pearl's all I needed to see."

True to his word, the old man urged his pony on and left Grit to help herself to as much as she cared to eat. She ate until she could eat no more, then secreted a round loaf of bread and as much of the produce as could fit into her leather pack.

Late in the afternoon, the man slowed the pony to a stop at a crossroad. Facing Grit, he spoke for the first time since she had joined him.

"There's a town a little ways down this road, Verrivale, where I'll be stopping for the night and unloading my wares on the morrow. You're welcome to travel on with me, but if you're set on reaching the Southern Sea, you'll want to continue down the road we've been traveling."

Grit gazed down the road to Verrivale, enticed by the thought of a bed to soothe her cart-rattled bones. The old man was undemanding company. She could certainly tolerate him a little longer, especially if he'd keep feeding her. But as she looked past the farmer at the road that continued to the Southern Sea, all possibility of remaining with the man and his cartful of food vanished.

"I'll get out here." Grit hopped from the cart and nodded to the man.

He tossed her a loaf of bread. "For your journey."

She caught the loaf and stared at it a moment, biting her bottom lip. It shouldn't matter—"Thieving's as easy as breathing," she'd told Seal and Oath—but her pack felt heavy on her back. She didn't think she could carry it one step, let alone all the way to the Southern Sea. She looked at the man's kind face.

"I already have food." The words tumbled from her lips unbidden. She couldn't stop the flow, awkward and foolish as she felt. "I mean, I took some. I filled my pack. While you were driving. I . . . I should give it back, shouldn't I?"

The man held up a hand and smiled at her. "It's yours, my girl. Keep it. Your honesty has come at quite a price to your pride and is worth far more to me than all the coins in Verrivale."

"But how can I pay you? I have no money."

"It's yours." The man waved his hand over the baskets of food. "Take more, if you need. Kinsmon has promised my cart will never empty. No matter how much I give to those who hunger, I'll always have plenty for myself."

Grit glanced at the baskets in the back of the cart, but shook her head and stepped away. Something inside her had broken . . . or been made right. She couldn't tell which. As the immensity of her debt to this man, to Harth, to Whisp, to Kinsmon, and to so many others who had given to her, voluntarily or unaware, dawned upon her, she knew she could steal no more. How many nights had Dame Dara shivered without a blanket?

"I should pay." She bowed her head and rolled a pebble under the toe of her boot.

"This is love, my girl, beautiful and illogical, wild and free. If you cannot embrace it, then let us exchange names that we may count this a gift from one friend to another. If we meet again, you shall say, 'Why, Jareh, how pleasant to see you again,' and I will respond, 'A pleasure to see you, too . . .'" He waited expectantly, his ear turned toward her.

"Grit." She raised her head to meet his gaze. "My name is Grit."

A smile spread across Jareh's weathered face. "May you travel safely and without hunger, Grit. I hope we meet again."

He shook the reins, and the pony started on. Grit stood in the center of the road until the cart was little more than a speck in the distance. Then she turned to continue her journey, her pack full of food and her mind full of wonder. Like a baby sparrow first taking flight, something beautiful and illogical, wild and free fluttered feebly in her heart.

# TWENTY

The midday sun beat upon Grit's bare shoulders. She sat on the side of the southward road, removed her tunic, and studied the unmarked skin. The absence of brands no longer disturbed her. In Port Colony, she had longed for something to identify her as belonging somewhere, though she no longer belonged in Thresh. Here in the Southern Realm, however, she needed no origin to placate Vell or anyone else. When she reached the Southern Sea, she would begin a new life, independent of Thresh, Port Colony, and all she had known in either place.

Jareh's food sustained her body, though her spirit flagged in his absence. *I almost wish I'd remained with the old man. If nothing else, he's a living, breathing human being.* Grit bit into her second loaf of bread. Across the road, the bushes rustled. Grit jumped to her feet and pulled her dagger, ready to meet any opponent.

A dog emerged from the shrubbery. Black and mangy, with hairless patches near his tail, he lay on the grass watching her. Scooting forward with his belly against the ground, he made his way across the road until he crouched just a few yards from Grit.

"What do you want, worm?" She'd stab the beast if he pounced on her.

He turned his head to one side and whined.

"Go away." Grit threw a piece of bread at his head, hoping to frighten him away. He opened his mouth to catch the bread midair. Wagging his tail, he inched closer. His ribs protruded from his sides.

Grit broke a larger chunk from her loaf. She tossed the piece to the dog, who devoured it in one gulp.

"I don't care if you're starving. That's all I'm giving you. Now get lost."

The wiggle started in his tail, but soon his entire body squirmed back and forth.

"I mean it, worthless creature! I've no use for a dog who thinks he's a worm. Anyway, you don't want me. I might eat you once I've run out of bread."

Grit sheathed her dagger, threw her pack over her shoulder, and sauntered down the road. After several steps, she turned. The dog had followed and stood in the middle of the road. He plopped to his belly and wagged his tail. She stomped her foot at him, turned, and refused to look back again.

The dog remained close when she sat to eat her evening meal. With each bite she took, his head tilted up, following the motion of her hand. Sighing, she tossed him the crust of her bread.

"You win, Worm."

He wiggled his way to her, nudged his head under her hand, and rested his chin in her lap. As she scratched between his ears, flakes of skin appeared in his dull, black fur.

"You're a nasty beast, and I doubt you'll be good company, but you may travel with me if you insist."

When Grit curled up under a shrub that night, Worm crawled under the bush with her. She cursed as he stepped on her hair and then her arm. Resting his head on her thigh, he settled with his tail near her face.

"Turn around, stupid dog." Grit reached for his neck to guide his head to hers. His body twisted, and soon the two were comfortably situated. Even if Worm's head smelled no better than his tail, Grit smiled as she laid her arm over his body. The presence of another living creature, even one as unpleasant as Worm, comforted her.

The next morning, Grit beckoned Worm to walk at her side.

"You may as well know, since you've attached yourself to me, we are headed to the Southern Sea." The dog's ears perked as Grit spoke. "I used to live along the Western Sea, you know. The waters there are frigid in winter, but perfect in summer, especially after a day of sparring. Coil and I used to . . ." She stopped, the memory of pleasant swims too painful to relive.

She frowned at Worm. "Do you know when I first noticed him, Coil of Dara? It was my Sixth Branding. He was standing in the front row, his hair spiraling in every direction and a smudge of jam on the tip of his nose. He was laughing, Worm, laughing at me as Dame Berth touched the rod to my arm. I swore he would never see me cry. He never did, either, not for the branding rod or for anything else. I never shed a single tear."

She realized she had stopped walking when she felt Worm lean against her leg and press his nose into her hand.

She patted his head and laughed. "No need to pity me, Worm. I've done perfectly well without tears. Look how far I've come. I'm almost to the Southern Sea, and I'm conversing with a dog."

She shook her head and closed her eyes to shut out the bitter reality of her loneliness. She yearned to spar with Coil, to listen to Sire Stone's careful instruction, even to snap at Dame Berth over the imperfect consistency of the porridge or whatever other complaint she might invent. *All of that is gone. Even if I were free to go back, the disgrace of failure and the shame of disownment bar my return. Thresh and all it holds are gone. Gone, gone, gone.*

She bent over, picked up a rock, and threw it as hard as she could against a tree. It hit the trunk with a thud and dropped softly to the ground. When she turned around, Worm sat waiting expectantly.

"Come on, Worm," she said, weary of her angry grief. "Let's go. It can't be too much farther."

**\*\*\*\***

Later that day, the air thickened. When the wind brought the scent of the ocean, Grit left the road behind. Breaking through dense scrub, she stepped over a twisted root and scanned the horizon. The Southern Sea stretched from east to west as far as her eyes could see, the sun reflected in its gentle ripples. She could almost taste the warm, sea-soaked air.

"Breath it in, Worm. It smells like the Western Sea, but warm."

She would stay until the memory of Thresh had faded, until she'd made a new name and a new life for herself.

She sat, removed her boots, and buried her toes underneath the warm sand. Worm sat beside her.

Ahead of them, a hundred yards from the shore, a small boat bobbed in the water. Near the boat, a man's head emerged from the ocean. The man reached a hand over the boat's side, then disappeared again under the water. Two minutes later, he appeared and disappeared a second time.

Grit wrapped her arms around her knees and squinted, intent on the spot where she had seen the diver plunge beneath the surface. He came up, reached into the boat, and dove again. He repeated the process every two minutes, never acknowledging Grit or even looking in her direction.

"What's he doing, Worm?" Grit asked.

The dog lay down in the sand and kept watch with Grit.

Finally, the man lifted himself out of the water and rolled his body into the boat. Seated in the middle of the small vessel,

140

he rowed toward shore. As he neared the beach, he jumped into the water and pulled the boat by a rope tied around his ankle.

He was Grit's height, slightly built with well-defined muscles for a man of his advanced age, and skin darker than any Grit had seen. Around his waist, he wore a cloth similar to what Threshan infants wore beneath their gowns. As he stooped to unfasten the rope from his ankle, the sun glinted off his scalp.

Without warning, Worm leapt forward and bounded across the beach. He circled the man, barking incessantly.

"Worm!" Grit rose and ran to the shoreline. "Get back, dumb dog!"

"He means no harm." The man laughed and knelt to let the dog lick his face. When he looked at Grit, his eyes were cloudy and white. She shuddered and looked away from his face. A thin silver band encircled his ankle.

"You are far from home," he said.

"I have no home."

"Your pearl says otherwise."

Grit wrapped her hand around the white sphere.

The man frowned. "I do not see much, but what I see, I see clearly. And, I see your pearl. No one wearing that pearl can rightfully claim to be without home."

He patted Worm on the head, rose, and pulled his boat further up onto the beach. From its hull, he lifted a basket filled with rough, oddly-shaped, gray shells. Both arms wrapped around the basket as he hugged it to his chest.

"Come, I could use your help."

"I didn't offer my help," Grit said, still clasping her pearl.

The man stopped and faced her, his milky eyes unfocussed. "What else have you to do?" With one hand, he gestured toward the sea. "It is not as though you can travel farther."

He turned and continued up the beach. Grit remained at the water's edge a moment, then trotted after him. He was right. She had nowhere else to go.

"The Southern Sea is a wonderful place," he said as Grit came alongside him, "especially for those who feel they have no home. There's an empty hut a hundred yards east of here. Inhabit it, if you like."

"I can build my own hut." She might have nowhere to go, but she wasn't so weak as to need to dwell in a hut built by another's hands.

"Wherever you have come from, you need not prove your worth here."

They had reached a modest structure of upright sticks bound together with twisted vines. A thatched roof covered a plank floor. The entire front was open to the sea. The man set his basket on a woven rug in the middle of the floor and faced Grit. "There is no honor in building a hut, nor shame in taking over an empty hut. The honor lies not in how or by whom the hut was constructed, but in the actions of the individual who lives within the hut."

Gesturing for Grit to join him, he seated himself on the rug and took a shell from the basket. Grit sat, her legs hanging over the edge of the raised hut, and surveyed the man's home. The furnishings were simple, a table and chair against the back wall and a bed in the corner.

"Do you have weapons?" she asked.

"Only this, and it can hardly be called a weapon." He held up the small knife with which he had separated the halves of the shell. A memory flickered in Grit's mind, but disappeared as the man continued. "I have no need of defense. Very few people, and even fewer of them unkind, come this far south. Do you have oysters where you come from?"

"No."

He scraped the inside of one of the shells with the knife and held something white out to Grit. "Try it."

"You first," she said.

He slid the meat from the knife into his mouth, pried open another shell, scraped his knife against it, and held the meat out to her.

Cautiously, Grit took the oyster from the knife's blade and put it in her mouth. It tasted fresh, like the sea with a hint of melon and a whisper of smoke. As it slid down her throat, all her senses awakened. She felt the soft breeze against her cheek, heard the man's gentle exhale and Worm's soft whine, smelled the sand and the sea and the flowers blooming outside the hut.

Grit opened her eyes. "It isn't awful."

"Someday, if you like, I will teach you to dive for them." He whistled, and Worm took an oyster from his hand.

The diver shucked his oysters, eating the meat of some and holding the meat of others out for Grit or Worm. Grit eased her hand away from her dagger. She wouldn't need it here. The man was no threat. On the contrary, he set her at ease. Peace washed over her with every wave of the sea, with every taste of his catch. She scooted closer to the basket. Watching his knife as he slid the blade between the half-shells, she caught her breath.

"Tell me about your knife. I have one just like it." Reaching deep into her pocket, she pulled out her Sire's Aid, the tiny dagger she had thought good for nothing.

The man smiled and hummed. "You must have been destined to come here and shuck oysters with me. Try it."

Grit shrugged, took an oyster from the basket, and mimicked the man's actions. Sliding the blade of the tiny knife into a small opening where the shells met, she wiggled the handle and pried the shells apart. The meat stuck to one shell.

She scraped her knife against the hard surface to detach it. At last, she held the meat on the edge of her blade.

"Your turn," she said.

Holding the man's wrist, she set the oyster in his hand. He slid his thumb over its mangled form, popped it into his mouth, and smiled. "Magnificent."

When the sun lay low in the western sky, Grit rose from the rug and looked to the east.

"A hundred yards?" she asked.

"Yes. Rest secure. You won't find another soul for miles."

She hopped onto the sand and whistled to Worm, who had fallen asleep under the hut. After several steps, she turned back to the man, who remained seated on the rug.

"Do you have a name?"

He looked up, and his cloudy eyes seemed to search the sky. "Ezekiel. Ezekiel of the Southern Sea."

The hut was just as Ezekiel had said it would be. One hundred yards to the east, nestled among the foliage lining the beach, with one side wide open to the ocean. Like Ezekiel's hut, this one contained a bed, a chair, and a table. A woven rug lay in the center of the raised plank floor. After wiping the sand from her legs, Grit climbed into the bed. Worm jumped in after her and curled at her feet. Despite Ezekiel's assurance that she could rest secure, she wrapped her left arm around her pack and her right hand around her dagger. She ruffled Worm's fur with her toes.

"Sleep well, my companion," she said. "We may stay awhile."

# TWENTY-ONE

When Grit awoke to a brilliant blue sky over a calm sea, the dog was gone. She sat up and searched the hut. Leaving her boots under the bed, she stepped onto the beach, bent over, and peered beneath the hut.

"Worm? Where are you, stupid beast?"

She straightened her back and looked around. Further down the beach, Ezekiel emerged from the water, a bundle in his hand. The black dog jumped in circles around him.

Grit trudged across the sand. "Fool dog can't stay where he belongs. Unless, he thinks he belongs with that old man instead of the girl who's fed him for days." As she neared Ezekiel, she called out to him. "He's an ungrateful beast. I'll take him away before he disturbs you more."

Ezekiel laughed, his face raised to the sky. "Nonsense. He's a magnificent animal, as true and brave as one might hope to meet."

"How can you say that? You barely know him."

"Ah, remember." Ezekiel pointed to his vacant eyes. "Though I do not see much, what I see, I see clearly. You couldn't ask for a purer heart than his."

"He's a dog." Grit put her hand on her hip. Perhaps the man's mind was as vacant as his eyes. "A dog, Ezekiel. You are praising a dog."

"Tell me, then, what fault you find with him."

Grit opened her mouth to speak, then shut it again. She gestured toward the dog. "He's filthy and mangy and stinks."

Ezekiel sniffed the air. "He's not the only one who stinks. Perhaps a dip in the sea would serve you both well."

"I don't . . ." Grit stopped, her nose close to her shoulder. "Fine. Come, Worm. The blind man says we stink. I say it has been too long since I had the pleasure of a morning swim."

She stomped as best she could across the sandy beach, Worm prancing around her with all the eagerness of a not fully-grown dog.

Behind her, Ezekiel laughed. "Come back when you are through with your morning swim. I should have cooked our breakfast by then. I hope you like fish."

Grit turned to scowl at Ezekiel. Realizing his blindness nullified her efforts, she said, "Only when it is cooked properly, and be sure to save some for my pure-hearted mutt."

She thought she heard him laughing as she muttered to Worm, "I sound like my dame. Only she isn't my dame anymore, not really."

She spoke the truth to the dog, yet it felt false somehow. The farther she traveled from Thresh, the more her tones and turns of phrase—even her thoughts sometimes—reminded her of Berth. How could she truly separate herself from the woman who disowned her? There was no immediate answer.

Grit shrugged and continued on. The dog bounded after her. Once at her hut, she stripped to her undergarments. Then looking around at the beach, empty of all but an old blind man, she shed those as well. Patting her hand against her thigh for Worm to follow, she rushed into the Southern Sea.

The warm water caressed her sore, weary muscles and cleansed her skin of weeks of sweat and dirt. Floating with her face to the sun, she tried to empty her mind of everything but the Southern Sea. She closed her eyes with no fear of Coil sneaking up to splash her in the face or dunk her beneath the waves. It would take time, many more swims like this, before she felt normal not knowing where Coil's body was in relation to hers. She would become a new person. She would exchange

Grit of Berth and Stone, or Grit of Stone, or whomever she had been until now, for Grit of the Southern Sea. And she would grow accustomed to swimming without Coil.

Worm's sharp toenails dug into her side as he tried to swim around her. She righted herself and put a hand out the support the dog. Rubbing his side with her other hand, she looked back to the hut and saw her clothes in a crumpled heap. She swam to shore, walked across the warm sand, picked up her clothes, and smelled them. *Little good my swim will do if I do nothing about my clothing.*

A few minutes later, she draped her wet clothing over the edge of the hut's floor, where the sun could dry them. She pulled the sheet from the bed, wrapped it around her body, and secured it with a knot over one shoulder. She wrapped her belt around her waist and tucked her dagger into it. *Only fools are found without weapons.*

When she returned to Ezekiel, he had a fire going. Grit's mouth watered at the scent of skewered fish roasting above the flames. The old man slid a fish from the skewer onto a plate. She took the plate from his waiting hand and found the courage to ask the question that had lingered in her mind since he first spoke to her.

"How did you know I'm far from home?"

Ezekiel slid another fish onto a plate and sat in the sand. "There are two reasons people come to Ezekiel of the Southern Sea. One, they are sent by Kinsmon to carry my pearls to Castle Concord. Two, they are driven here by a hunger to distance themselves from a home they no longer wish to claim. Since you did not identify yourself as one of Kinsmon's friends, I assumed you'd left your home far behind."

"But I am Kinsmon's friend. He gave me this pearl." The words tumbled unbidden from her mouth.

Ezekiel said with a gentle laugh, "Ah, but you did not say this at first. Be truthful. Has Kinsmon sent you here, or are you distancing yourself from your home?"

"Thresh . . ." Grit stopped, grimaced, and began again. It was no use pretending Thresh meant anything at all, either good or bad. It was better to forget the place as entirely as it had forgotten her. "I have no home."

"Thresh, you say?" His wistful voice demanded no reply. "It has been a long time, generations in fact, since a pearl from these waters has traveled to that village."

"What are you talking about?" She shook her head in confusion.

"Your pearl," Ezekiel said.

Grit remained silent, at a loss to grasp the man's meaning.

"Where do you think your pearl came from, if not from these very waters, discovered by my very hands?"

"You found my pearl?" Grit pinched the small orb between her thumb and finger.

Ezekiel nodded. "Found it and gave it to Kinsmon, like I do all the pearls I find. I never imagined it would make it all the way to Thresh."

"It didn't, actually." She could not deny the truth of her origins, now that it was out. Somehow, in Ezekiel's presence, the past didn't seem so horrid. "Kinsmon gave it to me some distance south of Thresh, on a promontory over the Western Sea."

"All the same, I never imagined it would have such a journey. Eat your fish before it grows cold." Ezekiel made a circle in the air with his fork.

She stayed with Ezekiel through the entire day, observing closely as he introduced her to the edible plants specific to the Southern Realm and cautioned her away from those leaves and berries that would cause illness or death. Whether she stayed

148

near him or followed the coastline many miles east, her survival depended in part upon a familiarity with the foliage.

Grit examined the veins of a new edible leaf Ezekiel had given her. "How do you do it? How do you see all of this when your eyes are useless?"

"I've learned to rely on senses other than sight. When a man cannot see with his eyes, he must rely on his nose, his ears, his hands, and sometimes, most frightening of all, his heart."

Grit nibbled the tip of the leaf. "How do you rely on your heart?"

"I have relied on my heart most recently by entrusting myself to a stinky, pugnacious girl who appeared out of nowhere with nothing to recommend her but a pearl around her neck." Ezekiel smiled and placed a hand on his chest. "Nothing but a pearl around her neck and an understanding, here in my heart, that I was to welcome her as a friend, though I do not even know her name."

*A stinky, pugnacious girl with nothing to recommend her.* That's what she'd become. Perhaps she'd always been offensive, but she used to have something to recommend her. She rubbed her arm. Would anyone in Thresh accept her on nothing more than a feeling and a pearl? No, they had cast her out. There was no going back, even if she wanted to.

When Grit did not answer, Ezekiel said, "You will understand someday, if you do not now."

"Humph! Kinsmon, Scarlett, and now you. All of you speak as if I'm a babe without a thought in her head."

"Perhaps you have too many thoughts in your head, or just not enough of the right ones. I'd never accuse you of having no thoughts." Ezekiel put a fist-sized, purple fruit into Grit's basket. "That's all for this morning."

He retraced his steps to his hut. Grit followed without speaking.

149

"It's Grit," she said as he gathered his fishing net. "My name, it's Grit of Berth . . . No, Grit of Stone. My dame disowned me."

"What does Kinsmon call you?" Ezekiel asked, his face toward the sea.

Kinsmon's voice was clear in her memory. "Grit of Berth and Stone. It's what they all called me in Port Colony, too, but it isn't true. Berth disowned me."

"If Kinsmon has called you Grit of Berth and Stone, then Grit of Berth and Stone you are. Let no one tell you differently. The blood of your dame runs through your veins, and neither she nor you nor anyone else can alter that."

# TWENTY-TWO

"How did you come to be here, Ezekiel?" Grit asked. Winter came to the Southern Realm, and though it arrived milder than in Thresh, the pair huddled close to the fire with Worm curled atop Grit's booted feet and three skewered fish propped close to the flame.

Ezekiel peeled a section of bark from a thin stick. "I was born here. I lived here happily for many years, in fact, watching the waves turn white against the sand and the evening sky turn every shade of red and orange and pink and purple."

"You haven't always been blind?" It had never occurred to Grit that Ezekiel might have once enjoyed sight.

"No." He hung his head, as if burdened by a truth he did not care to disclose. He sighed deeply and raised his chin. "In youth, my vision was perfect, except I did not value the things my eyes beheld. It was a flaw my patient dame never could correct. A beautiful woman with a cart of jewels is a fine thing in the eyes of a young man laboring after the rare pearl, but her appearance proved false and her riches cheap before my story ended."

"How did you lose your sight?"

An odd smile played at the corner of his mouth. "Do you really want to know, Grit of Berth and Stone? It isn't for the faint-hearted."

"I do want to know, and I'm far from faint-hearted."

Ezekiel poked the fire with his stick and waved the red-hot tip in a circle before plunging it into the sand.

"I burned my sight away. When I realized I couldn't trust my eyes, I took a stick like this one, held it in the fire, and

151

applied it to one eye and then the other. I would not have my foolish eyes deceive me yet again."

"Ezekiel, that was a dreadfully stupid thing to do." She clutched her arm where her sixteenth brand had been.

"It was painful, but I have not regretted it. I told you long ago I've learned to rely upon my other senses. They, together with a heart devoted to what is true and beautiful and good, have never failed me."

Grit stared into the fire, Ezekiel's words lingering in her mind. *A heart devoted to what is true and beautiful and good.* She had overheard the same phrase in Port Colony.

"What have you heard of this war in the north?" she asked.

"I've heard very little," he said, "but this much I know. If Chasmaria is to survive, her people must stand as one, each guarding another's back. It was infidelity that destroyed Chasmaria's ancient peace, and peace will come again only through the reversal of old Harmony's error."

"Who's Harmony?"

"The last great king of Chasmaria," Ezekiel said. "In his early days, when Kinsmon's banner flew above Harmony's palace, peace reigned all across this country. Harmony broke faith first with Kinsmon, and then with his closest ally, Queen Amity. It was the work of Havoc, and now she's at it again. That faithless creature would destroy the last vestiges of Chasmaria's glory. She's a vile creature, full of empty promises."

Grit ran her fingers through Worm's thick, black coat. "They spoke of her in Port Colony. I have met Havoc, if I understood them correctly. I don't care to meet her again."

"You have met that foul wench?" Ezekiel's back straightened. He turned his face to her, his milky eyes unfocussed. "Dear girl, tell me you haven't."

"Just once, on the Koradin-Thresh Highway. She . . . She cost me my test." Confusion as real as the moment Havoc tossed her into the wheelbarrow threatened to overwhelm her. She'd felt that fear once since, in the tree outside Peril and Zag's burning village. "I saw her again, Ezekiel. No, I *felt* her again in the Mid-Chasmarian forest. In the future, I'll do all in my power to stay as far from her as possible. I've no desire for hag's company."

"You may not have a choice. Some battles we may avoid. Others find us, however far we run, however cleverly we hide. Even now, Havoc scours the land, seeking to destroy the true, the beautiful, and the good." Ezekiel placed a hand on Grit's shoulder.

"Ah, blind man." She nudged him with her elbow. "You do not see I am perfectly safe. Whatever you think my necklace says, I am neither true, nor beautiful, nor good."

"You are not a liar, either, Grit of Berth and Stone." A grave expression came over Ezekiel's face. "At least, not a very good one. Why else would you remain here, if you did not possess these things in some measure?"

"You feed me, that's why." Grit rose, removed the fish from the fire, and sat back down beside Ezekiel. More confusing than Havoc was her own heart. She could name her hatred of the wench and her disgust with Thresh's council, but she couldn't explain the tug she felt when she looked at Ezekiel or Worm. Words failed entirely when she tried to express the sweet tumult accompanying every thought of Coil.

She pushed the golden-haired sireling from her mind, slid the fish onto two plates, and set one of the plates on Ezekiel's lap. "Take a bite of this and tell me it isn't worth sitting beside a blind man for an entire lifetime."

Ezekiel shook his head and laughed as Grit set the third fish on the ground for Worm.

Grit retired early, her mind wearier than her body. Ezekiel had condemned her as a coward, running and hiding from herself as much as from Havoc. Yet he also counted her among the true, the beautiful, and the good. Whether or not she could hide from Havoc, it seemed impossible to hide from the blind man's prying eyes. She pulled Sire Stone's blanket over her head and tried to sleep.

As winter progressed, Grit's swims became infrequent. She spent the first portion of each morning sitting on the beach, sometimes with Worm and Ezekiel, sometimes with only Worm, watching the waves lap against the shore. The birds were plentiful on this secluded beach, where no one rushed at them with shrieks and well-aimed pebbles as they did in Thresh.

"They are peaceful creatures," Grit said to Ezekiel one morning. "They care nothing for our activities, so busy are they with their own. It is strange I had to travel so far to see them as they really are."

A small gull waded along the water's edge. A second gull swept down and circled about the first bird's head, as if to urge her to take flight with him. Again and again, he circled high above, then swept down close, but she remained fixed on the shore, gentle waves lapping against her stubborn, twig-like legs.

Grit could not contain the scream that welled up from the core of her being. "Fly with him, stupid creature!"

Her fingers curled around the rock she'd been rolling in the sand. As she raised her hand above her head to throw the stone at the bird, Ezekiel's hand closed over hers.

"You aren't angry at birds, Grit." His finger gently pried hers apart, and the stone dropped to the sand with a thud.

She looked to the east, away from Ezekiel. The rising sun, that glaring orb of gold, seemed to shine on all her folly.

"It didn't have to be like this, Ezekiel, me flying alone to the very edge of Chasmaria. He told me to fight, but I didn't have the strength. He would have come with me . . ." Her voice trailed off, her energy spent.

Ezekiel's voice was quiet and unimposing. "Why didn't he come with you?"

Grit gulped, the gravity of her error tight as a rope around her neck. "I told him he was a fool."

Ezekiel released his hold on her and placed his hand on the sand between them. "It is strange, isn't it, the extents to which we must sometimes go to see ourselves as we really are?"

Grit looked into his eyes, vacant since he had punished them for their deception, and placed her hand over his. "Strange indeed," she said.

Over the Southern Sea, the two birds rose into the air, circling each other over and over until Grit could no longer tell one from the other. "It is all very strange indeed."

**\*\*\*\***

When Grit arrived at Ezekiel's hut the next morning, a dummy made of spare clothing stuffed with sand hung from a pole stuck in the ground.

"You were training to be a warrior, weren't you?" Ezekiel asked.

Grit rubbed her no longer branded arm. "A long time ago. I was good, too."

"It won't be the same as a sparring partner, but you'll enjoy using your dagger again." He plumped the dummy's torso.

Approaching slowly, Grit drew her dagger. As she circled the dummy, the sneering face of Turf of Elna and Bord formed in her mind—the dark, contemptuous eyes, one slightly higher than the other, the crooked nose broken in some childhood accident, the fat lips issuing threats he could not enforce, and the nick in his ear, a memento of the last time he'd dared challenge her to a match. She attacked the figure with all the rage of her banishment, slicing through fabric and sending sand spilling onto the beach. Shaming before the council was too good for Turf. The cheating coward's blood ought to flow from his body like sand from the dummy.

When she was through, Ezekiel unfastened the limp clothing from the pole, shook it free of sand, and handed it to her. She smiled broadly under a layer of sweat.

"You will find a needle and thread on my table. Repair the damage you have done," Ezekiel said.

Her smile faded as she looked at the tattered garments in her arms. "You want me to sew it back together?"

"Do you wish to spar again?"

"Of course I do." The satisfaction of destroying Turf still coursed through her veins. "I just didn't think the price of sparring would be an entire day of mending."

"Ah." Ezekiel clucked his tongue. "You did not think of the difficulty of restoring what has been lost, of repairing what has been broken. It is harder to heal than to wound and more noble to create than to destroy. It was many years after I burned my eyes before I was able to walk this beach and swim these waters without fear of the unseen."

He placed a hand on her shoulder. "Be thankful it will only take you the rest of the morning to mend your new sparring partner."

Their routine adjusted so that Grit spent her mornings sparring and mending while Ezekiel dove below the water's surface for oysters. In the afternoons, Grit scavenged for edible nuts, berries, mushrooms, and foliage. In the evenings, they roasted fish over the fire or shucked oysters in Ezekiel's hut, feasting together on the day's bounty. The busyness of her hands stilled her soul almost as much as Ezekiel's quiet understanding of the things she couldn't say. In time, he taught her to dive for oysters, to plunge to the bottom of the sea, to catch her breath at the surface, and to return again to the shimmering, underwater world. It was only there, beneath the waters, which stretched all the way to Thresh, that Grit allowed herself to think kindly of the village she left and the warrior who vowed to avenge her enemies. Did Coil swim alone now, or did he share the sea with someone else?

# TWENTY-THREE

One spring evening in Ezekiel's hut, Grit's knife struck against something hard in her oyster. A round, white pearl the size of her little fingernail rested in the oyster's flesh. She removed it and held it between her thumb and forefinger.

"Ezekiel, I've found a pearl."

He placed his fingers over hers and felt the smooth surface. "It is perfect, and it is yours by right."

"What do I do with it?"

"If you are willing to part with it, there is a young man at Castle Concord who would pay handsomely for this pearl. Take it to Dagger, and he will have all he needs to fashion an item of rarest beauty for the object of his deepest affection."

"Dagger?" Recalling the young leader who had so resembled her sire, Grit drew her hand from Ezekiel's. "I met him in Port Colony."

"Then you have met a miracle. Dagger's tender dame did not survive his birth. The midwife, young though she was, saw the danger in throwing Dagger to the mercy of his wretched sire and attempted to deliver the babe to his dame's sire. The cruel sire intercepted her on her way to the old man, wrested the infant from her arms, and tossed him into the river. It was there, above the swirling waters, that Kinsmon caught Dagger. The boy has lived at Castle Concord all his life, only venturing out across Chasmaria in recent years."

"What do you know of his affections?" Grit rolled the pearl between her fingers.

"Only that he saw her first when he was seven, and has never looked at any other girl."

LISA DUNN

"He'll pay a good price for this pearl?" For the right amount, she could forgive the proud sireling for being sheltered all his life. And if she was right about Dagger's affections, she might give Scarlet good reason to consider her a friend.

Ezekiel nodded. "He will, but you must take it to Castle Concord. Dagger rarely comes this way now that war has broken out in the north. I have several pearls for Kinsmon, as well, if you would be so good as to deliver them."

"I'll go tomorrow. I'll make it a quick trip, so we may feast together again as soon as possible. Can I bring anything back for you?"

"No. Only send me word when you arrive at Castle Concord. Send me word and a bottle of Kinsmon's special brew. I haven't had that in years." Ezekiel's voice held a sadness Grit had never heard. His cloudy eyes pooled with water. "And travel well, dear Grit of Berth and Stone, wherever your steps may lead."

Grit straightened her shoulders and sat back on her knees. She studied the old man's face. "You speak as if I will not return to you. Why would my steps lead anywhere but here?"

"Truly, I do not know, but I see it as clearly as I see your pearl."

"Foolishness, Ezekiel of the Southern Sea." She stood, crossed the rug, and hopped down the step onto the sand. "Utter foolishness you speak. Come, Worm. The blind man can't see the Southern Sea is where I belong."

****

"Ezekiel?" Grit sat up in bed and squinted at the man sitting at the edge of her hut. "What are you doing here?"

He stood and held a small packet out to her. "I didn't trust you not to leave without saying goodbye. Take this with you."

off

160

Grit stumbled out of bed and crossed her hut. She touched the silk packet in Ezekiel's hand. "Your sewing kit? Blind man, I have no plans to take up a needle while I am gone. Truth be told, I rather look forward to not sewing for a change."

He pressed it into her hand. "Take it anyway. There's no telling what might need mending during your journey."

"What if you need to mend something?"

"Take it."

"Fine." Grit avoided Ezekiel's eyes, sightless but ever-seeing. She thrust the sewing kit into her pocket and gathered her belongings. Throwing her pack over her shoulder, she whistled to Worm. The dog jumped from the bed and trotted to her side.

Ezekiel dangled a small pouch by its drawstring. "You're forgetting Kinsmon's pearls."

"Yes, the pearls. We mustn't forget Kinsmon's pearls." Grit snatched the pouch. Her fingers fumbled with the flap of her pack. Why did she feel so clumsy this morning?

Grit patted her thigh. "Come, Worm. The sooner we go, the sooner we may return. We'll bring back a new sewing kit for the old man—with silver needles maybe—since he seems intent on forfeiting his old one."

The dog licked Ezekiel's knuckles. The man crouched and took the creature's face in his hands. "Dear, sweet Worm, you are a companion like none other. How I wish we did not need to part company."

When he rose, tears moistened his cheeks. "Goodbye, Grit of Berth and Stone. I would say the same to you as I have said to Worm."

"Dry your tears, Ezekiel. It's not as bad as all that." Yet somehow, it felt it might be as bad as all that. What if Ezekiel was right? What if impulse took her elsewhere? Suppose Ezekiel left or offered her hut to some wayward traveler. What

161

then? Would she live the rest of her life without her blind man, without her Ezekiel?

The questions were too many and too difficult to answer. She turned from Ezekiel before she changed her mind. She could drop her pack on the sand and refuse to leave. The blind man had welcomed her in all her stench and rudeness. The sea and shore had fed them well enough. She didn't need Dagger's money, not really, but there was Scarlett to consider, too.

Though he could not see her, she refused to look at Ezekiel. "Guard my hut while I'm away. I'd hate to shed blood reclaiming it when I return. I will return, Ezekiel. Don't desert this place in my absence."

"Ah, Grit . . . I shall remain at the Southern Sea until it calls me home. You may count on that." He stretched out his hand and touched her arm. "Goodbye, Grit."

"Goodbye, Ezekiel."

With the dog at her heel, she walked to the edge of the beach. She pushed aside tree branches, stepped over roots, and kicked low shrubs to the side as she left, never looking back at Ezekiel, her hut, or the Southern Sea. *To hesitate is to waver, and to waver is weakness.* She laughed softly. *I suppose a little of Thresh lingers in me, after all.* Still, she could not bring herself to look back, even for the sake of proving her will strong enough to deny the memory of Thresh and to resist the allure of the Southern Sea. If she looked back, she might never have strength to leave this place.

At the edge of the coastal forest, she found the road that had brought her to Ezekiel.

"North, Worm." She pointed in that direction.

The dog trotted at her side through the morning and into the afternoon. In the evening, they slept under a shrub, much as they had on their first night together except this time,

Worm's ribs did not press against Grit's arm, nor did his fur cause her skin to itch. His smell also was less offensive.

"You've improved much since we met, wretched beast." Grit scratched between the dog's ears. He twisted his head to lick her face.

They had not been walking long the following morning when a cart rattled toward them from the south. Grit stepped to the side of the road to allow the cart to pass. As it neared, the driver pulled back on the reins. Grit recognized the farmer with whom she had traveled a day on her way south.

"Why, Grit, a pleasure to see you again." A smile spread across the old man's weathered face.

"A pleasure to see you, too, Jareh." A strange gladness filled Grit's heart. She looked back the way they had come. "Have your wares brought you this far south?"

"I made my annual delivery to Ezekiel of the Southern Sea this morning. He told me I might come across you on my way to Castle Concord." Jareh patted the seat beside him. "Will you accept a ride from an old friend?"

"Only if you will take Worm, too." Grit placed a protective hand on the dog's head. She wasn't leaving Ezekiel without him.

"Of course. Any friend of yours is a friend of mine. Hop up, both of you."

Grit pulled herself onto the wagon and settled herself beside Jareh.

"The Southern Sea has served you well," he said. "You appear healthier in every regard."

Grit shrugged. "I was not so unhealthy before."

As she leaned over to help Worm situate himself at her feet, she remembered Ezekiel's accusation, *You are not a liar . . . at least not a very good one.* Could Jareh see her falsehood as easily as the blind man had? The truth, which she would not admit to

Jareh or anyone else, was that her time at the Southern Sea left her feeling lighter and freer than she'd ever felt before.

Jareh reached into a basket behind Grit and pulled out a loaf of bread. "I acquired some fresh bread yesterday, if you're hungry. It's nothing compared to what my old woman bakes, but it'll fill your belly."

Grit shifted in her seat, her mouthwatering. "I don't have anything to offer you now, but I expect to come into some money soon. I can pay you this time, if you'll wait until we get to Castle Concord."

Jareh threw his head back and laughed heartily. "Now you sound like the girl I drove to the south! Have you forgotten my cart will never be empty? My old woman and I have always had enough to eat, and neither your money nor anyone else's could add to the peace we enjoy under our cozy roof."

"Wait." Grit gaped at the man. He must have misspoken. "Do you mean you share a home with your old woman?"

"A lovely little hut in the middle of a beautiful garden. Flowers in front, edibles in back. There we have lived forty years, and there we hope to live another forty. Seven children flourished there, and on our happiest days, each returns with a lovely dame and a brood of his own."

Grit took the loaf from Jareh's hand and bit into it. "You mean to tell me you and this woman of yours have shared a hut for forty years, and happily, too, and your offspring return to you, with dames and offspring of their own?" She swallowed and shook her head. "That just isn't done."

Jareh laughed. "Perhaps not where you come from, but it is not so uncommon here in the Southern Realm. I myself find it a most favorable arrangement."

"Do you never grow ill of her, though? Forty years is a long time."

The old man patted her knee. "Ah, Grit. When you find your heart bound up in the life and soul of another, there you find true treasure. Have I grown ill of her? Yes, from time to time, I've been ill of her, and she of me, but love, being kind, quickly cured each of us of our infirmity. We vowed at the beginning never to remain long in discord, and we have kept the promises we made to one another."

"But . . ." Grit stopped, not sure what objection she could make to Jareh's odd alliance with his old woman. It was even more peculiar than the alliance between Dame Berth and Sire Stone.

"But nothing. I don't expect you to understand, being so young and so fresh to this world, but it's a beautiful thing to be so connected to another person. I have never in forty years regretted binding myself to her, not even for an instant. Perhaps someday you will know for yourself what I mean."

Grit shook her head. "Oh, no. I am quite content to maintain my hut on the Southern Sea, alone except for Ezekiel and Worm."

Jareh turned to look at her. "You study those bushes as if even you do not believe what's just come out of your mouth. Have you had any visitors there at the Southern Sea?"

"No." Grit focused on the passing scenery, her eyes struggling to fix on one object.

"Hmm." Jareh returned his attention to the road, which split in two directions. He steered the pony to the right. "This way takes us right to Castle Concord's front steps."

A bush laden with delicate white flowers caught Grit's eye. She turned in her seat to watch it as they passed. A strange ache gripped her chest.

Jareh pointed. "Amity-berry blossoms. Prettiest flowers in all Chasmaria, if you ask me. The berries are something else, too, plump and sweet and the most glorious shade of pink you've ever seen. Even Kinsmon is partial to them."

"Tell me more about your old woman. How did you come to make such a close alliance?" *Anything to distract from the berries.*

For the rest of the morning, Jareh spoke of the woman he had adored for forty-five years, the offspring they had produced and raised, and the offspring of their offspring. Grit only half heard. The Amity-berry bushes, white with blossom, held a burgeoning harvest of bright pink berries. *Coil's berries.* She leaned over the edge of the cart to pluck one as they passed. As she pulled the delicate fruit from its bush, the pressure of her fingers crushed it. Dismayed, she threw the berry to the ground and watched as the back wheel rolled over it. She glanced at her fingers, now bright with berry juice.

Jareh's voice seemed to come from far away. "That juice doesn't wash off easily. You'll be stuck with pink fingers for a few days."

"I know," Grit said. "Coil never could wash the pink from his hair, either."

"Coil, is it?"

Grit turned, her breath caught in her throat, but Jareh focused on the road ahead and did not seem to expect an answer. Grit would not have given him one, even if she had known what the question was.

# TWENTY-FOUR

Jareh clucked at his faithful pony. The creature perked it ears and quickened its pace. A moment later, the trees thinned. They no longer traveled under a canopy of leaves, but verdant pastures opened before them, the sky above a pale blue. Castle Concord seemed more elegant and more imposing now that she was level with the structure. As they rolled closer, Grit studied the pure white walls. Bright red turrets topped each corner, and intricate latticework edged the rooftop and balconies. A multitude of tents littered the fields on the southern side of the castle. Like their surroundings, they were beautiful, but something about the tents unsettled her.

Grit turned to Jareh. "What are those tents? They weren't here a year ago."

"A year ago, Strike and Havoc were only getting started. Since then, young warriors have come from all over Chasmaria. Most of them were led by one of Kinsmon's scouts, but some of them . . ." Jareh chuckled. "Some of them, they couldn't tell you themselves how they came to this place, but come they have, some weary and wounded, others with weapons sharpened and ready to fight the evil that threatens to destroy their homes. Those tents, to answer your question, shelter the burgeoning army of Kinsmon the Great."

The cart rumbled to a halt. Grit looked from Jareh to the open doors of Castle Concord.

Scarlett appeared on the threshold. Her gaze turned from the cart to search the road that led down from the mountain. Exchanging her frown for a smile, she hurried down the stairs and rubbed the pony's muzzle.

"Jareh! How wonderful to see you again, and how wonderful to see you, as well, Grit! I trust your journey was pleasant. If you take the pony to the back, Jareh, one of the stable boys will get him a fine trough of oats. Then you may settle yourself in your usual room. Dear Grit, you must come with me. This is your first visit to Castle Concord, and I won't have you enter through the stables. Come, walk with me."

Scarlet offered her clean, even-toned hand to help Grit from the cart, but discontent showed in her green eyes. Grit looked toward the mountain road. *I'm not the friend she wants.*

Refusing Scarlett's help, she jumped to the ground and landed on her feet beside the cart. Worm, who had just woken from a long nap, stretched and followed. Scarlett cocked her head at the creature, as if unsure what to do with him.

"If I'm truly welcome here, so is he. Come, Worm." Grit sauntered toward the castle entrance without waiting for Scarlett.

By the time she reached the top step, Scarlett stood beside her. She put a hand on Grit's arm.

Sorrow laced the dameling's voice. "You will see people here who have been touched by Havoc, people haunted by the memory of things too awful to describe. Be kind to them, Grit. However awful you must be to me, be kind to them."

An odd discomfort struck Grit. "Am I awful to you?"

"You were less than genial in Port Colony. I'm sure you don't intend to be harsh or to ignore kindness, but you have a way about you that doesn't inspire comfort in others." How could Scarlett speak so bluntly and yet so gently all at once?

"But Worm . . ." Grit said. "And Ezekiel, Jareh . . ."

"All tender souls bound to embrace you despite, or maybe because of your imperfections. I cherish you, too, for all your rustic ways." With one last, longing look up the road, she squeezed Grit's arm. "Come, though. Castle Concord awaits."

She moved forward, but Grit remained outside, staring through the open doorway into the entrance hall. What did Scarlett expect her to do with these people? She wasn't like Ezekiel or Jareh or even Worm. She didn't know how to embrace others with all their weaknesses and imperfections. She wasn't sure why she should even try, except that Scarlett felt it was so important.

"I can hold my tongue, but I can hardly be genial. As for inspiring comfort in them, how on earth . . . why on earth am I to do that? The people in there, they are not my people."

Scarlett, standing in the open doorway, faced her. "But they are your people, Grit. As much as you are bound to Kinsmon, you are bound to them."

Grit fingered the pearl hanging on its delicate chain. She was, though she hardly understood it herself, bound to Kinsmon. She left him on the promontory long ago, yet at every turn, she heard his name. In every person, she felt his touch. As she squeezed the orb between her thumb and forefinger, Dagger's judgment echoed in her mind. *You wear that pearl around your neck. It means something, whether you acknowledge it or not. Every human being you encounter is someone in whose affairs you have an interest.* She willed herself to step forward, to meet without reservation these people Scarlett called her own.

From the red and white tile floor to the golden chandeliers, vibrant colors filled the entrance hall. On the far side of the room, painters added to a mural that stretched the width of the room. She could make out the beginnings of Port Colony, the chasm with its strange, half-way there bridge, and the shape of the castle. In the corner to her right, children danced to the cheerful song of a small band of musicians. Two children rolled a ball along one wall. Scattered around the room, pairs of individuals chatted quietly and larger groups laughed loudly. One man lay sleeping on a mat to one side of the fireplace. On the other side, the young dame, Laurel, stared vacantly at the ceiling, heedless of her avidly nursing babe. He had grown plump since Grit had held him under Laurel's disapproving glare.

The murmurs of their conversations filled her ears, and she longed for Ezekiel. How could she embrace these people? Their manners were so different from the calm of Ezekiel, different even from the boisterous Threshan villagers. Some appeared healthy and lively, smiling as words flowed from their mouths like water from a bubbly spring.

Others, like Laurel, looked haunted. Heads bowed, they huddled against the wall or shuffled about the room, keeping entirely to themselves. When Grit was little, Dame Berth had slit the throat of a dog like that, lest it spread its sickness.

Grit edged closer to Scarlett. "What ails them?"

A troubled expression crossed Scarlett's face. "Most have only recently escaped Havoc's grip. Some will heal in time and live lightheartedly. Others will bear Havoc's scars for life, turning their grief to others' consolation. They have such need of gentleness."

Grit did not respond. What might have happened to her, had Havoc not sold her to Turf? Might she, in the hands of Havoc, have become as distant, as troubled, or as vacant as the most desolate of these people?

Eager to leave the hall and her questions behind, Grit followed Scarlett into an outdoor passageway bordering an expansive courtyard. The image of Laurel's gaunt face remained with her, even in the sunlight. *What was she like before Havoc scarred her?* Grit shuddered with the relief one feels upon escaping disaster.

The courtyard was a cluster of intricately designed gardens with a gurgling fountain marking its center. A path of tiny pebbles circled the fountain. Trails wound away, first through shrubbery mazes, then through wildflower gardens, and finally to the castle's outer passages. Beyond the circular path around the fountain, a ring of trees offered shade. Grit noted the curve of the path, the shapes of pebbles, and the shades of flowers. As she passed the first shrub on her way to the courtyard's center, she veered off the path. *Surely not here, too . . .*

"Amity berries." She held a two-inch berry between her fingers, careful not to detach it from the bush.

Scarlett came to stand beside Grit. She plucked a berry and popped it into her mouth. "Their powers are astonishing. They ease pain and repair wounds, mostly of the body, but sometimes of the mind, as well."

"I know. There was a sireling in Thresh who knew where to find such berries."

Scarlett was quiet a moment, but when she spoke, her voice sounded wistful. "Do you miss him?"

Grit ran her thumb over the berry's skin. "I only wish he could see how large they grow here."

"Perhaps he will someday."

"Perhaps." Grit released the berry. She never considered Coil might exist anywhere but Thresh. She sighed, wiped her hands on the sides of her trousers, and looked around at the castle surrounding the courtyard. "Were you going to show me the rest of this place or not?"

They spent the afternoon exploring the interior of Castle Concord. Scarlett led Grit through long corridors, pointing out the kitchens, the dining hall, the library, various workrooms, and finally, Kinsmon's quarters. The place overflowed with things too fine for Grit's liking. Her dagger, blanket, and pack were sufficient. Standing in Kinsmon's spacious outer chamber, Grit remembered the pouch in her pack for the first time.

"I have a package for Kinsmon, and one for Dagger, too. Where are they?"

"We expect Kinsmon tomorrow evening," Scarlett said. "As for Dagger, I never know when he'll show up."

Scarlett turned her face toward the window. It was Dagger she'd hoped to welcome home. Grit wouldn't be drawn into the Scarlett's disappointment. She couldn't help not being Dagger. She looked around the room. What was she to do until Kinsmon and Dagger returned? *If I could give Kinsmon Ezekiel's pearls and sell mine to Dagger, I could leave this place and go back where I belong. But now who knows how long I shall have to stay here among these strange people with their peculiar manners and Scarlett with her unabashed sensitivity . . .* She clasped her dagger, comforted by the feel of its hilt against her palm.

"We'll find a room for you, of course. You won't have to sleep under a shrub or anything dreadful like that." Scarlett glanced at Worm. "The dog can stay, too."

"I'd like a room near yours." Grit struggled to make sense of her words even as they proceeded from her mouth. It was stupid, this feeling of being lost within the enormous castle after she'd made her way all the way across Chasmaria. Foolish to shrink from its occupants when she'd encountered so many strangers in her journeys. Perhaps, like an ill child clings to its dame, she had become attached to Scarlett in Port Colony.

Scarlett furrowed her brow and offered an odd smile. "You may have the room beside mine."

She led Grit to a spacious bedchamber overlooking the mountains to the north. Two comfortable-looking chairs flanked the middle of three windows in the castle's outer wall. To the left was a bed, a solid table beside it. In the far corner of the room, a curtain, partially open, revealed a metal tub. A wardrobe stood just outside the curtain.

Scarlett walked directly to the wardrobe and rummaged through its contents, muttering to herself.

Grit stepped to the tub and peered into it. "What is this for?"

"Hmm?" Scarlett turned, a lavender gown draped over her arm. "That? Why, it's a bathtub, silly! Haven't you ever taken a bath?"

She put the gown back and continued to look through the wardrobe. Grit ran her fingers over the smooth edge of the tub. How constricting, to bathe in something so small.

"Don't tell me you've never taken a bath," Scarlett said.

"I have." Grit fumbled to think of what to say next. "Only I've always bathed in the sea or in a river. This thing . . ." She flicked the tub with her finger. "It gives so little space, and takes up so much."

"A tub is a wonderful device. You should try it sometime, preferably before dinner. I'll fetch some hot water from the kitchens for your bath, and some clothing from the tailor. Nothing here seems to suit you." She glanced at Grit's trousers. "I'm sure you've almost worn those to shreds."

By late afternoon, after a long soak in a tub of hot water to which Scarlett had added fragrant oil and sprigs of lavender, Grit had undergone a remarkable change of odor and appearance. Her fingers, no longer stained with berry juice, were soft and wrinkled from the water. Her hair, after applications of creams Scarlett had passed through the curtain, felt light and smooth. Perhaps the dameling's method of bathing had its advantages. Grit splashed out of the tub and stood dripping on the floor.

Scarlett peered over the top of her book. She jumped to her feet, grabbed a towel, and threw it at Grit. "Dry yourself!"

Grit caught the towel and wrapped it around her body.

"I'm sorry. It's just that Ezekiel is blind, you see. It hasn't mattered in a year."

Scarlett shook her head and murmured something Grit could not decipher.

Once Grit was dry, Scarlett laid out the clothing she'd acquired from the tailor, black trousers and white undershirt and dark green tunic.

"It's the closest to what you wore here, but clean and without patches. I'm sure they'll fit much better. You must have been wearing those trousers for years." She gestured toward the foot of the bed. "A belt and boots. Have I forgotten anything?"

Grit suspected Scarlett rarely forgot anything when it came to personal attire. "No, that should do."

"Well, let's see, then. Put it on."

"I have no money." Grit ran her fingertips over the undershirt and tunic. The fabric felt softer, smoother, and stronger than that of her old garments. "Not yet, anyway."

"Who said anything about money? I'm authorized to outfit any who come to Castle Concord. These clothes and any others you need are yours, free of charge."

There was no sense in arguing. Grit shrugged and dressed. After transferring the contents of her pockets from her old trousers to her new ones, she slid her sheathed dagger onto her belt and faced Scarlett.

"When's dinner?"

"Don't you . . ." The dameling frowned and shook her head. "No, I'm sure you don't. Come here, Grit. Let me brush your hair."

Grit sat and allowed Scarlett to untangle her damp hair. The girl could have been gentler with Grit's head, but she was an exceptional conversationalist. Her lilting cadence soothed Grit's nerves, while her gentle hands soothed Grit's unkempt hair. Finally, Scarlett tied her hair back with a lavender ribbon and sat back, grinning at Grit's reflection.

"You're beautiful, Grit."

Grit opened her mouth to object, to argue her ugliness. The truth, which Ezekiel had noted and Grit could no longer deny, was that something in her being had shifted ever so slightly from the life she'd known before her exile. Some quiet force had begun its work the moment she set foot on the promontory. From Kinsmon's table to Harth's inn, in Jareh's wagon and nestled between Worm and Ezekiel, she had resisted its power. But it had worked, slowly and methodically, to change her. She glanced at Scarlett's reflection in the mirror.

She was a silly girl, so open and honest with her affection. How could Grit "inspire comfort" in one who took such pains over others' care? She felt through the fabric of her trousers, first for the oyster knife Sire Stone had given her and then the pearl she intended to sell to Dagger.

"Dagger misses you, too," she said. "And if you like, Scarlett, you may call me your friend, though I hardly think I'll make a good one."

Scarlett smiled and bowed her head. Her voice came soft and tremulous. "I'm sure you are already a fine friend, Grit of Berth and Stone."

# TWENTY-FIVE

The next afternoon, Grit stuck her head into the dim room in which Scarlett knelt beside a low cot. A putrid odor filled the air. Grit stumbled back into the corridor for a breath of fresh air. She coughed and looked into the room again, this time with one hand over her mouth and nose.

"How do you bear it?"

"I remember what they have suffered to come here, conditions much worse than filth, fever, and stench." Scarlett moved to the next cot and wiped a trembling patient's forehead. "This man left behind his home, his people, all he has ever known. He traveled far and under brutal conditions to escape the cruelty of Strike and discover the kindness of Kinsmon. I bear it because he has borne more than I ever hope to bear. But you needn't stay with me. The day is clear and fresh. Go outdoors. It will do you good."

Grit glanced down the hallway. She could remain with Scarlett in this quiet section of the castle where the weak, wounded, and ill convalesced or venture into busier areas. Encouraged by Worm's head nudging her leg, Grit nodded toward the far end of the hallway.

Stepping from the doorway, she said, "I'll find you at dinner."

"Kinsmon, too," Scarlett said. "I'm sure he'll want to welcome you."

Leaving Scarlett with her patients, Grit followed Worm down the corridor. She emerged on the eastern side of the castle. Passing an armory on her right, she slowed to study the various weapons. Bows, arrows, spears, daggers, and swords of every size lined the walls. A warrior sharpened his blade on a whetstone at the back of the large room. Grit wrapped her hand around her dagger. It would feel good to spar again.

Grit strolled beyond the tents she had seen the previous day. Rough warriors struggled to master precision moves demonstrated by their commander. Whisp, her long hair even blonder in the sunlight than it had been in Harth's inn, moved among the ranks, correcting poor form. Seeing Grit, she raised her sword in greeting and returned her attention to the warriors.

Grit sat on the edge of the training field, close enough to hear the commander shout instructions and to see the warriors' execution of each order. The warriors moved through stretching exercises and battle formations, working in pairs or trios to ensure no one's back was left undefended. These were moves she hadn't learned under Sire Stone. She closed her eyes and rehearsed them in her mind, but something felt wrong.

"I thought I might find you here." A familiar voice drew Grit out of a mental defensive maneuver. Kinsmon lowered his lean frame onto the grass. "Do you wish to join them?"

Grit watched the warriors a moment longer, then shook her head. "I only wish to return to the Southern Sea. Here . . . from Ezekiel." She pulled her pack onto her lap, withdrew Ezekiel's pouch, and offered it to Kinsmon, who took it without a word.

She looked back at the training field, where warriors were sheathing their swords and retiring to their tents. "I thought I wanted to join them, but now as I watch, I'm sure I'm not meant to be among them."

"No," Kinsmon said, his voice firm. "You are not meant to be among them. Walk with me to the dining hall. It's almost time for supper."

They walked quietly across the field and into the castle. In the elegant dining hall, all order of fare had been set out on a dark mahogany table running the length of the room.

"What's the occasion?" Grit asked. "You have enough to feed half of Chasmaria here."

Kinsmon laid a hand on her arm. "There is no occasion, Grit. Every meal I serve is a celebration."

He thread his way through the crowd, stopping to speak briefly with several individuals. Grit found Scarlett, who led her to two empty seats near the foot of the table.

Kinsmon seated himself and indicated for everyone to begin. The guests and residents of Castle Concord served themselves and one another, taking as much or little of whatever they desired. Some stood to eat, others sat at the table, and a few, like creatures frightened they might lose their meals to stronger animals, huddled in the corner.

After dinner, Scarlett stood near a side table, talking with Laurel in tones too soft for Grit to hear above the clatter of the crowd. Grit studied the dame's face. Though nervous and withdrawn, her eyes held an earnestness she hadn't noticed before.

A hand rested on Grit's shoulder. She whirled to face the young warrior with whom she had breakfasted in Port Colony. His sandy hair was longer now, hanging almost to his shoulders. The beginnings of a light beard marked his jaw line, but his brown eyes held the same quiet intelligence they'd held in Port Colony.

"You look like a captured bird," Arrow said. "Let's get you out of here."

He took her hand and pulled her toward the door. She followed readily. She'd had enough of the dining hall's clamor.

In the corridor, Grit pulled her hand from Arrow's. "I don't need to be led like a babe."

179

Arrow smiled apologetically. "I meant no offense. Castle life was shocking when I first arrived. I didn't suppose you'd move without encouragement."

Grit reached for Worm, but found only empty air. "Where's my dog?"

"Do you mean the beast cleaning up after all of us?" Arrow nodded toward the dining hall. Worm lay under the table, licking something from the floor. "He's a fine creature. Let him have his reward."

Grit looked from Worm to Arrow and back to Worm, her hand on her dagger. "I don't know how anyone stands it. I could hardly breathe in there."

Arrow gestured toward the exit. "This way. The north meadow is fine on a summer's evening. It reminds me of the Eastern Plains just enough to make me feel at home."

The grass on the northern side of the castle, where no tents stood and no warriors trained, grew thick and tall. Grit inhaled the sweet meadow air. The press of people in the dining hall had been stifling, but Grit hardly noticed Arrow's closeness, so natural and undemanding was his manner. She did not mind at all when he began to talk.

"Did you find the southern tip of Chasmaria? And have you eaten your breakfast in peace?"

"I did, and I have. I'm surprised you remember that."

Arrow's voice was pleasant, like a familiar game with an old companion. "People remember the strangest things. A girl in my village once told me nothing smells sweeter than a newly blossomed lily. Seven years later, though she has never again spoken of lilies, I cannot see that flower without seeing her face. That is the power of the spoken word at its very best, and that is why I try to choose my words carefully. The tongue can heal, but more often, it wounds more deeply than any weapon."

All her life, words had rolled off Grit's tongue so freely. Too few of them had been kind, but to try to change the established course of her tongue would be as ridiculous as Dame Berth trying to teach Seal to speak.

"Sometimes words are just words. It is weak-minded to give them too much importance."

"Perhaps you are right," Arrow said. "But perhaps it is cruel to give them too little."

## TWENTY-SIX

"**W**ar is an ugly thing, Grit. I hope you never see it. Even in the villages Strike and his men have not entered, fear grips the people. They stare at us, terrified of who knows what." Arrow's voice was low as they walked in the meadow the next evening. The sound of laughter came from the direction of the castle.

Grit glanced toward the open windows of the dining hall. "It will be over soon. Not even Strike can stand long against the armies assembled here."

Arrow looked at her, his face thoughtful. "It is not that easy. Strike's shadow darkens all Chasmaria. Minds are warped, to one extreme or another. Some people we liberate have taken on exaggerated pride and brutality, but most are fearful and timid. They won't meet our eyes. I never know which is worse, to be met with irrational outrage or with cowering timidity. I can't quite put it in words, but it frightens me. I am afraid I won't recognize my village when I return, assuming there's anything left to which to return." He fixed his gaze on some distant point to the northeast. "There is Havoc, too. Nothing is simple in this war."

They continued across the meadow. From time to time, Grit stole glances at Arrow. His face retained its pensive expression. Perhaps he believed watching his feet fall upon the earth might somehow solve the troubles plaguing Chasmaria.

"You remind me of a sireling from Thresh," Grit said. "Talon of March and Swot."

He looked up, a smile upon his face. "How so?"

Grit shrugged, her mind struggling to capture discarded memories. "I'm not sure. He was sincere, dependable. I never feared his betrayal."

"So far, the comparison is favorable."

"His sire was the laughing-stock of the council."

"My sire is dead." Arrow frowned, reached out his arm, and gripped Grit's shoulder.

"Refugees." He pointed toward the road that led down from the tunnel in which Grit had spent a night after crossing the Southern Chasm.

A small group of people approached, traveling too close together for Grit to count their number. Arrow urged Grit forward. His pace quickened, and she trotted to match his step. Who were these people? What had brought them to Kinsmon's castle? As they neared the refugees, Arrow slowed.

A middle-aged woman, a half-foot taller than Grit and with a fierce set to her scarred face, led the way. Behind her, three sirelings followed. One of the young men carried an elderly woman in his arms. Another cradled a small child who clung to him as if her life depended upon the strength of her grip. The third held a lethargic infant with cracked lips and sunken eyes. For all her harshness, Berth had threatened to shame more than one young Threshan dame over infants in such sickly condition.

"Where is that infant's dame?" Grit glared at each of them in turn.

Arrow stepped forward. "Welcome to Castle Concord. You must have traveled far."

The leading woman rested her hand on the hilt of a heavy sword. "Arborsedge."

The small village was located several miles north of Thresh, at the base of the Northern Mountains. Grit had never been there, but raiding parties visited Arborsedge during lean winters.

"You will find rest here." Arrow spoke as if he knew the struggles these strangers had faced. "Rest, and help for your people."

"There is no help for Arborsedge." The sireling carrying the elderly woman set her on her bare feet. Dark red stained his tunic as well as her shapeless dress. It could have flowed from either body.

"Calm yourself, Garnet." The old woman's voice cracked. "This man is not to blame for our misfortune."

"Was it Strike?" Grit clutched her dagger so tight her hand ached.

The first, stronger woman studied Grit. "Not Strike alone. We might have survived him. Several of us did, in fact, outlast his attack. It was the Golden Demon who destroyed Arborsedge, tearing apart the Inner Ring in search of some wretched hag who most likely doesn't exist. Only by chance did we escape his accursed sword."

"Tell me what happened." Arrow crossed his arms.

"It was the strangest thing I've ever seen," the old woman said. "While my neighbors implored his mercy, I poured myself a drink and sat at my table, waiting for the Golden Demon to enter my hut. I'd heard stories of him, how he enters villages, intent on destruction. 'Where is she? Where is she? Hand over the hag!' they say he cries while he cuts them down. Some claim it's a vow gone wrong, but who knows? I am old, as you can see, too old to fight, too old to question, and too old to plead for pity. I've lived long enough to welcome death, so when he kicked in my door, I raised my cup. 'To the Golden Demon.' I smiled, and he stopped, barely through the doorway. 'No.' He shook his head so that his golden curls went in every direction. 'You have it all wrong, old woman. The battle has never once gone to me. To her, always to her.' And that was it. He left as quickly as he'd come, sparing my life for reasons I'll never know."

"No." Grit looked from one wounded refugee to the next. It couldn't be real—the horrors her eyes beheld, the truth the old woman's story revealed.

"So, after Strike and the Golden Demon, you seven are all that remain? There are women here who will nurse the baby, and others who will tend to the rest of you. It will take time, but today your suffering begins to end." Arrow wrapped one arm around the elderly woman's back, stooped to place an arm behind her knees, and carefully lifted her into his arms.

Grit shook her head, her gaze fixed on the infant's cracked lips. "No, this cannot be. It has to stop."

"Grit, take the child," Arrow said.

"No!" Her vision blurred as she stared at the crippled woman's blood soaked tunic. The cruelty of the one who'd driven these people from their home was too terrible for her to bear. "No, no, no!"

She turned from Arrow and the refugees and ran, her legs straining to keep pace with the pounding of her heart, down the gentle slope to Castle Concord. She bounded up the stairs and raced through the open doors.

Where was Kinsmon? He retired to his quarters after dinner. She turned down a hallway on the north side of the great hall. At the corridor's end, she threw open two heavy wooden doors and entered Kinsmon's private quarters.

He sat at the rich mahogany desk in front of the grand fireplace.

She strode across the room and thrust her dagger into the dark wood, her face inches from Kinsmon's. "It stops now."

"Take your dagger out of my desk." He gestured to a chair on Grit's left. "Rest a moment, let your anger subside, and then tell me all about it."

She straightened. "I won't rest, not until the Golden Demon ceases his tyranny. You must make him stop, Kinsmon, before he destroys all of Chasmaria, before he destroys himself."

Kinsmon sat back, his arms folded across his chest. "So, that's it? You think I'm to blame for Coil of Dara's actions, do you?"

"You have amassed an army of warriors from every corner of Chasmaria. If anyone can stop him, it is you. Kinsmon, you must stop him."

Kinsmon leaned forward and rested his chin in the palm of his hand. "I think, my dear girl, it is you who must stop him."

"Me? This has nothing to do with me." Grit pulled her dagger from the desk. Pacing in front of Kinsmon, she clenched and unclenched her fist around the weapon.

"Doesn't it?"

She stared at him a moment, allowing his question to sink in. He met her gaze with tender understanding. Asking seemed to pain him as much as answering pained her. She fell back into the chair he had offered a moment before.

"Oh, Kinsmon, his vow. While I have contented myself to remain at the Southern Sea, he has raged to avenge my enemies. What am I to do?" With her dagger, she traced a flower in the armchair's upholstery.

His voice, when he spoke, was so low Grit could barely hear. "I think you know."

"You cannot mean it." Her dagger sliced through the fabric. "Anything but that, Kinsmon. I can't go back."

"You can if you choose to. It won't be easy. It will be dangerous, and there is a chance you will fail, but indeed, if you wish to see Coil saved from himself and, ultimately,

Chasmaria saved from Havoc, this is the path you must follow."

Grit sheathed her dagger and pinched the arm of her chair where she had slit the upholstery. "Can it not be accomplished some other way?"

"Yes." Kinsmon drew the word out. He walked around his desk and crouched beside Grit. Placing his hand over her fist, his fingertips touched the arm of the chair. "But if you wish to see it happen, if you wish to behold for yourself the most beautiful moments ever to be recorded in Chasmarian history, my dear Grit of Berth and Stone, you must return to Thresh."

He rose and walked to the door. "Consider it overnight. Dagger will come soon. If you choose to return to Thresh, he will accompany you, for he has impending matters to attend to in that region. If you choose not to go, sell your pearl to him and return to Ezekiel of the Southern Sea at your leisure. The choice is yours."

Grit stood to go, but stopped halfway out of her seat. The upholstery, torn a moment before, was whole again. Her stomach clenched with fear.

"Kinsmon, what have you done to my chair?"

He smiled an odd, charming sort of smile. "Just what I intend to do to everything, if you will but let me."

She stared at him as she walked across the room and passed through the doorway. In the hallway, she looked back at his calm, mysterious, beautiful face. Seeing the chair repaired frightened her enough. What plans did he have for Chasmaria, and why did he think to include her?

"Tell me in the morning what you decide," he said.

She did not need so long. By the time she reached the stairwell, Grit knew her answer. She couldn't dodge Kinsmon, nor could she deny her responsibility. She would return to Thresh, to the village that had shunned her, to the dame who had disowned her, and most importantly, to the warrior who had sworn to avenge her enemies. She had placed too little importance on Coil's words. If Arrow was right—if words indeed wound more deeply than weapons—the vows she'd extracted from Coil and the disregard she'd shown for his alliance were as cruel as all he had done to fulfill his vows.

## TWENTY-SEVEN

In the gray light of morning, Grit entered Kinsmon's quarters uninvited. Worm circled twice and lay on the floor in front of Kinsmon's desk. Grit fixed her gaze on a spot between the dog's silky ears.

"I'll go, but you must see Ezekiel receives a case of your special brew. Tell him where I've gone. Send Worm to Ezekiel, too. The old blind man shouldn't be alone, and Worm . . ." She squared her shoulders and looked at Kinsmon. "The beast would only slow my progress. Ezekiel knows how to care for him."

"You have my word it will be done." Kinsmon looked at Worm as if he understood all the affection and all the fear Grit didn't have the courage to voice, as if he knew she wasn't afraid of a slow journey, but of the journey's dangers rendering her unable to care for the creature herself.

"When do we leave?" Dagger's voice startled Grit. He came from the corner, a book in his hand, and sat on the edge of Kinsmon's desk. "And what is our plan?"

Kinsmon directed Grit to sit. She lowered herself onto the arm of the chair she'd sliced the night before. She swung one foot, just as Dagger did. She'd show him she wasn't just a bumbling village girl.

"Spend the day together," Kinsmon said. "Spar each other, learn one another's ways. Introduce her to Shriven."

"Who's Shriven?" Grit's foot hit the floor.

Kinsmon smiled. "You'll see soon enough."

"Are my orders, once we depart, what they have always been?" Dagger asked.

Kinsmon nodded. "Your time draws near, Dagger. Watch and wait."

Dagger picked an empty vase off the desk and turned it in his hand. "I do not wish to delay our business, but I had hoped at some point—"

"Go." Kinsmon's manner lightened. He took the vase from Dagger's hand. "I would hate to upset Scarlett by keeping you busy all day. Meet us outside the armory in an hour."

Dagger was at the door almost before Kinsmon finished speaking. Once he left, Grit leaned against the back of her chair and folded her arms over her chest. "How am I to stop Coil? If you recall, I was banished from Thresh. I doubt they'll let me past the village gate."

"My dear Grit of Berth and Stone, I ask only one thing of you. Do what is in your heart. I call you my heart and hands. Your heart will guide you truly. Listen to its whispers and dare to act upon them."

"That's hardly a plan at all." Fine words and wishful thinking wouldn't solve the problem of Coil.

For a moment, the thin lines in Kinsmon's face appeared much deeper. "It is all the plan you need."

She glanced at the door through which Dagger left. "I have a pearl to sell."

"Why didn't you offer it while Dagger was here?"

"It hardly seems the time for such a transaction. Here we are, discussing a journey that may well end in death. Pearls and fortunes seem rather irrelevant, don't they?"

"There you are, my girl. You listen well to the whispers of your heart. Hold on to the pearl until the moment either pearls or fortunes seem relevant. He won't miss the pearl, but will appreciate it all the more when the time is right for him to possess it. You, too, will be richer when that time comes than you would be if you sold it to him today."

An hour later, after breakfast in the dining hall, Grit and Kinsmon met Dagger outside the armory. The sireling circled Grit, his chin resting in his hand.

"We'll start with a dummy. I'd like to see for myself what she can do."

Dagger left and returned a moment later with a dummy much like the one Grit had battled at the Southern Sea. When he had set it up, he turned to her.

"Show me what you know."

As Dagger shouted commands, Grit attacked the dummy, her mind and muscles rejoicing in the familiar exercise. Now it was not Turf of Elna and Bord whom she fought, but Coil of Dara, his round face no longer smiling, his blue eyes wide with alarm as Grit thrust her dagger into his midsection. Ruthlessly slicing and stabbing, she jumped, spun, and ran at the human form, the memory of Ezekiel's sewing kit ensuring the precision of her maneuvers. *By whatever means necessary.* As she pulled her dagger from the dummy's heart, her gut tightened. *If it kills me to do it, I will stop his treachery.* She suppressed the memory of the pinkish-gold curls that haunted her, waking and sleeping, since she left Thresh. Tender remembrance would only complicate her task.

Kinsmon watched intermittently, his gaze often drifting over the bands of warriors training to the south. Dagger watched intently, arms half crossed and chin resting in one hand. From time to time, he pointed without a word or traced invisible lines in the air. *He is marking my movements, to correct or commend, just as Sire Stone did all those afternoons.* She jabbed at the dummy's navel. She hadn't trained four years, with both Sire Stone and Coil shouting at her, to be shamed by a castle brat who'd probably never met the sharp end of a stick.

"Stop," Kinsmon said.

The dummy was in shreds. Grit's hair hung free of the lavender ribbon Scarlett had given her, and sweat dripped down her face. She wiped her blade on her trousers as if she'd just engaged in bloody battle and pointed her weapon at Dagger's heart.

"Shall we spar now?"

Kinsmon turned his attention from the training warriors. "Sit. You must learn you do not always need to destroy your opponent. You fight with flawless precision and accuracy, but your heart is intent on annihilation. While there is a time to kill, there are also times to wound, spare, and even heal. There are also, dare I say it, times to lay aside all you are for another's sake. You won't achieve your goal through rage."

"Go on." Sheathing her dagger, Grit fixed her attention on his solemn face.

For an hour, Kinsmon explained, demonstrated, and finally guided Grit through maneuvers designed to defend without injuring one's opponent. She took care to learn the maneuvers precisely. Ezekiel's sewing kit lay at the bottom of her pack. If Kinsmon made her repair his dummy, she wanted it to be a quick job.

Finally, Dagger stood before her, his weapon raised. Kinsmon gave the command, and their blades struck, sending a delightful, almost forgotten tremor up Grit's arm. She was sparring a real person. She laughed aloud as she blocked Dagger's next attack.

"To the left!"

"Stop!"

"Twist!"

"Thrust!"

Grit's dagger pierced his tunic, just over his heart.

"Whoa!" Dagger leapt back, eyes stern. "Rein it in. You aren't supposed to kill me!"

"I know!" Grit threw her arms up in the air. "I couldn't help it. Your blade came too close. Am I to let you kill me?"

Kinsmon's calm voice broke in above their yelling. "No. You are not to let him kill you. You are to value his life and seek to preserve it as you preserve your own. You must learn to hold back, Grit. The time is near when precious lives, yours included, will depend upon your mastery of this skill. You can and must keep your weapon from rushing ahead of sound thinking."

Grit stood still, breathing hard and staring at the mountaintops to the north. Kinsmon asked too much.

Dagger kicked at the ground and raised his eyebrows at Kinsmon. "This is not going as smoothly as I had hoped it would. Perhaps someone else should go."

"That won't do." Kinsmon frowned as he looked from Dagger to Grit. "Put away your weapons. It's time Grit became acquainted with Shriven."

Together, they headed to the stables in the northeast corner of the castle. Kinsmon passed several stalls and stopped before one containing a white horse with a multitude of small reddish-brown patches. The animal stretched his neck over the stall door, threw his head back, and let loose a cantankerous neigh.

Grit stepped back. "I don't think I like this beast."

The horse bobbed his head at her and blew a blast of hot air through his nostrils.

Kinsmon ruffled the horse's forelock. "Ah, but Shriven likes you. In time, you will come to adore him, too. Spend some time getting to know him. He'll carry you much more quickly to Thresh than your feet. I've other matters to attend to, but Dagger will help you with anything you need."

He left Dagger and Grit standing on either side of Shriven's head. Grit kept one hand on her weapon. Either the horse or the sireling might compel her to use it. Dagger watched Kinsmon go, then peered at Grit over the horse's nose.

His face was like a child's. "I wasn't trying to kill you. I had control of my weapon at all times and would not have so much as scratched you."

Grit stroked Shriven's neck. She didn't mean to slash Dagger's tunic. She just got carried away with the fever of the fight. She glanced at him. "I am accustomed to sparring for blood, and more recently, to sparring a man of sand, whose wounds could be easily, if tediously, repaired with needle and thread. It's difficult to hold back."

"But you will try?"

"I will."

After a brief silence, Grit nodded at Shriven and said, "This beast can't possibly like me."

Dagger ran his fingers through Shriven's mane. "Kinsmon understands creatures, and he understands people. He would not have paired you with Shriven if he didn't know you will get on well together."

Grit wasn't so sure. The horse stomped a foot on the straw and bobbed his head in her direction. She reached her hand up to trace the outline of a rust-colored patch on the side of his face, and he leaned his head into her hand. All apprehension evaporated. She placed her other hand full on Shriven's velvety nose. She'd found the courage to accept Worm. She'd do the same with Shriven.

Dagger took a bridle and lead off a hook beside the stall door. He fastened the bridle on Shriven and led the horse out of the stall. Grit took a step back as the enormous animal pranced past her. Recovering, she followed a few paces behind Dagger as he led the horse into the stable yard. This beast demanded more courage than Worm, but she wouldn't be found a coward.

For the next half hour, Dagger taught Grit how to bridle and unbridle the horse and encouraged her as she walked him around the stable yard. After a quick lunch brought to them by a young boy, Dagger led a chestnut mare from the stable. He helped Grit onto Shriven's back, mounted the mare, and led Grit to the northern meadow, far from the clamor of sparring warriors. There he guided her through the horse's gaits. Riding wasn't as difficult as she'd expected. She fell into an easy rhythm with Shriven.

On the far side of the northern meadow, the horse broke into a gallop. Leaning over Shriven's neck, Grit squeezed with her legs and clung to the reins. There was no stopping the beast. She closed her eyes and willed herself to stay atop the horse.

"Ride with it, Grit! Ride with it!" Dagger's voice rose like a battle cry over the pounding of her heart and Shriven's hooves.

She'd spent her life training to be a warrior who would not shy away. She pushed herself off Shriven's neck and straightened her back. Her body moved with the horse, rising and falling. They sped across the meadow, her heart pounding with exhilaration, even as the sweet scents of horse and grass eased her mind. They rounded the meadow and neared the castle again. Grit eased the reins back, bringing Shriven to a halt in front of Dagger.

"You ride well enough, all things considered," he said. "Do you suppose you can travel on him?"

Grit nodded.

Dagger looked at the mountains. He seemed to see something beyond their tops. "We leave tomorrow, first thing. Back to the castle, now. It will be a difficult farewell, and I'm sure you have things to do before we leave."

They returned to the stable, with Worm trotting along behind the horses. Grit glanced at the odd green pendant

Dagger wore on a black cord around his neck. "Did Kinsmon give you that?"

Dagger held the triangular piece between his thumb and forefinger. "He took it out of the river from which he rescued me. It's a shard of glass, worn smooth by the passing waters."

"Unless I am very much mistaken, it is also the color of Scarlett's eyes."

He glanced at her, and for the first time, Grit sensed humor in his expression. "It is exactly the color of Scarlett's eyes. Never mind getting along with Shriven. You and I, Grit of Berth and Stone, we may get along all right, after all."

## TWENTY-EIGHT

Kinsmon tossed a heavy saddlebag across the Shriven's flanks and fastened it to the rear of the saddle. "There's enough to sustain you until you arrive in Thresh. Remember the promise I gave you, Grit. You'll endure harsh treatment for a time, but in the end, when a new age dawns in Chasmaria, beauty will shine like the summer sun."

Leaving Grit standing with Shriven's reins in her hands, he turned to the right and held his arms out. "Dagger."

The sireling released Scarlett's hands and took a step toward Kinsmon, his jaw set. "I will serve your interests wherever my path may lead."

Kinsmon wrapped both arms around Dagger. Grit imagined a younger Kinsmon holding out his arms to receive an orphaned infant. But Kinsmon was not young, and Dagger was far from infancy. Despite his youthful features, Dagger appeared weary, somber, and much older than his twenty years. He stepped from Kinsmon's embrace and turned once more to Scarlett.

"Your hands . . ." She stood so close to Dagger their bodies almost touched. Her strained voice sounded of desperation. "You use them so sorely. They'll be dreadfully calloused before you return again. Once more, before you go, before your hands are damaged beyond help."

Trembling, she removed a small jar from her pocket, opened it, and dipped two fingers inside. Her head bowed, she took Dagger's hand into her own and massaged the cream into his hand in widening circles, paying close attention to his knuckles and the spaces between his fingers.

Dagger bowed his head, and his forehead touched hers. "My hands are never without help, nor are we. My dear, dear Scarlett, we are never without help."

"Must you leave me again?" she whispered, a tear falling onto his other hand as she took it in hers.

"You know I must."

Neither spoke again, but both followed the movement of Scarlett's fingertips long after she smoothed the last of the cream into his skin. Her fingers lingered on Dagger's a moment before she pressed the jar into his palm. Dagger touched his lips to Scarlett's forehead.

Grit looked away with a pang of guilt. She shouldn't have watched. This sacredness belonged to them, not her. Weeping over Dagger's hands was the highest foolishness, and yet Grit ached for Scarlett, for Dagger, and inexplicably, for herself.

"I heard you were leaving." Arrow had approached unnoticed. "Keep well, my friend. And may we live to share another evening's beauty."

"May we live . . ." What dangers might come to herself, to Arrow, to all Chasmaria? Horrific images filled Grit's mind, and she could banish none of them.

"Grit." Scarlett held her arms open. Grit accepted the dameling's embrace, and the ache intensified. *Perhaps this is the beginning of missing someone.*

In a low, breaking voice, Scarlett whispered in her ear, "Keep Dagger safe."

Releasing Grit, Scarlett forced a smile. She nodded to Dagger, who had already mounted his mare, and pressed Grit's shoulder. "May peace lead and joy follow. Now, go!"

Grit stooped down to set her cheek against Worm's soft fur. "Be good to Ezekiel, Worm."

She stood, ruffling the dog's fur one last time, and mounted Shriven. When she was situated in the saddle, Kinsmon passed her a folded blanket.

"Take this, in case you have need of it." A faint, familiar sparkle lit his eye.

Grit looked at Kinsmon, blinking for lack of understanding. Sire Stone's blanket had served her well. Why should she need another? She took the blanket, though, and crammed it into her pack atop of her blanket from Sire Stone. Far be it from her to pass up a spare blanket, especially one as warm as this.

At a shout from Dagger, his mare, Fealty, started into a brisk walk. Shriven sidestepped and rushed to catch up with the mare.

Moving in rhythm with Shriven, Grit followed Dagger up the road. She scanned the pastures, dotted with horses, cattle, and creatures whose names escaped her, and peered into the trees, looking for raptors and other of Kinsmon's feathered messengers, counting each time she spotted one. From time to time, she glanced at her companion.

Dagger fixed his attention on the path ahead, only occasionally turning his gaze to the right or left to check the motion of a horse through the pasture or the wind through the trees. Halfway up the mountain, he slowed Fealty and spoke for the first time since leaving the castle.

"Kinsmon has told me many things, but he hasn't told me why you decided to return to Thresh." The sireling sat erect in the saddle, giving the impression of surety and precision. He seemed aloof, harsh even, but there was something else in his manner. *He doesn't know what to do with me. I frighten him. But why?*

"What do you know of the Golden Demon?" Grit asked, coming even with him.

"The Golden Warrior, Grit. I refuse to call him a demon, and you should, too." His voice held a passing note of irritation. "He is ruthless in his pursuit of destruction. He works alone or with a single witness, attacking villages only after Strike has devastated the Outer Rings. The Golden Warrior pays little heed to the few strong who remain, only shedding their blood if they stand between him and the Inner Ring. There, upon the defenseless, the weak, and the aged, he unleashes the full strength of his power, demanding of them information they don't possess and denying their claims of innocence. His origin and his name are both unknown."

"He is my sparring partner. You say his aim is destruction, but it is not as broad, nor as simple as you describe it." Grit steeled herself to tell the rest. "I was banished from Thresh. You may as well know, since it will make our reception rather challenging. Before I left, Coil of Dara vowed to avenge my enemies. The Arborsedge refugees prove he goes too far in his pursuit of vengeance. He must be stopped. I compelled him to this treachery, and I will not rest until he rests."

"How do you intend to stop him?"

Grit didn't need to feel her dagger to know it was there, so heavily did it weigh upon her mind. "By whatever means necessary."

When they reached the rocky terrain just outside the entrance to the tunnel leading to Sages Bridge, Dagger turned his mount east.

Grit slowed Shriven. "Shouldn't we cross here? It's the quickest way, isn't it?"

Dagger shook his head. "There's another bridge a few hours east. We cross there. On the other side is a village in which we spend the night. After that, we follow the roads to Port Colony, and then on to Thresh."

202

He eyed Grit before continuing in slow, measured words. "After that, I cannot say what your future holds. Kinsmon calls you his heart and hands. I'm uncertain what that means, but I know you're under his protection. Remember that as we go forth. You are under Kinsmon's protection."

Grit cared little for talk of the future and her need of protection. "What's your business in the Northern Forest?"

"To return you safely to Thresh."

Grit sat a little straighter in her saddle. What did Dagger think she was? "I can get to Thresh just fine on my own."

He laughed and shook his head. "No, that's only a small part of it. Mostly, I am to watch and wait."

"For what exactly are you to watch and wait?"

Instead of answering, Dagger bowed his head and spurred his mare on. As Shriven fell in behind Fealty, Grit glared at the sireling's straight back. He may have been raised in a castle, but his manners matched those of a village babe. Did he imagine Scarlett's civility covered the both of them?

They crossed Legions Bridge in the mid-afternoon. The wide bridge spanned the chasm at a point more shallow and narrow than Sages Bridge. Its sturdy planks had been designed to withstand the pressures of crossing armies. Without breaking pace, Shriven and Fealty carried Grit and Dagger over the chasm and into the heart of Chasmaria.

## TWENTY-NINE

The village of Harding was located at the base of the Southern Mountains. Grit and Dagger arrived just as its busy residents were returning to their huts for the evening meal. At the entrance to the village, an armed sireling barely old enough to have passed his test greeted Dagger with stiff formality.

"Dagger of Castle Concord." He stuck out his chest, but his small brown eyes looked everywhere but at Dagger. "Name your traveling companion and state your destination."

"What is this, Bard?" Dagger sat back in his saddle, his eyes stern as he glanced from the curly-haired youth to the village beyond him.

The boy relaxed, letting his spear tilt as he exhaled. "It's Strike's fault, really. Since they heard he was sending out raiding parties, the council has required a constant guard at the village gates. We're supposed to check everyone who enters and find out why they've come. My sire and I think they might be making a bit much of it all, what with us being but a day from Castle Concord, but others think we can't be too cautious with visitors."

"They are not making too much of it all. Be on your guard, boy. Strike would hold all of Chasmaria in his power if he could, and he is neither your only enemy nor your worst." Dagger nodded at a small, silver flute suspended from a silver chain around Bard's neck. "Play it often, Bard. Sing Kinsmon's promises boldly through the coming darkness."

He took a deep breath and let it out slowly, gazing on Bard's downcast head. "Come now. You needn't write dirges in your head. You must play something jolly for us this evening, in the home of your dear sire. For the sake of your report to the council, Dagger of Castle Concord and his companion, Grit of Berth and Stone, travel to Burrow's hut in hope of a warm meal and shelter for the night."

Bard smiled, and it seemed his entire being came alive. "If that be the case, our parting shall be short. My watch is almost at its end."

He stepped to the side and motioned Dagger and Grit through the gates of Harding. Watching them pass, he tilted his head as though trying to hear a barely audible strain. Meeting his gaze, Grit frowned. Was he a fool? No Threshan would accept Dagger as easily as Bard had accepted her.

Outside a hut in one of the middle rings, Grit and Dagger dismounted and tethered their horses to a post. A stooped man came out of the wooden hut. Over his entire person, a haze of dust seemed to hover. Grit fingered a strand of her smooth, clean hair. Perhaps Scarlett should have sent some cream and a comb for the man. Who knew what vibrant shades hid in his scraggly locks? A broad grin spread across the man's pocked face as he shuffled over the stony path.

"Ah, Dagger! Come in, come in. No. On second thought, stay where you are. The light's much better out here."

The man retreated into the hut. He rejoined them a moment later and held a closed fist out to Dagger.

"She'll love these, she will." His bushy eyebrows wiggled as he spoke. His fingers, the nails of which were cracked and broken, uncurled to reveal two pale, purple gemstones. "Amethyst, they're called."

Dagger picked up one of the stones and examined it in the light of the evening sun. A proud, tender smile crept over his features. "You've done exceptionally well, Burrow. Scarlett will adore these. Thank you, old friend."

Burrow bowed his head and dug his toe into the pebbled ground. "It's nothing. I sent a whole bag of them to Kinsmon last week when Pledge passed through." He eyed Grit cautiously. "Who's your friend?"

Dagger slipped the gems into his pocket. "Ah, yes. Burrow, this is Grit of Berth and Stone. Grit, meet Burrow, an old friend of mine and a seeker of Kinsmon's promises. If you see something sparkling on a chain, it is quite possible Burrow unearthed it. His careful hands pluck these gems from the mountain behind us and deliver them to Castle Concord with the utmost devotion."

"You have known each other long?" The beginnings of discontent played in Grit's mind like distant, almost indiscernible music.

"Aye, I've know the lad since he was a babe. You're Dagger's friend. You shall be mine, as well. Come in now, both of you."

Burrow placed a gnarled hand on Dagger's shoulder. The young man walked beside the older into the dimly lit hut. Grit followed, keenly aware that their reception among her people would be quite different from Burrow's heartfelt welcome. She would have to fight her way into Thresh, and it wouldn't be an easy one. Even if she won, she did not count on Dagger being admitted solely on the basis of his association with her.

Inside, Dagger and Burrow dished out bowls of chicken stew and chunks of bread. Bard entered the hut just in time to eat, and the four sat to dine together, the three men discussing the more pleasant affairs of the village. Grit had nothing to contribute. She listened quietly and chewed her food slower than necessary.

*They are happy together.* She mashed a soft carrot against the roof of her mouth. *Burrow, Bard, and Dagger, they are like the children who have not yet learned to guard against making easy alliances.* Yet their freedom, the way they listened to one another and laughed together, only amplified the discontented murmurs of her heart. She stabbed her fork into a thick piece of chicken, stuffed it into her mouth, and chewed fiercely.

"Sire," Bard said as they finished eating. "Dagger thinks the council is not making too much of Strike."

Burrow stared hard at Dagger. "Is that so?"

Dagger nodded.

"Is he working alone?" the older man asked, his gray eyes alert.

Dagger answered with a slight shake of his head. "Strike has yet to venture this far south, but it is only a matter of time. For now, watch and wait." He paused, seeming to communicate some secret to Burrow. After a moment, Dagger slapped the table with both hands and spoke in a firm, jovial voice. "And play music! Yes, I think it is time for some of Bard's magic."

Within minutes, the four had cleared the dishes and sat comfortably around the hut. Bard lifted his flute to play. At times, the tune was soft and gentle as the lullabies Grit had heard the dames hum throughout Castle Concord. Other times, she closed her eyes to see warriors moving in synchronized motion across a grassy field. Then a sad strain brought the dame Laurel to mind, wrenching Grit's heart until she thought she would collapse under the pain.

Through it all, like a chord of hope, played a melody Grit could only call Kinsmon. From time to time, Bard exchanged his flute for his voice, a rich instrument more exquisite than any Grit had heard before. Occasionally, Dagger joined him, his tone deep and soothing. Burrow hummed along now and then, nodding his head with drooping eyelids and upturned lips.

Grit alone found no solace in Bard's song. The hum of dissatisfaction that had begun in her heart formed into a soft, rhythmic beating. As she realized her ignorance of the beautiful songs the others sang, an emotion she had not felt so strongly since the day the Threshan council had decided her fate rose in her heart, and she accurately dubbed her troubled song *Injustice*.

Bard's song became anguished, yet joyful, as if his soul sank to the depths with only a thread of peace to rescue it. Grit looked at her companions. Their eyes were squeezed shut, yet hope shone through the pain etched on their faces. Dagger clutched his weathered green glass, Bard's fingers danced over his flute, and Burrow wrapped one rough hand around a copper band on the opposite wrist. As battles threatened all Chasmaria, they held fast to Kinsmon's promises, like grasping that single thread of hope dangling in every note of Bard's sad song.

Grit studied the pearl hanging from her neck. Running her fingers over its smooth, delicate surface, she willed her spirit to rest in the promise of something beautiful, but it was no good. Try as she might, she couldn't overcome her rising sense of injustice.

She took out her dagger and tossed it in an arc so that it stuck fast in a wooden timber on the opposite wall. The music stopped, and Bard lowered his flute. He, like Burrow and Dagger, stared at her.

"What?" Grit shrugged and rose from her chair. She crossed the hut to retrieve her weapon, turning in a circle so that she faced each man in turn. "Why have these songs never reached Thresh? You've kept them hidden here, as if they are your special prize. You've known each other many years, an entire lifetime even. You've dined at Kinsmon's table, enjoyed his protection, and relished his friendship so much that you are at perfect ease in one another's presence. Why has Thresh been excluded?"

She plucked her dagger from the beam and pointed it at each of them before sheathing it. "Tell me what justice you see in this."

Dagger dropped his hand into his lap and stared at her, a blank expression on his face. Likely no one ever asked the castle brat a question he couldn't answer.

"Grit." He shook his head and sighed. "Do you suppose you are going to Thresh only to stop the Golden Warrior? Has it not occurred to you your return to Thresh may carry implications far beyond restraining a warrior's madness?"

Grit sheathed her dagger. "No, it never did, and if you suppose I'm to carry this music to Thresh, you're a greater fool than I've ever met. I hardly know this music myself."

Burrow leaned back in his seat. "It's not the music, nor the words even that are important, my girl."

"It's the song of the heart." Bard spoke over his raised flute. He blew one sweet, single note and smiled, his eyes closed. "Once you learn that song, Grit of Berth and Stone, carrying it to the ends of the earth is no burden at all."

"You speak nonsense." Grit flopped back into her chair, one leg draped over the arm.

But, she trained her eyes on Bard's nimble fingers and tried to anticipate each note as it proceeded from his flute.

# THIRTY

"Bard was not completely honest," Dagger said as they left Harding the following morning.

"I'm surprised you tolerate deception in your favored poet," Grit said. "I should think a poet, by nature, could sing only truth."

Dagger snorted lightly. "It's easy enough for poets to hear and to sing, but for the rest of us . . . For the rest of us, the song of the heart can be difficult to learn, let alone sing. There's some comfort, of course, in knowing you never strive alone. Many have struggled before you, and many struggle alongside you. Take solace in that."

He stole a glance at Grit, who rode beside him beneath the shade of ancient trees. "I see in your face you doubt me."

"I hear in your tone you doubt yourself. Anyhow, I have no need of solace. I survived a year on my own without the consolation of others. Before that, I may as well have been on my own for all the kindness shown in Thresh."

Concern softened Dagger's angular features. "Has it been that bad? Has no one ever shown you mercy?"

"No one, and I've never asked for pity." Grit spurred Shriven to a trot.

Even as she spoke the lie, she recognized it as such. Her leather pack bounced against her back, weighted with blankets from Sire Stone and Kinsmon, her Sire's Aid, Ezekiel's sewing kit, a brush from Scarlett, and the small wooden bowl Coil had filled with berries. The pack itself was a gift from Coil, who had spared her life in the tree, refused a share in Turf's glory, and vowed to repay those who had shamed her. She glanced at her dagger, a gift from her dame upon her Twelfth Branding, and felt for the first time in her life reluctant to draw it. *I hope it does not come to that.* Grit pushed back images of Coil's blood dripping from her blade.

Dagger slowed his horse at Shriven's side. "Have you heard of Strike's youth?"

"What of it?" Grit asked.

"Well . . ." Dagger winced. Clearly being conversational didn't come as easily to him as to Scarlett. He gave Grit a strained smile. "There's a story often told among Castle Concord's warriors."

Grit leveled her gaze at Dagger. "In that case, I've not heard it. Stories travel to Thresh even slower than music."

Dagger's expression hardened into something more familiar. "I thought I might tell it to you to pass the time, but perhaps you would prefer to remain ignorant of your enemy."

"Do regale me." Whatever Dagger's story was, it had to be better than imagining Coil's death.

"I thought you might like to hear it." Dagger sat straighter in his saddle, a genuine smile on his face. He licked his lips and took a deep breath.

"Forty years ago, twins were born in the mountain village of Summit Colony. Fierce and violent tempered, the older lived by the will of his impulses; the younger demonstrated a more pensive nature. Even before they could sit up, the older twin would strike the younger, who bore his sibling's assaults indifferently."

Dagger spoke in a voice tender and distant, as if he'd memorized the story in his childhood. "As the boys grew, the younger became as able a fighter as the older, albeit with a style contrary to his older brother's erratic blows. The younger twin was slow, sure, and when he didn't hold back, close to lethal. Working together, they could thrash any who stood against them. They were accomplished combatants by the age of fifteen. Warriors placed wagers and offered bribes a full year prior to their test."

"A full year?"

"A full year."

"Unheard of. Go on."

"When their test came, they traveled together to increase their chances of survival. They eluded their hunters the full sixteen days. On the last day, as they traveled the mountain path toward Summit Colony, they came upon a dameling whose lamb had slipped into a ditch and become entangled in a thorny shrub. Intending to steal the sheep and carry it into Summit Colony as a triumph feast, they scrambled to free the creature. When they regained the path, the older twin wanted to harm the dameling; the younger, seeing no gain in assaulting her, argued against this plan."

"A waste of energy, assuming they'd secured the lamb," Grit said. "It isn't as though they could eat the dameling, and it would hardly add to their honor to capture a girl too weak and dumb to rescue her own lamb."

Dagger raised an eyebrow. "Yes, well . . . To continue, their dispute became violent. While they wrestled one another, the lamb wandered away. Then, the dameling blew each twin a mocking kiss and retreated behind the mountain boulders. She disappeared, and the twins' four hunters emerged from behind the rocks. The twins battled fiercely, but their hunters overpowered them and led them, bruised and bound, into Summit Colony.

"When the twins related their story, the council became uncomfortable at the mention of the dameling. They wished to interview her, but she couldn't be found. A slaughtered lamb supported their tale, but the council decided against them, banishing them from Summit Colony."

Grit turned to face Dagger, heat rising in her cheeks.

He hesitated. "Councils do not always rule justly."

"I'd be the last to claim they do. Get on with your story."

Dagger watched her a moment and then continued. "The twins traveled south and made it as far as a promontory three or four days past Thresh. There they stumbled into a clearing and found Kinsmon and a grand feast. He offered each a seat at his table, but they tried to bargain with him. The older twin in particular sought Kinsmon's food on his own terms. He questioned its quality, offered a trade of a weapon for a plate, and dared to ask for a sample. Kinsmon warned against taking one bite, but each accepted that single bite. When the food touched his tongue, the older twin spat it out, cursed, and labeled his twin a fool to stand so long contemplating the bitterness of what he called poison. He stormed into the woods, swearing and kicking at shrubs."

Grit yawned, feigning disinterest. "I suppose the younger twin remained to feast."

"Wrong. The younger twin remained only long enough for Kinsmon to promise to feast with him another day. Then he fled into the woods to rejoin his twin. The older twin, however, refused to accept the younger, citing his hesitation as a grave weakness with which he would not associate himself. He disowned his twin, swearing to utterly destroy him in time."

Grit turned in her saddle. "Why did he not destroy him then and there?"

Dagger flashed a smile. "Ah, that's the question. What would possess a cruel man to postpone his treachery?"

"Distinction. What's victory without an audience to observe one's triumph? He'd have been a fool to return to the village that banished him, even with a mangled body, and no honor could be gained elsewhere. Who'd be impressed by one stranger's victory over another? No, Dagger." Grit shook her head, a proud smile on her face. "The older twin had to allow himself and his sibling time to establish reputations elsewhere. Waiting was his only choice if he wished more than the simple satisfaction of destroying the younger twin."

"Perhaps you understand too well." Dagger studied her with a curious expression. "But, yes, Strike preferred a cruel, well-planned destruction that would bring him widespread recognition. Now that he's gathered an army and the support of Havoc, we may expect his full wrath to fall upon his twin."

Grit let out a gruff laugh. "Well, then, let's hope the younger twin, however slow he may be, has remained sure and lethal."

# THIRTY-ONE

From a distance, Port Colony was beautiful. Golden lights sprinkled the dark outline of buildings. Beyond the city, the setting sun cast a pink glow across the sky and over the sea. Dagger reined in Fealty and waited under the cover of the forest's edge for Shriven to carry Grit to his side. He whistled, and an eagle soared down from the top of a gigantic pine and rested on his outstretched arm.

"To Vell!" Dagger raised his arm, and the eagle took flight once more, headed into the heart of the city.

Dagger turned to Grit. "Port Colony is hostile territory. We'd made small gains in this city, but Strike and Havoc together have sown fear and confusion. Their spies and servants work to undermine all Kinsmon's scouts have labored to accomplish. Vision reports brutal acts against friends of Kinsmon, but nothing has been confirmed. Be on your guard. Reveal nothing of yourself to anyone."

They waited a full hour, Grit's ears attentive to every rustle and snap of the forest around them and her eyes fixed on Port Colony. She shifted her weight in Shriven's saddle.

"We could go around," she said.

Dagger shook his head, but did not look at her. "Messages to deliver."

A bird's shrill call broke the silence. Dagger repeated the sound, still but for his lips. A moment later Vell stepped from behind a tree. In one fluid movement, Dagger dismounted, his feet touching the ground with a soft thud.

"Escort Grit to Fellows Inn, Vell," Dagger said. "I'll join you once I've delivered the most pressing of my messages."

Grit glared at Vell. She had no desire to repeat the pain of his arrow in her neck and the days of confusion and weakness that had followed.

He returned her distrustful stare. "I vowed not to kill you and not to raise my pipe at you, but I didn't say anything about knocking you out some other way. If you're planning to put up a fight, I won't hesitate to employ a branch to secure your life."

"That won't be necessary." Dagger shot Grit a warning glance. "Put away your dagger. His job is to protect you, not harm you."

Grit sheathed her dagger and rested her hand on her hip so that her fingertips just touched the hilt. "I don't need protection. Least of all from him."

"I'm sure you'd have said the same last time you entered Port Colony, and look at all the trouble you got yourself into then," Vell said. "We're on the same side, you and I, but the other side doesn't know that. They think I serve Strike. With me at your side, you'll have safe passage to Harth's inn. You'd be hard pressed to make it on your own. Port Colony is a much darker place than it was on your last visit. I wouldn't let a dog wander the streets unguarded."

A dog. Worm. Had he made it home to Ezekiel yet? She was glad she'd left him in the Southern Realm, where she needn't worry what strangers might do to him.

"Okay," she said. "I'll go with you, but I swear, if I so much as see your pipe, I won't hesitate—"

"You have a deal. We'll see you at the inn, Dagger. Tether the horses, and I'll make sure they're cared for and waiting on the other side of the city when you're ready to go." Vell gripped her arm tight and led her into Port Colony. It seemed she couldn't escape being his prisoner, but she didn't resist this time. The city's residents watched Grit hungrily.

218

"That's a pretty one you've got, Vell." A stooped man wrapped a bony finger around a strand of Grit's hair. "Care to share?"

She spit in the man's face as Vell yanked her closer to his body.

"Paws off." Vell's voice was harder than Grit had ever heard it.

Her back pressed against Vell's thick body, and his arm wrapped around her ribcage. He brushed her hair out of her face and held it in a ponytail at the back of her head. His whiskers scratched her ear; his breath warmed her cheek. "Stay close and let me be the foul one. They are starving tonight, and you must not entice them."

Fear rose in Grit's chest, fear deeper and more raw than she'd ever known. In this city of ravenous men, her security was entirely in Vell's hands. Vell, who had almost killed her once, held her so close and so tightly she could barely breathe. *He is afraid. Afraid of things more awful than I dare imagine.*

She turned her head so her lips almost touched his neck. "Could you at least not pull out all my hair?"

"Forgive me," he whispered, his gaze darting from shaded space to dark corner. He let go of Grit's hair, but kept his hand on the top of her head.

She was relieved when Vell turned down an empty alleyway and led her to the backyard of Harth's inn. They passed a small stable and entered the inn through the kitchen door. The kitchen bustled with activity as Scarlett's dame barked orders at various individuals stationed around the room.

"Don't let that burn!" Harth waved her towel at an absentminded old man tending a pot over the fire, then turned to a slender girl. "Refill the mugs in the dining room!"

Vell released Grit and cleared his throat. "I have a guest for you."

Harth tucked her towel into her apron. "Grit, isn't it? It's good to see you again, and good to see you looking so well. Sit in the dining room. Put your feet up. Have a drink on the house. I'll send your dinner as soon as I've seen to everything in here."

Vell and Grit passed through the kitchen and into the dining room. Every table in the room was full, so they sat at the counter. The barkeep filled a mug for each of them. A few minutes later, the girl from the kitchen brought their dinners.

As they finished eating, Dagger came out of the kitchen. Harth followed, looking like a dog waiting for a choice morsel to drop from the table. She set a plate on the counter and waited for Dagger to sit.

Vell scooted from his stool. "Take my seat, Dagger."

"Thank you. A good evening's work, Vell."

"I'll be about my business, then. A safe journey to you both." The guard bent to Grit's ear and whispered, "I'm sorry about the arrow last time you were here."

Harth leaned on the counter. "How is my precious girl, Dagger? Is she well? How sorely I miss her."

"Scarlett is well. Here." Dagger pulled a folded paper from his pocket. "She sends you a letter. I can read it to you now or later, if you prefer."

"Oh, do read it now." Harth rested her chin on her folded hands and looked at him expectantly.

"Excuse me a moment longer, Grit." Dagger unfolded Scarlett's letter and leaned closer to Harth. "My dear dame . . .

Grit swirled the cider in her mug while the bartender filled mugs for other customers. A dameling, perhaps sixteen or seventeen years of age, slid onto the stool on the other side of Grit. The dameling's long, golden curls were tied back with a bright pink ribbon. Clear blue eyes and delicate pink lips adorned her round, youthful face.

"May I have a juice, barkeep?" Her voice was as innocent as her smile. She took her mug of juice from the barkeep and turned to Grit. Her eyes widened in amazement when she saw Grit's pearl. "What is that round your neck?"

Grit took a swig of cider. "It's a pearl."

"Where did you get it?" The girl squinted for a closer look at the orb.

Remembering Dagger's warning to reveal nothing of herself, Grit straightened her back and chose her words carefully. "An ally gave it to me as security for a future service."

The girl sat back, her pink lips drawn into a frown. "It must be quite a service for your ally to have given you such a magnificent pledge."

"It's nothing much." Grit shrugged her shoulders and stared into her mug. Eventually, the girl would have to lose interest in the pearl.

The girl leaned closer. "Its surface looks so smooth." Her voice cracked as she reached a hand out to touch Grit's pearl.

"No!"

Dagger's voice rose above the clamor of the dining room. He pulled Grit back by the shoulder. His other arm shot across Grit's chest and knocked the dameling's hand away from the pearl.

Grit jumped off her stool, sending it crashing to the ground. Dagger stepped over the stool to place himself between Grit and the girl, who glared at the dark-haired sireling.

Her eyes flashed cold and unfeeling, and her hair, gold and shiny a moment before, was now gray and brittle.

Grit stumbled backward, grasping for her dagger. *It's her. The hag. So far from the Koradin-Thresh Highway.* Bile rose in her throat.

The hag extended a wrinkled hand. "Ah, Grit, we're old friends, aren't we? Would you despise a poor, aged woman?"

Dagger's voice trembled with rage. "Do not touch her, Havoc! Grit of Berth and Stone is under Kinsmon's care. If you would so much as lay a finger on her, or on anything that belongs to her, you must speak to Kinsmon first. Leave here and return to whatever hole you crawled out of, you foul, miserable wretch!"

Havoc returned Dagger's fierce gaze. A smile crept across her twisting features. She laughed coarsely. Peering around Dagger to address Grit, she asked, "Is that what Kinsmon calls you? Grit of Berth and Stone?"

"Silence, Grit!" Dagger glared at Havoc as her hair lightened from gray to gold and her eyes recovered their soft, sky blue shade.

The dameling spoke again to Dagger, her voice steady despite her shifting appearance. "You blunder, River Rat. Her dame disowned her over a year ago. She is merely Grit of Stone now. Unless Kinsmon thinks her dame still matters . . ."

Grit stepped from behind Dagger. "My dame is inconsequential."

Havoc raised a questioning eyebrow. Dagger roughly pushed Grit behind him and held one arm out to keep her from moving forward again.

"How charming. The river rat guards Stone's cherished possession."

Dagger placed a hand on the hilt of his sword. "I told you to leave, wench. If you do not do so immediately, I will summon Kinsmon himself."

222

Havoc's blue eyes filled with frenzy. Through gnarled lips, the wild creature, half dameling, half hag, sneered. "I'll go, River Rat, but only because you've given me something to consider."

She backed away from them, shuffling all the way to the entrance of the inn. There she darted through the open doorway and was lost in the crowded street. Dagger wheeled to face Grit.

"I told you to hold your tongue." Grabbing her by the elbow, Dagger steered Grit across the dining room and marched her up the narrow stairway. She struggled against his grasp, but he clenched her arm tighter.

At the end of the upstairs hallway, he threw open a door and slammed it shut behind them. Crossing to the far side of the room, he nearly shoved Grit into a stiff, wooden chair. He ran the fingers of both hands through his hair like he meant to pull out the jet-black strands in fistfuls. Breathing deep, irate sighs, he paced the length of the room. Every few steps, he stopped to look at Grit and shake his head.

Grit crossed her arms over her chest. "What exactly is your problem? I fail to see what grievous act I have committed to make you behave like a madman."

Dagger stopped mid-stride. "Do you know nothing of the danger you're in?"

"I know woefully little of the danger I face." Grit leaned forward in her seat and rested her elbows on her knees. "You people seem to think all I need to know is what is in my heart. Perhaps you ought to tell me what's going on in the world outside my heart, as my heart doesn't seem to serve me as well as it should."

Dagger's anger abated. His hands fell to his sides and his shoulders drooped as he walked to the table and took the chair next to hers.

"There's some truth in that. Allow me a moment to think. There is so much you ought to know."

# THIRTY-TWO

G rit ran her fingernail along a scratch in the table's smooth, wooden surface. Dagger kept his face buried in his hands. From time to time, he peered through his fingers to look at Grit. Then he'd close his eyes and move his head up and down or from side to side, as if scanning the pages of his mind. She thought he was tightly wound at their first meeting, but she had no idea how tightly wound.

At last, with a deep sigh, he turned his chair so it faced hers. His face was grave, but all traces of anxiety had vanished. "You never asked what happened to the younger of Summit Colony's twins."

Grit shook her head, disbelieving. "Havoc has visited us, and you speak of stories decades passed? It hardly seems important what happened to the younger twin."

"It is of utmost importance, especially to you." He leaned back in his chair and crossed his arms over his chest. "While the older twin first traveled south to Port Colony, then east to Koradin, and then here and there, never making one place home for long, the younger twin retraced his steps north to a humble seaside village. There he earned a mostly favorable reputation, attached himself exclusively to one unlikely dameling, and sired four remarkable offspring, one of whom was not long ago banished for some sort of infantile folly surrounding her test. You'd know more about that sort of thing than I. Rumor has it the younger twin frequently wanders the forests in search of a nourishing feast and has never removed from his neck the smooth, white stone Kinsmon gave him as a seal of his promise to feast with him another day."

Grit's chest tightened. "My sire. But how can it be?"

She rummaged through a lifetime of memories, snatching up and replaying any in which Sire Stone existed. Could Dagger's story be true? She couldn't deny Sire Stone's strange affiliation with Dame Berth and his partiality toward her above all other women, nor could she ignore the facts of her banishment, Sire Stone's walks through the woods, or the stone she'd admired from her earliest days.

"There's more." Dagger drew in his breath and folded his hands in his lap. "The older twin. While in Koradin, he sired a child. Willow was the dame's name, offspring of Sage Frost, leader of Koradin. Willow of Echo and Frost."

"Get on with it. It can't be that hard to tell."

Dagger looked up from his hands and spoke with deliberation. "Upon Willow's death, the older twin threw his newborn infant into the river Jubilee."

Speaking slowly, Grit pieced together the stories she'd heard. "You are Strike's offspring. Your sire, the older twin, has vowed to destroy his younger twin?"

Dagger nodded, his face solemn.

"And my sire, Sire Stone, is the younger twin?"

"That's correct."

"Then you and I, as their offspring, should by all rights be enemies." Grit traced the curve of her dagger's hilt with her forefinger, her gaze fixed on Dagger's impassive face.

"Do you consider me your enemy?" he asked.

"It depends on your purpose. What exactly do you plan to do in the Northern Forest?" Grit pursed her lips and wrapped her fingers slowly around her dagger. She could take him, if it came to that.

"I intend to dissuade my sire from destroying his twin and all his twin holds dear. I have sworn to demolish his hold on Koradin, and I will do all in my power to ensure he does no more harm to Chasmaria or to himself. By whatever means necessary, I will stop him."

Dagger studied her face, his intense blue eyes unblinking. As he leaned back in his chair, a sardonic smile played at the corner of his lips. "Shall we proceed as enemies, Grit of Berth and Stone, or as allies?"

She shook her head. "'By whatever means necessary,' you say. Then why do you care whether he harms himself?"

"The creature you met downstairs, Havoc, seeks to spread fear and discord all over Chasmaria. Given the opportunity, she would destroy Kinsmon and all who call him friend. She cannot achieve any of this on her own, however." Dagger leaned forward. "She has made a deal, Grit, with my sire."

"What sort of deal?"

"She helps him destroy Stone and all he loves; he conquers Chasmaria village by village until he can hand the entire country over to her destructive power. There's no telling what darkness will fill this land when that day comes."

"So Strike and Havoc have set their sights on Sire Stone?" Grit asked. Was that why Havoc had ambushed her on the Koradin-Thresh Highway? Was that why she had appeared in Harth's inn? Was Grit's death the first step in destroying all Stone cherished?

"You know I speak truthfully." Dagger seemed to struggle again with thoughts he did not wish to express.

He folded his hands between his knees and looked into Grit's eyes. "They will pick you off, one by one—you, your dame, your younger siblings, all your sire cherishes—leaving Sire Stone to fall at last by Strike's own hand. That is why I told you to reveal nothing of yourself to anyone. I made a grave mistake when I revealed your name."

Grit twirled her dagger. She needed a moment to think.

Dagger continued, "Strike cannot win this game. Even if he succeeds in destroying Sire Stone, he will lose when he hands Chasmaria over to Havoc. She has no loyalty; she knows no favorites. She'll destroy him as soon as she's exhausted his usefulness. You understand now, I hope, why, as much as I despise my sire, a part of me pities him. You ask why I care if he harms himself. It is because he is a mere pawn of a greater power, because forces beyond his control compel him to do what sane men find reprehensible. I wish to spare him the full effect of his errors. Because he cannot keep himself from harm, I would do it for him. Perhaps you feel the same for your Golden Warrior."

"Do not speak of my Golden Warrior." Grit sheathed her dagger and studied the castle brat. He'd no right to bring Coil into the conversation, but he was honest, if nothing else.

Leaning forward, she spat in her hand and offered it to Dagger. "Allies?"

He looked at the spittle pooling in her palm, raised his hand to his mouth, spat, and took her hand in his.

"Allies."

Wiping his hand on his trousers, Dagger rose. He secured the lock on the door, extinguished the lamp, and crossed to the window, where he looked out over the darkened street. "This city has become a foul place. Take the bed. I'll lay out a mat. I don't wish to leave you alone tonight, not here."

Tired as she was from their journey and the excitement of their encounter with Havoc, Grit did not argue. She crawled into the bed and pulled the covers to her chin. She needed all the rest she could get.

Dagger remained at the window. He took from his pocket the small jar Scarlett had pressed into his hand at their parting. He opened it, reached a finger in, and set the jar on the windowsill. His gaze searched the street as he massaged the cream into his hands.

"A foul place indeed," Dagger said as he slid Scarlett's jar of cream into his pocket. He took a mat from under Grit's bed and pulled it to the side of the door.

As Dagger settled to sleep, Grit slipped a hand underneath her covers to assure herself of her weapon's presence. *Never approach a stranger without a ready weapon*, that's what Dame Berth always said. There were strangers aplenty in this awful city, and Grit wouldn't be found unarmed tonight.

Sometime in the night, a commotion in the hallway awakened Grit. Throwing back the worn patchwork quilt, she drew her dagger and waited, perched on the edge of the bed, her heart pounding. Had Havoc returned for her?

Dagger stood at the door, sword ready. Urgent knocking joined the sounds of shuffling feet and muffled voices that had woken Grit.

Harth called through the door, her voice constrained. "Dagger! Open up!"

Grit rose and stood beside Dagger as he hurried to open the door. Harth bustled past them, ushering a small group of people into the room. There were eight of them, wild-eyed and smelling of earth, sweat, and blood.

Harth bent over the side table to light a lamp. "I thought you'd want to speak with them, but it's best they be seen by no one else. Spies are everywhere these days, after all."

# THIRTY-THREE

Grit sat on the edge of the bed and inspected the group Harth brought into their room. She remembered Oak and Vision from her last visit to the inn. They seemed different somehow.

The hint of the warrior Grit had detected in Oak was no longer a mere hint. Now he was the consummate warrior, broad and tall with stern eyes that seemed to take in every detail of his surroundings and a chiseled face whose expression betrayed nothing of his inner thoughts.

Vision, whose sharp eyes had missed nothing at their last meeting, seemed incapable of focusing on one thing for more than a second. His gaze darted about the room, stopping only when the need to speak forced him to relax his vigilance. From time to time, his muscles twitched, as if at any moment he might explode into action.

Grit clenched her dagger tight.

The other six individuals, three men, two women, and a girl not much older than Grit, moved across the room as one. Filthy, emaciated, and unarmed, they positioned themselves in a semi-circle behind Oak. Tattoos marked each of their arms. The girl had only one tattoo, but others' arms were darkened wrist to elbow by what Vell had called "the Ink of Koradin."

Harth waved them toward the table on the far side of the room. "Sit, sit! I'll bring up some food and drink and whatever else you require."

Oak glanced at the refugees. "They've suffered long and traveled far. Bring mats and blankets, whatever you can spare for their comfort."

231

As Harth hurried from the room, Oak turned to Dagger. "I beg you to forgive our intrusion. The rigors of travel are inconsequential compared to the harsh treatment they received in Strike's dungeon. I would prefer not to stop, but they cannot continue without a day or two of rest and recovery. As there is no place between Koradin and Castle Concord as secure as this inn, we judged it best . . ."

"Say no more. Harth was right. I do want to speak with them." Dagger assumed a commanding air as he addressed the man who remained standing behind Oak when the others had settled themselves around the table. "You've come from Koradin, have you?"

The man puffed out his chest. "We are among the faithful of Koradin. Strike's held our village for several months now. Many oppose him, but few have the courage to do so openly. Those who do are either killed or imprisoned. We considered ourselves lucky to have landed in the Western Dungeon. We escaped with help from Vision and Oak, who have long followed our plight." He glanced at Oak, standing with his arms crossed over his barrel chest, and coughed. "Only one prisoner remained, a mad old woman who refused to come away with us. We tried to persuade her, but she wouldn't budge. We go to Castle Concord to seek Kinsmon's protection and plead for military reinforcements that we may reclaim our village from Strike. There are those still in Koradin who would rise against Strike if they thought their numbers could support a battle."

Dagger rested his chin in his hand. "That's good to know. What's your name, good sire?"

"Forge."

"I expect to visit Koradin soon. Could you sketch a map of your village?" Dagger asked.

The man hesitated, scrutinizing Dagger as if he almost recognized him. He glanced at Oak, but the warrior was engaged in conversation with one of the women.

"Never mind the resemblance, Forge." Vision, silent since ushering in the refugees, spoke from his lookout by the window. "You'll find none better to serve the interests of Koradin."

Sire Forge turned back to Dagger. "I'll make you that map."

Dagger rubbed his hands together. "I want every detail, however insignificant it seems. Include every building, every room, every passageway."

"You'll need her, too." Sire Forge nodded over his shoulder at the dameling seated at the table. "Scullion!"

At her name, the dameling looked up. Pale and petite, like the weakest dameling of the Inner Ring, she scurried in her bare feet to Sire Forge's side. Facing Dagger, she bowed her head, a tangled mess of stringy, brown hair.

"Scullion, is it?" Dagger asked. The dameling nodded. "Can you sketch the interior of Koradin's fortress, from the lowest dungeons to the highest towers?"

Scullion raised her scarred face, brown eyes sparkling, and spoke with a confidence at odds with her quiet voice. "As a kitchen slave, I've spent my entire life inside the fortress. I know every room, every hallway, and every secret passage. I daresay I know the fortress better than Sage Frost himself."

"How is Sage Frost?" Dagger looked from one refugee to the next with unflinching intensity.

Sire Forge winced. "He hardly knows how unwell he is. His council disbanded, and I fear his mind has failed him as well. He no longer recognizes those he knew before Strike defeated him, but spends hours each day imagining himself in conversation with his long deceased offspring. Died in childbirth some twenty years ago. They say Strike dashed the infant's head against the rocks."

Dagger's face remained impassive before the veiled question in Sire Forge's eyes. "A pity about all of them. I've heard Frost and Willow were decent folk."

He gestured Sire Forge and Scullion toward the end of the table, where Oak had placed a pen and a roll of parchment. Grit cocked her head to the side as Dagger leaned over the developing map. *No wonder Kinsmon rescued him from that river. See how sure he is of himself, how he commands others, and they obey. He'd have done well in Thresh.*

After a few minutes, Grit left her perch on the side of the bed and crossed the room. Her bare feet pressed softly into the grooves of the worn wood planks. She sat among the fugitives at the end of the table opposite Dagger and watched the sireling study the parchment upon which Scullion drew.

His dark brows came together. "What are you drawing now?"

"A passageway."

Sire Forge put a hand on Scullion's bony shoulder. "He won't be needing that one, not unless he intends to break into the dungeon. It's how we escaped, but there's a trick to the door, and it won't do him any good coming or going."

"Draw it anyway. I want everything," Dagger said.

Grit leaned closer to the men and women seated at her end of the table. "Tell me about our enemy. Who is this Strike of the Northern Mountains?"

Three of them answered at once.

"A vile man."

"Evil to the core."

"He is more clever than any foe you will encounter."

This last description came from the woman seated beside Grit. She continued, "He drew our youth into his ranks during their tests. We didn't realize this, of course, until it was too late. When an army from the east attacked, Strike pressed an alliance with Koradin based on the memory of Sage Frost's long-dead offspring, Willow. It was a segment of Strike's army, mainly of warriors of the Northern Mountains, which attacked Koradin. Strike stood with us until the enemy pressed most firmly. Then, he commanded his men to take the fortress. The warriors he'd brought into Koradin and many of our own youth turned against the faithful of Koradin."

"In the end, we were forced either to accept Strike's rule or to face imprisonment or death," said one of the men.

The second woman, who had remained quiet the whole time, looked at each of her companions. "He had ears everywhere. Not three hours after speaking his name with disgust, I was awakened in my bed. This is the least of the pain Strike's men inflicted upon me." She pulled up her sleeve, revealing a pattern of crisscrossed scars running the length of her tattooed forearm. Grit had nicked her share of Threshan youth and branded her own arm, but to inflict such brutality on another without cause was unthinkable.

She reached across the table and touched the woman's scarred arm. "Do you know whether the Golden Demon has visited Koradin?"

"The Golden Demon? No, no. I've never heard of him. Who is this Golden Demon?" The woman pulled her arm back and looked uneasily about the room.

"No one. I'm sorry to disturb you. Think no more of it," Grit said.

She sighed, relief flooding her heart. Coil was unknown in Koradin. There were limits to his cruelty, places his name was not as accursed as Strike's.

"What of the village of Thresh?" she asked, remembering Strike's vow to avenge his twin. "Has Strike attacked Thresh yet?"

"No. At least, he hadn't as of our departure." A sly smile lit the first woman's stern features. "We learn a lot in the dungeon from warriors who think no one listens. Strike has prepared many times to attack Thresh, but has yet to follow through with his plans. Instead of sending his army to Thresh, he sends them off to capture some distant, unimposing village. The warriors do not understand why he sends them off to the plains or into the mountains when they might at last subjugate their ancient rival."

Grit had forgotten the enmity between Thresh and Koradin. She was supposed to hate these people. Why was she glad they'd escaped? Her relief went deeper than knowing Strike had left Thresh alone. She frowned at the woman's scarred arm. He should pay for his abuse.

One of the men spoke up. "It won't be long. They say Strike grows increasingly agitated by his altered plans. I suspect he'll soon defy that woman of his."

"Defy her?" Dagger jerked his head up from the map he had been studying. His hands gripped the edge of the table.

The refugees looked from one to the other, confusion on their faces. At last, the young woman with the scarred arms answered Dagger. "Some whisper it is she, not Strike, who commands the army."

"And you suppose he will defy her soon?"

The woman traced the scars on her arm. "I wouldn't be surprised if he throws her off any day now. He doesn't enjoy being controlled by a woman."

Dagger's blue eyes shone with cold determination as he rolled up the map and rose from the table. "Pack your bag, Grit. We mustn't delay."

The alliance between Strike and Havoc was unraveling with potentially disastrous results. Time was not to be wasted, neither on gathering information from refugees nor on debating their course. The best course, the only course, led immediately to Thresh. Grit would release Coil from his vow, by force of her dagger if necessary. Then they would warn Sire Stone and the council to prepare for Strike's certain attack.

As Dagger packed his bag, Grit rose from the table, pulled on her boots, and collected her few belongings, cramming them into her pack. She stood at the door, her hand clutching the knob and her foot tapping the floor while Dagger took leave of Vision, Oak, and the refugees.

"Brave men and women of Koradin. I thank you for your help and wish you peace in Port Colony and safety as you proceed to Castle Concord. I trust we will meet again under more pleasant conditions. Oak, Vision, guide these people with every caution to Castle Concord and add my name to their petition." Dagger clutched the glass shard hanging from his necklace. He looked from one refugee to the next, his eyes glistening oddly. "May the throne of Koradin prevail."

With a curt nod of farewell, Grit swung open the door and entered the hallway with Dagger right behind. Passing through the kitchen, they bid farewell to Harth. They did not speak to one another until they reached the forest north of Port Colony. Vell proved as good as his word. Their horses were tethered and waiting.

Dagger mounted Fealty and turned in his saddle to face Grit. "We must hurry to Thresh. If Strike and Havoc quarrel, there's no telling what either might do. We must think quickly and act carefully. If Thresh and Koradin fall together into the hands of Havoc, there will be no hope for the rest of Chasmaria."

## THIRTY-FOUR

Leaving Port Colony behind, Grit and Dagger followed Chasmaria's undulating western coastline. After several days, they reached the Koradin-Thresh highway.

Grit spied Thresh first. The afternoon sun blazed above the village, creating a haze over her former home. She eased the reins back to bring Shriven to a halt and willed her fingers not to fidget. The training fields were empty. Dagger slowed Fealty beside her.

Grit squeezed her legs to Shriven's side to stop their shaking. "They may kill us on sight. I'm not exactly a favorite among the council members."

"That isn't hard to imagine," Dagger said. "Perhaps you should try being pleasant."

"Pleasantries may work in Castle Concord, but they won't restore what Thresh stole from me, nor will they restrain the Golden Demon."

"Golden War—"

"Golden Demon, Dagger. Stop softening the truth. Let's call it what it is." She spurred Shriven on, not wanting to discuss Coil any longer. She couldn't afford a second failure on the Koradin-Thresh Highway. This time, the consequences extended far beyond the loss of her honor. *Lives. Innocent lives. That's what's at stake. I must stop Coil. If I turn back now, I'll deserve every shame I've borne and more.*

When they came to the place where she'd struggled with Havoc over a year before, Grit reined Shriven in. Horrific images of the wench tumbled through her mind.

Grit pointed a shaking finger toward the sand. "She was right there. Havoc. I was a fool to offer help."

Dagger leaned over and placed his hand on her arm. "She's not there now. And, she cannot touch you or anything that belongs to you without Kinsmon's permission. Remember, she has no right to you."

Grit stared at Dagger's hand and resisted the impulse to shake it from her arm. The rare tenderness in his voice and the firmness of his touch only intensified her terror of the creature who had torn apart Thresh and Koradin, who had pitted Strike against Stone, who had twice attempted to harm her, and who had vowed to destroy Chasmaria and Kinsmon. *I never knew fear to be so close, a fiend within my veins, devouring me from heart to limbs.*

By force of will, she stilled her trembling muscles. Leaning forward with a hand on Shriven's muscular neck, she spat in the sand. "May the wench's blood soak the earth upon which she falls. I won't be fooled again."

Dagger drew back. "Anger sickens the soul. Let Kinsmon's promises strengthen you and know you aren't alone. Whatever lies ahead, I'll do all I can to aid you, as will Kinsmon himself if need be. He won't abandon us when we are in need."

"What of Coil? What of his need?"

"That's not my decision to make." Dagger studied her a moment before continuing in measured words. "Have we not discussed the importance of discerning the times to kill, wound, spar, and heal? It's up to you, Grit, to determine which of these Coil requires."

Dagger could speak so easily. He had no real attachment to the sire he hoped to overthrow. How would he feel if it were Scarlett he rode to oppose?

They traveled several yards before Dagger spoke again. "I would not admit this to many, but there are things I fear, not the least of them being what lies ahead. We'll both have to pretend to be braver than we are. Can you put on a good show?"

Grit rubbed her upper right arm, memories of her Final Branding flooding her mind. "Oh, I can put on a good show."

She fixed her gaze on the village ahead.

"This is new." Warriors stood at intervals around the Outer Ring, with one on either side of the road leading into the village. "That guard, on the left, is Turf of Elna and Bord, coward of cowards. Allow me to handle him. We have a history, Turf and I."

She spurred Shriven forward, her head held high and her hand on her dagger, daring Turf to bar her entry into Thresh.

"Halt!" He thrust his spear out to block their passage. The guard opposite him did the same.

Both horses stopped. Turf advanced toward them, his face expressionless. When he recognized Grit, he scowled.

"My prey returns." He cast a glance at Dagger. "What rubbish hangs about her now?"

Grit sat tall in her saddle. "Why, Turf of Elna and Bord, you've made it all the way to the station of village guard. I'm mildly surprised you climbed so high, but the council must be shocked you haven't climbed higher. Tsk. Tsk." She shook her head in feigned disbelief.

Turf thrust his spear at Shriven. "State your business, Grit of Stone."

Grit grew serious under Turf's cruel glare. She could not back down, but did not wish to fight with him here on the outskirts of the village. A band of warriors might easily form out of the scattered guards.

"I demand you escort my companion and me to the meetinghouse, where we will present ourselves to the council. If you have anything to say to me, you may say it there. If I choose to say anything more to you or of you, I will say it there. I haven't forgotten your cowardice as a hunter."

"Ha! Say what you will. You and your unclaimed ally have done all you can to hold me back, but neither of you can keep me from the honor rightfully mine." Turf snorted in derision. "I doubt the council will be pleased to see the trash they threw out a year ago come back to stink up the village, but have it your way. Present yourself to the council. You know the way."

He moved his spear aside to let them pass; the other guard mirrored his actions. Grit glared at Turf as she passed him by.

He shook his spear at her. "You can't touch me, foolish girl!"

She led Dagger past the huts of the Outer Ring, into the heart of Thresh, and toward the meetinghouse. All the while, Turf's manner nagged Grit's mind. Something in his bearing unsettled her. Unable to figure out the cause of her discomfort, she noted the activity around her.

Thresh was much as Arrow suggested it would be. It was the same, yet changed. Something wasn't right. Youth jostled one another in the street, but not with the same vigor. It was as if they knew they played a foolish game and wished to save their energies for something more urgent than childish brawls. Dames trod with heavier feet, watching their babes closer than she remembered. More sires and sirelings strolled through Thresh this afternoon, all of them wearing grave expressions.

Several children stopped to watch Grit and Dagger proceed through the village, but most of the older Threshans shuffled out of their way, stealing circumspect glances at the intruders and clutching their possessions tighter. Instinctively, Grit kept one hand on her dagger and wrapped the other around the reins. *Perhaps I should have returned sooner, though what I could have done to prevent this melancholy air is beyond me.*

She searched the faces, but nowhere did she find Coil. On the other side of the street, a dame with straw-colored hair grasped the hand of a curly haired girl. The dame's other hand supported the bottom of a baby resting in a sling across her chest. Seized by regret, Grit steered Shriven in the trio's direction.

"Dame Dara!" Grit dismounted, fumbled with her pack, and withdrew the blanket Kinsmon had given her. She held it out to the woman. "Take it."

Dame Dara released the girl's hand and snatched the blanket from Grit. She studied Grit suspiciously. The child stroked the blanket with her grubby hand.

"It's so soft," she whispered.

Grit's gaze lingered on the clean wool. "I hate to part with it, but a wretched girl stole your dear dame's blanket some time ago. It is right that she have a new blanket, and a much nicer one at that."

The girl's blond curls bobbed as she nodded. Dame Dara pulled on the child's arm, dragging her onward. The dame would never like Grit. Dagger smiled oddly.

"What? It's only a blanket, and I have another one." Grit threw her pack over her shoulder and proceeded toward the meetinghouse on foot, leading Shriven.

After tethering her horse, Grit stood in the open doorway of the meetinghouse with Dagger close behind. The council was in session. Some members were seated around a long table set on the stage; others stood leaning on the backs of their chairs.

Sire Stone paced the far end of the low stage, his voice raised. "Allow me to go to him. He's my twin, after all. Perhaps I can bargain with him for Thresh's safety."

Berth leaned back in her chair. "And what bargain could you make with the mighty Strike? What do you have that he couldn't take by force if he so desired?"

"I don't know, but . . ." Sire Stone fell silent. The other eleven council members followed his gaze.

"Grit." Sire Stone exhaled, taking a step toward her with arms outstretched. "I thought I'd never see you again."

"Wait!" Sire Pierce said. "Who accompanies her?"

Dagger stepped forward. Squaring his shoulders, he raised his chin and addressed the council.

"I am Dagger of Willow and Strike, rejected by my sire and reared by Kinsmon's hand."

"Kinsmon!" Sire Swot leapt from his chair and scurried toward Dagger. "Do you mean *the* Kinsmon, who defeated Havoc in the great quake that rent Chasmaria into thirds? And Willow . . ." He repeated the name to himself, trying to place her. "Willow, Willow . . . Would that be Willow of Echo of Ardor of Parch and so on all the way back to Koradin of River of Harmony?"

Grit threw up her arms. At least Sire Swot hadn't changed. "Does it matter? When Thresh may be days from falling to Strike, does it really matter who reared this stranger or who birthed him?"

"The same Kinsmon and Willow." Dagger spoke in a low, steady voice, and leveled his gaze at each council member in turn. "I beg you to overlook the rash speech of my ally. She forgets too easily what her hand has agreed to."

The words stung, but Grit could make no argument. She'd called Dagger a stranger, a dangerous error to make when they sought admittance to the village.

Sire Swot wrung his hands. "Are the stories true, then?"

Dagger gave one decisive nod. The wiry man sank into a chair, clutching his chest.

"We must accept him. He's a true child of Harmony, a direct descendant of Koradin, and our only hope of making an ally of what remains of that village."

"Someone tell me what Swot is babbling about now," Sage Brakken said.

Grit struggled to remember a story she was sure she'd never heard.

"He refers to an old saying that when a child of Thresh and a child of Koradin reign in the villages bearing their names, peace will return to Chasmaria," Dagger said.

"Yes, yes. And he is a child of Koradin. I vote to accept him into the village. We'd be fools not to . . ." Sire Swot's words became completely unintelligible, his mind having descended into the deepest depths of thought where all that proceeded from his mouth was garbled mumbling.

Berth rose from her chair. "He may be a descendent of Koradin, but he is also the offspring of our enemy, and I don't recall anyone saying we want Koradin for an ally. Perhaps his death would serve us better."

Bitterness tinged Dagger's voice. "My death will do you no good. I already told you my sire rejected me. He hasn't seen me in nearly twenty years, let alone established an alliance with me. I'm sure he already thinks me dead and is grateful for that mistaken fact. My demise will be of no consequence to him. My life, on the other hand, may prove very useful to you. Little would satisfy me more than to destroy Strike's power over Chasmaria."

Dagger spoke with easy confidence and looked each council member in the eye. It seemed not a challenge, but a pledge of honesty.

He would win them, just as he won everyone—Scarlett, Kinsmon, Burrow and Bard, all the scouts in Port Colony. They'd listen. They'd do as he commanded. They would count him the most honorable of men. Grit stepped back from the council. Dagger didn't need her to stir up the usual altercations.

"You wish to usurp your sire's throne, then?" Sire Pierce asked.

"I wish to see the day when Chasmaria is free of treachery. I'll do all in my power to speed the coming of that day."

"What pledge can you give that you will not betray us if we accept you?" Sire Pierce asked.

The room fell silent. What could Dagger offer? Sire Stone studied the sireling, perhaps to discover traces of Strike in his rejected offspring. Following Sire Stone's gaze, Grit noted, in the face that resembled her sire's in all but age, nothing of deception or brutality. Instead, a reflection of Kinsmon's bearing that she didn't notice before shone in Dagger's noble features. He stood before the Threshan council, calm and unhurried in the urgency of the moment.

"He pledges the life of his sire's twin," Sire Stone said.

Grit cocked her head at her sire, but Dagger simply bowed his head at the older man.

Sire Stone faced Sage Brakken. "I second Sire Swot's vote to accept Dagger of Willow and Strike. I offer a place in my hut should he require a bed. Should he betray Thresh, you may do to me what you would do to him."

"We decide the girl's fate first. Have you all forgotten she has no right to enter Thresh?" Sage Brakken leveled his gaze at Grit. "We banished you."

"I came back."

On the other side of the table, Dame Berth paced in front of the fireplace, the branding rod in her hand and a cold stare fixed on Grit. "What gives you the right to set foot in this village?"

Grit advanced toward the low stage. "I give myself the right. And, I defy anyone to bar my way."

"Why is she here?"

Grit did not need to turn around to know Coil stood in the doorway. His footsteps sounded firmly on the wooden floor as he circled to stand between her and the council. From his heavy boots to his broad shoulders, he looked every bit the seasoned warrior. His face, too, spoke of grueling battles, hardness etched in every feature. What had Arrow said? *Words can wound more deeply than one might imagine.* Is this what her tongue—and the cruel vows she demanded of him—had wrought?

Grit gulped and looked Coil in the eye. "I have come to dispel the terror of the Golden Demon."

# THIRTY-FIVE

"You've come to dispel the terror of the Golden Demon?" Sage Brakken's laughter filled the meetinghouse. He waved his hand as if to shoo away a bothersome insect. "Let the Golden Demon be, girl. He holds no terror over us. You still haven't answered. By what right do you enter Thresh?"

Grit looked again at Coil, the memory of his desperation at their last meeting at odds with the hardened warrior standing before her. He studied her through stern, blue eyes that held none of the mocking mirth she'd hoped to find.

"I claim the right of an outsider to challenge the champion for admittance to Thresh," she said. It was what Coil had wanted her to do in the first place, way back on the rocky shore when he'd begged her to stay.

Sire Stone pounded his fist on the back of Dame Berth's empty chair. "Utter foolishness! She cannot be permitted to do this."

Dame Berth threw the branding rod. It clanked against the stone fireplace before thudding onto the wood floor. Red-faced, she turned on Grit. "Have your way, fool girl, but don't say I didn't teach you better. Let her fight the champion. Death alone will compel her to control her foolish impulses."

"Berth." Sire Stone's voice was an anguished breath.

Dame Berth wagged a finger at Sire Stone. "No! I'll not be dissuaded by any of your talk of what was or what might yet be. That goes for you, too, Swot. She fights the champion."

Sire Stone shook his head. "This is unwise, Berth. Think of the consequences."

Coil turned from Grit to the council. "I stand with the dame. Let her face the champion. Should she succeed against him, dispelling the terror of the Golden Demon will be an easy task to complete. Should she fail . . ." He glanced over his shoulder. "Should she fail, I myself will see that the Golden Demon is laid to rest."

"The matter is settled, then," Sage Brakken said.

Sire Stone stared at Coil, his eyes filled with dismay. "It is foolishness, utter foolishness."

Sire Swot sat up as though physically pulled from his reverie. "But what about him? Can we at least accept the descendant of Koradin?"

Like a cat deciding between two prey, Coil looked from Grit to Dagger. "If she triumphs, his fate is in her hands. If she fails, his fate rests upon the mercy of the champion. I believe, Sire Swot, this is standard procedure in such situations."

Sire Swot shuffled the parchments on the table in front of him. "As far as I have read or heard, Coil of Dara, such circumstances, just as we have before us now, have never occurred. Or at least, they have never been recorded as having occurred, but I suppose it is a just proposal you make, if Sage Brakken agrees."

Sage Brakken nodded toward Grit and Dagger. "Lock them up for the night, and alert the village of a sparring match in the morning. Few will want to miss this one."

Grit resisted the urge to fight when Sire Pierce pulled her arms behind her back. Next to her, Dagger offered his wrists to another council member. All the while Coil watched placidly, his gaze never straying from Grit's face. She wanted to spit at him or scream at him or laugh and tell him that the pair of them would win in the end, but she and Coil were no longer conspiring against Turf in some childhood game. He had supported her claim to fight the champion and had sworn to lay the Golden Demon to rest if she failed, but he looked upon her as an enemy carefully measuring her for any hint of weakness.

Sire Pierce shoved Grit toward the door.

"Fool! Never imprison an armed warrior!" Dame Berth marched across the meetinghouse.

Sire Stone stepped in front of Berth and reached for Grit's dagger. She'd have fought him, but her sire appeared already defeated. Her dagger looked smaller in his hands than in hers. She felt a thousand times smaller herself without her dagger at her hip.

"I'll keep it safe until morning," he said.

Coil passed Grit without a glance. Apparently, he'd seen enough of her. His voice was cold and calculating. "Sire Stone, I require your aid."

****

Later that evening, Grit sat beside Dagger in the small hut in which the council had locked them.

Grit leaned her head against the earthen wall. "I suppose you won't tell me to restrain myself now that it's not your chest in danger of my blade. Surely you won't advise me to hold back in this sparring match."

"I cannot tell you to kill another human being. It's a brutal arrangement into which you rushed." Dagger sighed deeply in the semi-darkness. "Still, you may fight for your survival . . . Mine, too, come to think of it."

In the silence, Grit rehearsed in her mind all she had learned at the Southern Sea and Castle Concord. Only half-aware of her actions, she sliced her empty hand through the air, imagining Varlet of Dara advancing upon her.

"You must sleep." Dagger leaned forward, his arm outstretched. He held her hand steady, his palm smooth and cool against her skin. "You won't be fit to face the champion,

251

whether to destroy or to spare, if you do not first rest your mind and body."

She curled on the hard, dirt floor, her head just touching Dagger's knee. If this was to be her last night of life, she didn't wish to be entirely alone. As Dagger sang tenderly of Castle Concord, weariness overcame anxiety, and Grit fell asleep to dream of Worm and Ezekiel, then of Scarlett, Dagger, Arrow, and Kinsmon.

She awoke in the middle of the night, a strange tightness in her chest. Had it been only a dream, walking with Coil through the gardens of Castle Concord and showing him berries twice the size of any he'd picked in Thresh? His laughter had rung so clear, but now only the sound of Dagger's breathing filled the darkness. The castle brat must have felt her start. He brushed her hair from her face, whispered something incoherent, and hummed one of Bard's songs as she drifted back to sleep.

When she woke again, light entered the hut through a small window high in the wall. It would be tight, but could she fit through the window? Eight small fingers wrapped over the window ledge and two eyes peered into the prison hut. Grit scrambled to her feet.

"Psst! Grit! It's me, Oath!"

"What are you doing, child?" Grit reached up to touch her sibling's fingers, but they were too high.

"Bringing you breakfast. You can't very well best a champion on an empty stomach."

Oath pushed a parcel through the window. Grit caught it as it fell. Her mouth watered at the smell of fresh bread as warmth spread through the cloth wrapping into her palms. She squinted at Oath.

"Where'd you get this?"

Oath lifted one finger from the window ledge. "Never mind that. I have ways of acquiring what I need. I have to go now. Seal's shoulders can only bear so much."

The girl disappeared from sight, a soft "oomph" confirming her dismount from her twin's long-suffering shoulders.

It was mid-morning when Sire Pierce and Dame Berth retrieved Grit and Dagger from their hut. Leading them to the rear of the meetinghouse, they left Grit with an armed warrior at one end of the sparring circle and continued with Dagger around the perimeter fence. With a solemn nod, the warrior handed Grit her dagger. The champion had not yet arrived, but a small crowd began to gather, hungry to watch the banished girl battle the village champion. Grit vaulted the fence into the circle. Let the show begin.

Eager spectators sat on tiers of planks erected on the opposite side of the fenced circle from the meetinghouse. More villagers arrived, and the crowd overflowed the tiers and spread around the circle. Villagers leaned against the wooden fence, peering at the challenger awaiting the champion's arrival. Grit paced along the eastern curve. From his seat in the stands between Dame Berth and Sire Pierce, Dagger frowned. His gaze met Grit's and shifted to the west.

A horn announced the arrival of Thresh's champion. Sire Stone and Sage Brakken stepped to either side of the gate to allow him to enter the circle. He narrowed his eyes to scrutinize his challenger. Grit faced him, barely able to mask her horror.

Coil of Dara moved gracefully despite his broad frame, as if he might vault a fence or curl into a somersault without warning. His cold, blue stare bore into Grit's as he proceeded to the center of the circle.

He called over his shoulder to Sage Brakken. "Allow us to settle our terms of combat." He did not wait for the elderly man's approval, but approached Grit with firm, determined steps and led her to a section of the sparring circle unpopulated by spectators.

With his back to the villagers and an arm resting on the fence, he leaned forward and spoke in a low voice. "So, in your esteemed opinion, may Thresh rightfully boast possession of a warrior worth fighting? That's what you wanted, isn't it?"

Desperate, Grit searched his face. Did he hate her? Or had he truly done all this to please her? Her will, so strong against Kinsmon's dummy, faltered. *So this is the emptiness Scarlett feels apart from Dagger.*

Her shoulders drooped, and her voice came as a whisper. "I've no desire to spar you."

"And yet it didn't bother you to leave me."

There was a new hardness to Coil, a bitterness that hurt more than all her dreams of pink-streaked curls. Her chest ached, her heart nearly crushed under the weight of the change in him. The golden curls that had refused to leave her memory shone immaculately clean in the morning light.

"Your hair," she said. "It isn't pink."

An awkward smile broke the firm line of his lips. "I . . . I thought you hated it that way."

She reached to touch his hair, but drew her hand back. The council watched their every move. "Through all my journeying, it was the one thing I could never banish from my mind."

Relief, pity, and all she had never dared hope to find in her old companion flooded Coil's eyes, washing away the bitterness that had nearly crushed her heart a moment before and filling her with hope.

"You've gotten us into a fine predicament, and we haven't time for pleasantries," he said. "You must listen carefully and do exactly as I instruct if we are to survive this match. Blood-thirst grips many on the council, and they won't be satisfied until one of us lies in a crimson pool. I will slash and cut you,

Grit, but I will not kill you." He took Grit's dagger from her hands and held it in his as if inspecting it. "You must plant this dagger in my chest, or you will kill us both. Only be sure to miss my heart by a hair, if you will, and don't plunge too deeply. Now that you are back, I'm able again to breathe without pain, and I rather wish to continue doing so. Can you do this?"

She snatched her dagger from Coil's hand. "You want me to stab you? Is this your idea of a good plan?"

"I would prefer another way, but we don't have one. You aren't safe unless you defeat me. Trust me, Grit. I know what I'm doing. Can you follow my instructions?"

Grit gulped hard. After a quick glance at Dagger, she looked into Coil's earnest eyes. She struggled to reconcile the familiar youth before her with her memory of the Arborsedge refugees. *How could he have done all they claimed? And yet I saw them . . .* Countless thoughts she could not voice swirled through her mind. Whatever was true, whatever was false, she could sort through it later. Now, she must decide whether to trust Coil or operate independent of him. *Do what is in your heart to do.* Kinsmon's words echoed in her mind. She raised her dagger and pointed it at the only boy she'd ever thought worth sparring.

"To Coil."

A relieved smile played at the corners of Coil's lips as he repeated his part of their old refrain. "To Grit."

He turned on his heel and crossed the sparring circle. When he reached the far side, he removed his sheathed broadsword and passed it over the fence to Sire Stone. Then Coil drew a dagger from his boot and faced Grit. Sage Brakken blew a long note on the horn.

On opposite sides of the circle, Grit and Coil raised their daggers high. The crowd fell silent as challenger and champion roared as one, "Prove yourself!"

# THIRTY-SIX

G rit and Coil circled the sparring ring, drawing ever closer to one another until they met in the middle. Grit made the first move. Thrusting at Coil's right arm, she sliced just below his elbow; he twisted his arm to nick her in return. She reached for his cheek; he slashed her tunic from shoulder to wrist, barely missing the flesh beneath it. Grit leapt to the side; Coil pounced after her. Back and forth they went, Grit attacking boldly and Coil returning wound for wound, but to a lesser degree, until blood stained them both. It was as if no time had passed. She knew his moves before he made them, even as he seemed to know hers.

After an hour, Sage Brakken called for an intermission. Wiping the sweat from her brow, Grit stalked to the fence, grateful for the rest. Across the circle, Sire Stone passed a flask to Coil, who drank greedily from it. Slate, sneaking through the crowd that had gathered around Grit's side, passed her a small flask. Grit took it and drank slowly, keeping one eye on Coil at all times.

A movement to her right caught her attention. She jerked her head toward the fence. Seal and Oath leaned over the bottom rail. Seal gestured oddly with her hands, as if tracing circles and figure eights on an invisible table. Jabbing motions punctuated the smooth flow of her delicate hands.

"What's she doing, Oath?" Grit asked.

"She's reenacting the match." Oath watched as first Seal's left hand, and then her right, jerked toward the meetinghouse. "See? Coil just pounced after you."

Grit studied her youngest sibling. As Oath had said, Seal was reenacting the match through her hands. Every step, every leap, every twist, every jab . . . Seal's deft hands omitted nothing.

"Make her stop. It's disturbing." Grit thrust the empty flask at Oath.

Sage Brakken blew the horn, and the bloody dance continued. Grit slashed Coil's side. He thrust his dagger into her left shoulder. Drawing his arm back, he pulled the knife from her flesh. Her body screamed in agony, but his chest was wide open, unprotected. The opportunity might not come again.

Grit threw herself toward him.

In the instant her dagger pierced his flesh, Havoc's hideous face appeared behind Coil, her eyes ablaze with evil triumph. Horrific fear overwhelmed Grit.

Her concentration broke. She thrust her dagger an inch deeper and not as far from Coil's heart as she had intended.

He stood still, looking at Grit with an odd expression in his eyes.

"Too deep, Grit." He collapsed.

Grit fell at his side and reached for the dagger, her hands trembling. She had to undo the damage.

"No!" Coil's arm shot from his side and grabbed her wrist. He shouted, but his voice was barely louder than a whisper. "Leave it there, or I swear by my broadsword, I will kill you with your own dagger."

His other hand reached into a pocket and withdrew a silver flask. He handed it to Grit.

"Drink this, vicious girl." He gave her a weary smile.

Grit opened the flask and took a gulp of its contents. How could this be? Staring at Coil, she took another drink and swished the sweet juice around her mouth. She hadn't been mistaken. Kinsmon's special brew, or something very close, rolled over her tongue.

Coil's face was pale. Blood oozed around the blade of her dagger in his chest. *No, no, no! It can't have come to this.*

She spat her mouthful of juice over his chest, aiming it at the wound. She could think of no other remedy. Maybe, just maybe, Kinsmon's brew or Coil's berries or whatever the flask held could undo her error. Propping his head in her lap, she put the flask to Coil's lips. While she waited for him to swallow, she splashed juice directly onto his wound. Then she gave him another drink.

"Move aside, Grit. I'll tend him in his hut." Sire Stone crouched at Grit's side. "Give me your dagger."

Grit moved her hand between Sire Stone and the weapon protruding from Coil's chest. "He said to leave it there."

"Not that dagger, child. Your Sire's Aid. Give me your Sire's Aid. Tell me you still have your Sire's Aid, and tell me it does what I think it does."

Grit dug in her pocket for the oyster knife and passed it to him. Sire Stone scooped Coil into his arms, rose, and walked out of the sparring circle.

He stopped only for a moment to speak to Sire Swot. "It was foolish to set them against each other. If she has killed him, we may consider our doom sure."

Sire Swot followed Sire Stone. As they rounded the corner of the meetinghouse, Sage Brakken waved Sire Pierce forward. Sire Pierce stood on a raised platform at the edge of the sparring circle. The crowd hushed. Dagger stood at Grit's side. She hadn't noticed his arrival. Had Pierce and Berth released him?

"Dagger, I feel rather weak." Grit clenched her jaw. The world seemed slow and distant. Sounds and sights dulled and blurred all around her. Her legs felt as wobbly as they had when Whisp ushered her from Vell's prison to Harth's inn.

Sire Pierce's voice grated against her mind like the screech of a thousand dying seagulls. "The match goes to the challenger! The council of Thresh accepts Grit of Stone, formally disowned by the dame who bore her, and with her, Dagger of Willow and Strike. They may move about the village as a free dameling and an able sireling."

Dagger took her hand and raised it above her head like some gesture of triumph. The crowd grew loud again. Fools, all of them, to think they looked on victory. Dagger draped her arm across his shoulders, wrapped his arm around her back, and held her steady.

"Lean on me and cling to Kinsmon's promise." He took her left hand and eased her fingers over her pearl.

He walked her through the gate and away from the sparring circle. Grit's lips quivered as she replayed the match in her mind.

"What have I done, Dagger? I've killed him, haven't I? Take me to his body. I have to touch him. He'll be in the Outer Ring, seventh hut from the main road on the right." She spoke in a distant, shaky voice. Her eyes barely focused as her steps fell clumsily in with Dagger's. She could still feel the resistance of Coil's flesh as she'd plunged her dagger into his chest. Had it been fear or triumph in his eyes?

The smells of sweat and blood and rosemary seemed to hang in the air, even though Coil had gone. She bent over and retched until her stomach felt as empty as her heart. She stared at the puddle of bile tinged pink by the swallow of juice she'd taken. Dagger urged her onward. Her feet moved, but she replayed the final moves of the match over and over, as if reciting them would reverse their damage.

"I nicked his rib, poked his side. He got my shoulder, and I flew at his chest. A hair to the left of the heart and higher . . . Dagger!" She clutched his shirt and tried to turn back to the sparring circle. "She was here, right behind Coil. Did you see her?"

"Grit, you are talking nonsense. Come out of it." Dagger grabbed her shoulders and shook.

The confusion left as Grit focused on Dagger's face. Her limbs still trembled, and her injured shoulder felt as though on fire, but she spoke calmly now. She'd never been surer of anything. "I'm not speaking nonsense. Havoc was here. Did you not see her? She stood right behind Coil as I stabbed him."

Dagger wrapped his arm around Grit again. She was not fool enough to decline his support.

"We must get you to Coil before either of you suffers more," he said.

He walked briskly toward the Outer Ring, lifting Grit to her feet when she stumbled. When they arrived at Coil's hut, Dagger didn't bother to knock. The door was cracked. He pushed it open and led Grit inside.

Berth had trained her to make careful note of her surroundings, but Grit marked only one detail of Coil's hut. On a bed pushed into the far corner, Coil of Dara was stretched out on blood-stained sheets. His shirt had been torn open, and Sire Stone stood over him, one hand on the dagger protruding from the sireling's chest and one holding a bloody, balled up cloth.

"Wait!" Grit ran across the room, pushing her way past Sire Swot to stand beside Coil's head. Sire Swot passed Grit her oyster knife, with the cap removed from its hilt. She dug her finger deep into the ointment and held a glob of it above Coil's heart. "Remove it quickly, sire, and let us hope this medicine is strong enough."

Sire Stone tightened his grip on the dagger. "On the count of three. One. Two. Three."

In one smooth, quick motion, Sire Stone pulled the dagger from Coil's chest. Grit dropped the glob of ointment deep into the wound. She thrust her finger back into the knife's hollow hilt, scooped out more ointment, and smeared it into Coil's bleeding wound. A little more pain from her hand didn't matter now. The ointment ran dry, but still she scraped the inside of the hilt, desperate to give Coil all the help he could get. He had no other hope. How she wished he were a dummy she could simply sew back together.

"Dagger! My pack!"

She nearly dropped the bag taking it from Dagger's hand. She fumbled over the engraved flap, cursing the clumsiness of her hands. She couldn't shake like this when Coil's life was in the balance. Ezekiel's sewing kit had fallen to the very bottom of the bag. She pulled it out and spread it open on her lap. The feel of the needle between her fingertips steadied her. The strongest thread slid easily through the needle's eye.

Pinching Coil's wound closed, she whispered, "This might hurt, but you and I are used to pain."

Carefully, with deeper concentration and greater precision than she had ever applied to Ezekiel's dummy, Grit pierced Coil's skin with her needle. Blood slipping between her fingers, she marked his chest with tiny, methodical stitches. When she was through, Grit laid her crimson hand firmly over Coil's heart and waited, her attention fixed on his pale face. If her stitches worked, she'd gladly mend ten thousand shredded dummies.

Blood ceased seeping from underneath her hand. Coil's chest rose slightly and then fell. The tiny movement beneath her hand sent a trill of hope through Grit's spirit. His chest continued to rise and fall in almost imperceptible rhythm. His eyes fluttered open, then rolled closed again. Grit did not move. She couldn't look away from Coil's pale face.

She could hear Dagger, Sire Stone, and Sire Swot whispering behind her. Slate, who had followed Grit and Dagger from the sparring circle, entered the hut and joined the others in waiting.

Hours passed, but finally Coil's eyes opened and did not close. He looked at Grit for a full five minutes before speaking.

"I thought you weren't coming back," he said weakly.

"So did I."

"You said Thresh held nothing for you."

Grit lifted her hand and checked the stitches. She dared not meet Coil's gaze. "Perhaps I lied."

"You look horrid, you know."

"You're one to talk." Grit looked up from Coil's chest and forced a frown. "I said I like pink hair, not crimson."

Coil winced at the effort of a gentle laugh. Sire Stone placed a hand on Grit's uninjured shoulder.

"Coil is very weak, Grit. You mustn't wear him out. Besides, we should have dressed your wounds hours ago." He helped Grit to her feet and guided her away from Coil's bedside. When they were at the door, Sire Stone turned to Dagger. "Will you stay with him through the night?"

Grit's back was turned, her full weight on the doorknob, and though her ears still rang with the echo of steel upon steel, she heard Dagger's quiet answer. "I won't leave his side, not when Havoc hunts him."

Grit whirled to face Dagger, her jaw clenched. He had not spoken quietly enough. She looked from Dagger to Coil, then marched to the latter's side.

"I will not have him suffer at that creature's hands." Sitting on the side of the bed, she reached behind her neck to remove her pearl on its golden chain. She leaned over Coil, slipped her hands beneath his neck, and fastened the clasp of the necklace. Her fingers traced the line of the chain and lingered to caress the pearl, which sat in a pool of blood on Coil's chest. For an instant, the image of Scarlett's fingers lingering over Dagger's flashed across Grit's mind. She met Coil's gaze with stern tenderness.

"If Havoc comes to you, Coil of Dara, tell her Kinsmon's heart has claimed you for Castle Concord and send that hag away."

She turned to Dagger, who sat with a puzzled expression on his face as he looked from Grit to the blood-stained pearl around Coil's neck. The wound in her shoulder, which had not bothered her while she tended Coil, now seared with pain. She pressed her hand against her arm and glared at Dagger.

"And you . . . If any ill befalls him in my absence, it'll be my dagger through your heart with no salve to heal. I'd stay to defend him myself, but as you know, I could barely walk here. Sire Stone . . ."

Her sire wrapped an arm around her waist and helped her to her feet.

"Come, my girl. Let me care for you."

# THIRTY-SEVEN

In the hut next to Coil's, Sire Stone dressed Grit's shoulder. As the sticky, dark brown mixture he'd applied to her wound dried, he arranged a mat for her in a corner of his hut. While Grit settled on the mat, Sire Stone knelt and covered her with a light blanket.

"I imagine you'll want to build your own hut soon enough, but you're welcome to stay here as long as you like," he said.

Grit propped herself up on her uninjured arm and stretched her neck. Her shoulder throbbed, but her entire body ached. "What exactly happened this morning?"

Sire Stone laughed softly. "This morning, though he fell by your dagger, Thresh's champion won his most perilous battle. Coil has fought in many skirmishes, but none so dire as his struggle against himself. Since you left, I've often wondered if he were losing that battle, if he might follow the way of Strike instead of seeking a better way. I strove to guide him, but pain will drive a man to madness more quickly than reason can restrain him."

"He isn't mad. He never threw in his lot with Strike. He can't have done that." It was horror enough that he'd been the Golden Demon.

"Coil alone knows what he has and hasn't done," Sire Stone said. "He disappeared for days, but never spoke a word of where he went or what he did. Talon may have some knowledge, but he isn't as chatty as his sire. Unpleasant rumors of Coil's business beyond Thresh are all I've heard. "

Grit shook her head. She didn't care about the past, not with this day still so jumbled in her mind. "He saved us both. I almost killed him for it."

Sire Stone laughed again. "It was a mad plan, to be sure, but he was in his right mind the moment he found you in the meetinghouse. He saw the council required blood and determined to spill his rather than yours. He'd brook no objection. Indeed, I could offer no alternative. I'm not sure his herbs and berries would've been sufficient without your dagger's salve, though. I'm relieved you had it with you still."

"I only hope we've done enough to restore him completely. He's badly wounded." Grit flexed and relaxed her sore leg muscles.

"Time will tell. Sleep now, Grit. You're exhausted."

Grit closed her eyes, but only for a moment. Fear swelled in her heart. She sat up and stared at the empty mat near the foot of Sire Stone's bed.

"Where's Slate?"

"He's in Coil's hut," Sire Stone said. "He'll sleep there tonight. He's intrigued by your new ally, and Dagger consented to his company."

"What about Dame Berth and the babes?"

"I assume they're in their mats by this hour. Why do you ask?"

"Strike." She wanted to tell Sire Stone that his twin intended to destroy everyone he held dear, but the words would not form on her tongue. The day's events had drained her energy, dulled her senses. Too numb to think clearly, she lay back on her mat. "They must be on their guard."

"Sleep, Grit. Dagger will defend both Coil and Slate. As for Berth and the girls, your dame is fierce enough to guard them all. I don't think even Strike would be so brave as to face that woman in battle."

Grit shook her head slowly, yawned, and closed her eyes. Before falling completely asleep, her hand grazed the hilt of her dagger.

Sleep brought turbulent dreams. First Havoc chased Grit from the Southern Sea to Thresh, from Thresh to worlds unknown. Then Grit swam with Coil from the Western Sea to the Southern Sea, the water cool, then warm against their flesh. At the Southern Sea, with Ezekiel watching through his clouded eyes, a creature, half-snake, half-human swam circles around Coil. Its face took form, and Havoc's cruel, laughing mouth expanded to swallow Coil alive. Clutching her dagger, Grit swam against the current that pulled her from Havoc. The snake tail whipped through red saltwater, slashing Grit's shoulder open.

Grit awoke with her hand clasped tightly around her dagger and her wounded shoulder burning with pain. She relaxed her grip on the dagger and wriggled the ache out of her fingers before sitting up. There was nothing to be done about the shoulder. Dim light filtered through the windows. Sire Stone had already risen and departed from the hut. His bed was neatly made, and a plate of food lay on a footstool next to Grit's mat. She ate, willing the memory of her dreams from her mind with every bite, then rose and straightened her mat.

Three damelings were passing in front of Sire Stone's hut as Grit emerged. They stopped when they saw her. The tallest, a willowy girl with eyes as green as Scarlett's, stood with one hand on her hip. Her fine face twisted into a sneer.

"Grit of Stone," she said.

"Aren't you a little far from the Inner Ring, Merit?" Grit pulled Sire Stone's door shut behind her.

Merit let out an irritated breath. "You know as well as I do, I don't live there. Tell me, though, how does it feel to have

267

destroyed your only ally in Thresh? Do you suppose you'll ever find another ally?"

Grit glared at her. "Merit of Shore and Brakken, are you sure you didn't spend your training years with your sire? You are almost as much a fool as he, speaking so surely of what you do not know."

Merit narrowed her green eyes. "We all saw what you did to Coil. You can't deny your dagger in his heart."

"I can if I choose to. Anyway, Coil is much stronger than you credit him. His heart could survive much worse than a nick from my dagger."

She pushed past Merit and her companions and headed for the hut next door. This time, she took in every detail of Coil's hut—the bundles of herbs above the stone fireplace, the pots stacked in neat rows, the table covered with jars and vials, some empty and some full of unidentifiable substances, but all stained with various shades of pink.

The rumpled mat on the floor at the foot of the bed must be Slate's. Dagger would never sleep while on guard. Despite its disheveled condition, an underlying orderliness marked the hut, as if someone had subjected a particularly tidy space to frenzied activity, with no time to restore its accustomed state.

Grit nodded to Sire Stone and Dagger, who sat on stools behind the table, deep in conversation, then turned her attention to Coil. He was half-sitting in bed, propped up by pillows and rolled blankets. His face was pale, but his chest rose and fell with greater ease than it had the previous night. He opened his eyes and looked Grit's way.

He gestured for her to draw near. "Let me see your wound."

"Sire Stone dressed it last night." She sat on the edge of the bed and pulled back the strip of cloth Sire Stone had wrapped around her upper arm. Coil frowned at the gaping wound.

He pointed to a jar on the bedside table. "Pass me that poultice."

As he twisted the lid, he winced in pain.

Grit took the jar from him, removed the lid, and gave it back.

He dipped his fingers into the poultice and gently dabbed it on her wound. She clenched her jaw as he repeated the process. Before long, he had coated the area surrounding her wound with a thick layer of the sticky, mud-like goo.

When the door clicked shut behind Dagger and Sire Stone, Coil looked up momentarily. "This wound looks awful. Sire Stone should have been more liberal."

His finger brushed over her wound, and she grimaced.

"What is that?" she asked.

Coil's blue eyes sparkled as he leaned closer to Grit's shoulder.

"Just a little something I concocted from berries, honey, and a handful of herbs I found lying around. In the time you were gone, I discovered several uses for my berries, as well as a few ways to enhance their potency. For example, when you boil them . . ." He gave Grit's shoulder a final dab. "There, that should do. Your wound should heal quickly, now that you have the benefit of a generous application."

Coil gazed at his handiwork a moment before shifting his eyes to Grit's right arm. He leaned closer, his eyebrows knit together.

"Your brands are gone," he said. "How did you do it? One bowl of berries couldn't have been enough to erase all traces of an act as foolishly brutal as your Final Branding."

"My Sire's Aid came from Kinsmon. It contained the same salve that preserved your life."

"Sixteen years of fortitude, and nothing to show for it. What's it like, Grit, life without brands?" Coil shook his head as he traced two imaginary lines down Grit's unmarked arm.

His fingertip lingered near her elbow where her sixteenth and most severe brand had been. Her skin tingled beneath his gentle touch, and she dared not meet his eye, for fear he would become uncomfortable and take his hand from her arm.

"It was frightening at first, like plunging into a world in which one knows none of the rules," she said. "There, in that strange world, honor is won through restoration rather than destruction. They tell you it is easy to wound others or even to wound oneself, but healing is harder. It is much harder, Coil, and I am just beginning to understand what this means."

Coil leaned back on his pillows. An involuntary groan escaped his lips, and his face contorted with pain before he recovered himself.

Grit inhaled sharply. "I didn't intend to wound you so gravely. I promise I didn't." Her arm ached from the absence of his fingertips.

"I've felt worse. You're home and not too stubborn to listen to someone who knows what he's doing. I was afraid one way or the other you wouldn't heed my instructions yesterday."

"You were a fool to trust me to follow such instructions. You nearly got yourself killed."

Coil studied her for a moment. "Dagger speaks highly of you."

"If you think he speaks well of me, you should hear him speak of Scarlett."

Coil smiled. "I have. From the stories he tells, she's a bit of a silly dameling. And yet, I would like to meet her. Kinsmon, too, I think."

"You would like Kinsmon." Grit's gaze drifted to Coil's chest. Beneath layers of dried blood, ointment, and herbal paste, the faint outline of her stitches showed. "As for Scarlett, if you met her in your current condition, she'd be sure to send you to bathe in lavender scented water."

Grit reached for the bowl and cloth on the table. Placing the bowl on the bed, she dipped the cloth into the water and began to wash away the blood that had dried on Coil's chest, as she had seen Scarlett do with the wounded at Castle Concord. She worked without speaking, focused entirely on the task at hand. Coil watched her work. As Grit drew closer to the wound, he closed his eyes and clenched his jaw against the pain.

When at last Coil's chest was clean, Grit covered his wound with a fresh layer of the herbal concoction. She leaned over and lifted the pearl. She rubbed the orb with the cloth, trying to remove the blood from the opalescent surface. Try as she might, Grit could not remove the bloodstains.

"Where did you get all these necklaces, Grit?"

"All these necklaces?" She placed the back of her hand on Coil's forehead to check for fever.

"How many do you have?" Coil asked.

"Just the one. Except, I gave it to you, so I suppose I have none."

"No." He shook his head slowly.

She followed his gaze. A pearl dangled from a thin gold chain around her neck. She dropped the towel, grabbed the pearl between her fingers, and studied it from every angle, comparing it to the one she'd given Coil. The only difference was in color. Hers was iridescent white; Coil's the deep crimson of dried blood.

"Dagger!"

# THIRTY-EIGHT

The door to Coil's hut flew open, and Dagger rushed into the room. He scanned the hut's interior, his eyes fixing at last on Grit, who stood by Coil's bed with one hand at her chest and the other hovering just above Coil's chest.

"What is this?" Her hands shook, but she released neither pearl.

Dagger strode to Grit and took her pearl in his hand. He studied it closely, turning it in his fingers as she had done. He glanced at the second pearl, which rested in Grit's outstretched hand.

"Where did you find it?" Dagger nodded toward the pearl around her neck.

"It was just there," Grit said. "What is it, Dagger?"

He stood still a moment, saying nothing as he examined the new pearl. He stepped from the bedside, crossed one arm over his chest, and rubbed his fingers over his lips.

"Kinsmon's promises cannot be counterfeited. The pearl you wear now is as authentic as the one you placed on Coil last night. Why did you give your pearl to him?"

"To protect him from Havoc." Grit blurted the first clear reason that entered her mind. "You said Havoc couldn't touch me or anything belonging to me without first asking Kinsmon. I thought if I claimed him as my own or better yet, as Kinsmon's own, Havoc would not dare come near him."

She glanced at Coil. "Also, Jareh, the farmer . . . He said if we met someone who had need of the promise Kinsmon gave us, to give it away freely. Dagger, I gave Coil the pearl because I had to. He needed it. Why should I have kept it from Coil in his need? Would you keep your shard of glass if another needed its promise?"

Dagger looked thoughtfully at Grit. "I can't say what I'd do. I've never seen anything like this. I have, however, studied Kinsmon's promises and the signs of his promises enough to know these pearls are both true seals of Kinsmon's word. However the duplication has occurred, both are authentic."

"What does it mean, though?" Grit asked.

"Who can say?" He gestured toward Coil. "He looks famished, not to mention almost as exhausted as I am myself. Give him something to eat, Grit, and then leave the poor sireling to rest. Sire Stone will watch over him while I catch up on my sleep."

"What am I to do?" Grit asked.

Dagger stared at her, weariness written in every feature. "Must you ask so many questions? Surely you can find something to do."

Without another word, he left Coil's hut for the quiet solitude of Sire Stone's.

After serving Coil oatmeal and eggs, and ensuring he was comfortably situated, Grit set out for Dame Berth's hut. She had no desire to see the woman, but the image of Scarlett lavishing praise on Harth pressed upon Grit's memory. She didn't aspire to such affection toward her dame—that would be foolishness—but she'd do what she could to warn Berth of the threat to her life.

So Grit stood in Dame Berth's doorway, laden with a fish, a basket full of the forest's bounty, and a loaf of bread purchased from a young dame in the Inner Ring.

"What do you want?" Dame Berth snarled, her hand on her hip. "The council may have accepted you, but I haven't rescinded my disownment."

"I've come to serve your midday meal." Grit gently pushed past Dame Berth, who offered less physical resistance than verbal. She laid her offerings on the table and counted to three in her head, waiting for Dame Berth's abuse.

"A lousy meal won't buy back the honor of my name," Dame Berth said.

Grit did not immediately look at the dame. There was no point arguing with Berth. That had never ended well. She'd serve the meal, say her piece, and leave. What Berth chose to do wasn't up to Grit. When she'd emptied her basket, she looked up and met the eye of the brooding woman.

"I do not wish to buy the honor of your name," Grit said. "Rather I wish to add honor to your name, whether or not you share it with me. I know a dameling who speaks of her dame with music in her voice and tenderness in her features. If I had not met Harth in the flesh, Scarlett's treatment of her in her absence would compel me to admire her dame. That, Dame Berth, is the honor I would add to your name, the honor of one's offspring's high regard. I do not expect ever to speak as glowingly of you as Scarlett does of Harth, knowing both you and myself as I do. But I will give you what honor I can, beginning with this luncheon. You may take it or leave it, to your honor or shame."

As Grit sliced the bread, Dame Berth reached out her hand and took a grape. She took another and another. Grit placed a slice of bread on a plate and pushed it across the table to Dame Berth before turning to cook the fish over the fire.

They ate in silence. Grit chewed slowly, studying the woman who had raised and discarded her. The dame ate like she hadn't had enough to eat in years. Maybe she hadn't. Maybe that was why she was rail thin.

After second helpings of everything, Dame Berth leaned back in her chair. "I'm still not claiming you."

"I haven't asked you to claim me. I ask only one thing. Be alert. You and your babes are precious to Sire Stone. As such, Strike seeks to ruin all three of you. Be on guard at all times, ready to defend yourself and them. Warn Seal and Oath as well, that they may not wander naively into his clutches."

Dame Berth narrowed her eyes at Grit. "How do you know all this?"

"It doesn't matter how I know it. Swear you will guard your offspring with your life, and that, for Sire Stone's sake, you will protect yourself as well."

"I'll swear nothing to you," Dame Berth said. "You should leave now."

Grit rose and collected her things. Pausing in the doorway, she turned to Berth.

"Whether you swear or not, I sincerely hope you heed my warning. You'll receive no mercy from Strike." She glanced at the dame's arm and thought of the refugees from Koradin. "Butchering your flesh will be the least of his brutality."

Grit left and made her way to Coil's hut, where she spent the afternoon in more gratifying conversation, despite Sire Stone's suggestions that the poor warrior ought to rest.

Coil seemed to have no interest in rest. He listened intently to Grit's tales of the world beyond the Northern Forest. He was eager to hear of all she'd encountered in Port Colony, at the Southern Sea, and at Castle Concord, but he told her little of his activities during her absence. What he did reveal to her, he shared with a vigor that raised Sire Stone's alarm.

"Sit back, Coil," Sire Stone said as he placed a clean towel and a bowl of fresh water on the table next to the bed. When he reached the door to leave, he turned back to Coil. "I don't believe you're ready to get up yet."

Coil pulled his errant legs back onto the bed. "I suppose you will have to collect my jars if you wish me to tell you their contents. I can do so much more than erase dagger wounds now."

Grit ran to the table, returning to Coil's side a moment later with several jars cradled in her arms.

"This," he said, holding up a jar of ground leaves, "will cool a fever when steeped in hot water and drunk by the sufferer. I gave my dame's littlest babe some this spring. Within minutes, her fever left, and she rested serenely. This one here will ease a headache. This one, a stomachache."

"How did you do all this, Coil? I would have thought becoming Thresh's mighty champion would have consumed all your energy, to say nothing of your time. And if you engaged in any other activities . . ." Grit pursed her lips and studied his face. She would know the truth, however awful it was. "I can't imagine your fame was easy to win."

"It wasn't easy." Coil's muscles tensed, his eyes grew cold, his voice more agitated with every word. "Shall I tell you about it? Would you like to hear how dames shrieked and babes wailed as I walked past their huts drenched in the blood of their sires? Would it please you to hear how old women howled in fear as I ransacked inner rings, how the names they call me echo in my dreams every night? I could tell you tales that would send you cowering back to your Southern Sea. Would that please you, you who left with neither regret nor inclination for company? What would you have had me do, Grit, but spar away your memory and hope against hope that you might someday return and find me reason enough to stay?"

Grit had not expected Coil's outburst. She sat back, staring at him. She considered snapping back at Coil, telling him he'd been a wretched fool, but bit her tongue. His tone held a desperation she had not observed in him before.

He sat against his pillows, defying her to answer. Sweat beaded on his forehead, and his breath came in short gasps, labored under the pain of his wound. He stared at Grit, oblivious to the objections of a body crying for rest.

"So they are true, all these tales of the Golden Demon?" she asked.

"All of them and more."

As Grit studied Coil's face, she saw Scarlett, on that last morning at Castle Concord, holding Dagger's hands and gently massaging soothing cream into them, quietly devoting herself to the tiniest details of Dagger's welfare. Looking deep into Coil's agitated eyes, Grit sympathized with Scarlett. Desperation nearly overwhelmed her as she realized that Coil's distress ran much deeper than sorely used hands. No cream would soothe Coil's soul.

He waited expectantly for her to speak, his eyes never wavering. Silently and with all the confidence of a babe's first step, Grit took his hands in hers and ran her thumb over each finger of each of his cold, trembling hands. As she reached each fingertip, she imagined it as memory demanded, warm with life and stained with berry juice. From time to time, she glanced at his hair. It still bore the reddish brown hue of spilt blood. Grit did not see blood. Instead, she saw Coil's hair as she had so often seen it in her dreams—golden, streaked with pink, and filling her with an inexplicable ache. Her shoulders drooped as she studied Coil's rough hands.

"Coil of Dara," Grit said, her voice barely audible, "though I have not understood this fully until now, you have always been enough for me."

She looked up to meet Coil's eyes, only to find them closed. His head leaning back on his pillows, his shoulders relaxed and his breathing slowed. Without opening his eyes, he asked, "Will you release me from my vow?"

Grit leaned toward the table to dip the cloth into the water. Squeezing the excess water into the bowl, she cleared her throat. "Only if you promise never again to ask me to put a dagger in your heart."

"If Talon of March and Swot were here, I would swear it to you on oath." Coil wrapped his fingers tightly around the small hand that still held his. Grit squeezed back and did not loosen her grip as she wiped Coil's forehead with the cool cloth.

Soon after, Sire Stone returned with a basket of food. He frowned at Coil, still reclining with his eyes closed while Grit wiped his forehead and cheeks with the damp towel.

"Does he have a fever or have you exhausted him?" he asked Grit.

"I'm fine. Let her be," Coil said.

Sire Stone set about preparing plates for Grit, Coil, and himself. Dagger and Slate entered the hut just as Sire Stone was serving Grit and Coil. After preparing two more plates, Sire Stone sat on the stool behind the table and began to eat.

"Did you rest well, Dagger?" he asked.

"Yes. I'm ready to guard our invalid through the night."

"Is that really necessary?" Coil asked.

"Yes." For once, Grit and Dagger were in perfect agreement.

****

As darkness descended upon the village, Grit joined Dagger outside the hut.

"Have you spoken with Dame Berth?" he asked.

Grit kicked at a pebble. "Fool dame ignored my warning."

"She ignores it to her own peril. Did she not consider the girls?"

Slate slid through the half open doorway. "What's this? Are Seal and Oath in danger?"

279

"They're in no more danger than foolish boys who eavesdrop," Grit said. "Go to bed, Slate."

"You're all in danger." Dagger, arms crossed over his chest, studied the boy. "Grit has warned Dame Berth to protect herself and the twins against an attack by Strike, and you should do the same. Stay alert always, young man."

The thin boy straightened his back, squared his shoulders, and nodded his head at the tall sireling. Slate had learned his lessons well. He would cower before no one. Pride welled up in Grit's heart

"I understand," Slate said. Without another word, he walked toward Sire Stone's hut.

When Grit entered the hut a minute later, Slate met her in the doorway. He bowed his head and passed out of the hut. Grit watched the door close behind him.

"Is he sleeping next door again?"

"Yes," Sire Stone said. "I believe he'd follow Dagger to death, if given the opportunity."

"Let us hope Dagger doesn't lead him there," Grit said, as much to herself as to her sire.

Sire Stone laid a blanket over the mat he'd prepared for Grit. "I wouldn't have let him go if I didn't trust Dagger to protect him. If I could convince Berth to send me Seal and Oath, I'd feel surer of their safety. If I could convince Berth to come here as well, I might even sleep in peace. I have never liked having you all so scattered about the village, and I like it even less tonight."

"You know, then, that Strike aims to destroy all of us before killing you?" Grit asked.

Sire Stone nodded gravely. "I have suspected as much. This morning, Dagger confirmed my deepest fears. I slept earlier today. You sleep now. I'll guard you while Dagger guards Coil and Slate. We must hope Berth performs her duty valiantly.

She is neither as harsh nor as proud as she leads you to believe."

Grit settled onto her mat, her hand securely over the hilt of her dagger. Two hours passed before she fell into a fitful sleep.

Dreams of Havoc and Strike disturbed her slumber. Twice she called out in her sleep, sharp, indiscernible syllables that brought Sire Stone to her side. After assuring her of her safety, he returned to his chair by the cracked door, where he peered into the outer darkness, fingering the gray key that had hung at his neck for nearly twenty years.

# THIRTY-NINE

"**B**erth!"

Sire Stone's cry pierced through the sounds of the battle raging in Grit's dreams. Her eyes flew open. She threw back her covers and pounced to her feet, dagger in hand.

Sire Stone raced from the hut, leaving the door swinging on its hinges. Grit rushed after him.

In the middle of the street, Sire Stone clung to Dame Berth, his thick arms wrapped around her chest, his legs spread to steady himself against her crazed flailing. The anguished dame alternated banging her head against his chest and throwing her head back to howl obscenities. She kicked his shins and spat in his face, but still he held her fast.

"Let me go! Strike! He has him! He took my Slate! Let me go!" Dame Berth scratched at Sire Stone's arms.

"You can't defeat him, Berth," Sire Stone said. "Let an army form, but don't rush into battle against that man."

Armed Threshans emerged from the huts on the Outer Ring and formed a line on the southern side of the village. Over their murmurs, Dame Berth shouted the direction Strike had taken when he left her hut with her bound offspring.

Grit followed a group of young warriors to a position just behind Coil's hut. The light of torches revealed a disorderly band of Threshans straining to see the retreating enemy in the darkness beyond the village. The warriors of Thresh argued with one another over the best course of action. They cursed the misfortune of having their champion laid up with a dagger wound to the chest. None could decide whether to pursue the enemy or guard the village.

Several yards to the west, Sire Stone restrained Dame Berth, his head resting against hers.

"Don't let him get away. The boy only wanted to protect us. I should've sent him away. If none of you will go after him, let me!" Tears streamed down Dame Berth's twisted face.

"No, Berth," Sire Stone said. "You don't know the danger we face."

Then the darkness was no more. In an instant, the blaze of a thousand torches rose as one flame across the horizon. As far as the eye could see in either direction, foot soldiers and mounted warriors held blazing torches aloft.

Grit shuddered at the enormity of Strike's army. Several Threshan warriors stepped back, terrified by the army facing them. There was no way for Thresh to defeat them.

Halfway across the training field, Strike turned his enormous white steed to face the rough band of Threshan warriors. Fire reflected in his silver helmet. A small figure mounted in front of Strike writhed against the warrior's hold.

"Slate!" Unable to contain the wave of emotions that overwhelmed her, Grit cried out to her captive sibling, a sound deep and foreign, yet as close and raw as her very soul.

Dame Berth wrenched herself from Sire Stone's grip and charged at the mounted enemy.

Grit chased her dame, her muscles burning and her head swimming. *He will pick you off one by one, Dagger said, and it's begun. One by one. No, no, no!* Her feet pounded against the ground to the beat of the screams in her head.

Slate leaned toward Dame Berth, shouting incoherently. With all the force of his young body, he slammed against Strike's chest, nearly unseating both captor and captive. Strike wrestled the boy back into the saddle, and Dame Berth rushed at the great white horse. Strike's left arm tightened around Slate's neck.

Grit screamed as the warrior raised a spear over his head and plunged it into Dame Berth's heart. Slate slumped in Strike's arm as his dame staggered backward.

"Shame to you, Strike of the Northern Mountains." Berth lurched forward and spat. Bloody phlegm stuck to the horse's shoulder. "Stone's the better man by far."

As the dame fell, Grit stretched out her arms to receive her broken body. They crumpled as one into the grass. Grit placed her hand over the wound, trying vainly to stop the blood. She was not ready to see death so close. Dame Berth laid her hand over Grit's.

"You are the only one who stood with me." Dame Berth gasped for air. "Grit of Berth and Stone, my offspring, my ally, my honor."

"You reclaim me?" Grit wiped a tear from her dame's cheek.

"Yes, fool girl, I do." She clasped Grit's hand and with her last breath, sighed her firstborn's name. "Grit of Berth and Stone."

Somewhere west of Thresh, a horn sounded. Dame Berth's hand fell limp on her bloody chest. As Grit hung her head over her dame's lifeless from, Strike's mount reared and whinnied.

Shielding Dame Berth with her body, Grit looked up to take in her dame's murderer, from his weathered boots, to his scarred hands, to the silver-black hair brushing against his broad shoulders. He was just as she remembered. He wore the same silver helmet she saw the day she let Peril and Zag pass beneath her. What lay behind the helmet? Had brutality tainted the features she'd come to cherish in the faces of her sire and siblings? Was Dagger's pride amplified in his sire, without the tempering effect of a tender heart? Grit had no desire to see Strike's face, for fear the sight would warp her perceptions of Sire Stone, Slate, Seal, Oath, and Dagger.

As Strike galloped away with Slate, Grit pushed Dame Berth's body from her lap and rose to her feet. She stumbled forward, rage surging in her heart. *I'll hunt him to death before he takes another one of us. I'll pry Slate, dead or alive, from his arms, and do to that coward whatever he has done to Slate.*

Her legs denied her will. She tripped to her knees. Glancing over his shoulder, Strike pumped his spear in the air. Grit pushed herself from the earth and scrambled to her feet.

From behind, arms wrapped around her waist. Pulled back, her body slammed against a strong, solid figure. "Do not pursue him," Dagger said.

Grit struggled against his hold. "He murdered my dame. Shall I allow him to do the same to Slate? Shall I leave his deeds unpunished?"

"Slate's as good as dead, and you will be, too, if you chase after him. Look at Strike's army."

She trained her eyes on the retreating army as Dagger spoke in her ear. "If you would honor your dame, do not do it by rushing to join her in death. Turn around, Grit. Honor your dame with your life."

Strike and his army disappeared into the darkness, and Grit turned to gaze upon her fallen dame. Dagger released her, and she dropped to her knees beside Dame Berth's body. She ran a finger across Dame Berth's cheek and traced the line of her jaw. She appeared peaceful in death, as Grit had never known her in life. Perhaps Sire Stone was right. Perhaps Dame Berth was neither as harsh nor as proud as Grit had believed. Perhaps there was, after all, something in her worth admiring. Were she a weaker dameling, like Scarlett perhaps, Grit might have cried. But she was Grit of Berth and Stone, who had sworn at the tender age of six never to cry.

"I'll honor you as I know how." Grit slipped one arm under Dame Berth's neck and the other under Dame Berth's knees and stood on shaking legs, cradling her dame in her blood stained arms. Without a word and heedless of the dull, lingering pain in her shoulder, Grit marched across the training fields and past the quiet spectators. She neared Sire Stone, and he reached out his hands to accept her burden.

"I claim this task, Sire Stone," Grit said. "She will be sent to sea with high honor. Someone, please, fetch a burial ship."

Sire Stone stepped aside to allow Grit to pass, directed two sirelings to meet him at the seaside with a burial ship, and then fell in behind Grit and the lifeless Dame Berth. Dagger, Seal, and Oath followed behind Sire Stone, Seal leading Oath by the hand. With her free hand, Oath hid her eyes from the crowd's view.

Coil sheathed his sword and followed with uneven steps behind the somber twins. Dagger fell back to lend him support. Others joined the procession as it made its way toward the Western Sea.

Grit stood on the pebbly beach, still cradling Dame Berth's body. When the sirelings arrived with a long, narrow boat, she gently laid her burden in it. Her heart felt no lighter for the emptiness of her arms. She crossed her fingers over each of her dame's sightless grey eyes, closing them forever. As she arranged Dame Berth's arms over her chest, she paused a moment with her hand over the wound. Finally, she straightened Dame Berth's garments, the fabric so worn it felt like gauze between her fingers. How long had she been without new clothing? Grit stooped and picked a smooth, round pebble from the beach.

Grit raised the pebble to the crowd that had gathered, then leaned over Dame Berth and placed it deep in the gaping hole left by Strike's heavy spear. She straightened, wiped her hands on her trousers, and moved to the head of Dame Berth's burial ship.

"Let any who would give this dame honor come forth and do so," she said.

Sire Stone was first to answer Grit's call. He reached behind his neck and removed the leather cord with Dame Berth's key and the stone he had received from Kinsmon so many years before. Fumbling with the cord, he loosed the stone from its hold. He held the small stone in his hand a moment, then fell to his knees at Berth's side. Carefully, he tucked the stone under her hand and remained on his knees a full minute before rising and walking to Grit's side. He was shameless in his grief, but Grit could not bring herself to condemn him.

Dagger nudged Seal and Oath, who stooped with him to collect pebbles from the beach. Each placed a pebble on Dame Berth's chest. Coil limped forward next, laboring to breathe as he knelt to place a stone on Dame Berth's still form. When he struggled to rise, Dagger stepped forward to aid him to his feet. Others followed, each placing a pebble on the lifeless Threshan, until her body was nearly covered with pebbles.

When no more came forth, Grit closed her eyes, placed her hands on the edge of the boat, and pushed. Straining against the weight of the boat, slivers of timber scratching her palms, she dug her toes into the rocky beach. If she could get Berth to the sea, they might both find peace.

The burial ship edged forward, slowly at first, but gaining speed as she applied more force and began to run. She was waist deep in the Western Sea, salty spray kissing her face, when she finally let go of the boat. By the light of a full and brilliant moon, Dame Berth sailed into the eternal night.

# FORTY

The crowd dispersed, leaving Dagger, Coil, Sire Stone, and the sire's three female offspring scanning the horizon for one last glimpse of Dame Berth's burial ship. Coil stood apart from the others, leaning on his broadsword. He turned to look toward Thresh, rocks grating together under his shifting feet. The movement drew Grit's attention from the sea. She followed his gaze. She'd thought nothing could surprise her now, but Kinsmon stood in a swath of light at the edge of the forest. He started toward them, moving with grace.

Coil did not wait, but set off across the beach to meet Kinsmon. When he came within a yard of Kinsmon, Coil collapsed. He lay on the ground, a crumpled heap of curls and cloak. Grit broke from the group by the water. She raced across the beach and fell beside Coil. He convulsed beneath her soothing hand.

"Kinsmon, what ails him?"

"There is much that ails him." Kinsmon crouched at Coil's side, one hand on the sireling's shoulder, and gestured for Grit to move back. She refused to leave, but sat on her heels while Kinsmon whispered in Coil's ear so softly she could not discern his words. Then Kinsmon helped Coil into a seated position with his legs crossed in front of him and placed Coil's broadsword across his lap. Coil's head was bowed, but he no longer shook. Kinsmon took Grit's hand, helped her to her feet, and led her a few paces away.

"You heard the cry of battle tonight. Coil has heard sharper, more brutal cries than those which filled your ears. Not only this, he has extracted from Thresh's neighbors cries

289

that would make your blood run cold." Kinsmon looked hard at Grit. "You have pierced his heart twice, most recently with your dagger, but first with your words. The second wound will heal easily. It may even serve to heal the first wound. The first wound . . . The first wound has borne consequences of which you need know no more than you already do."

"How am I to repair my error? Ezekiel's sewing kit can only do so much." Grit closed her eyes, her error too great to bear.

"You are to do nothing, my dear, little Grit, but what is in your heart, the heart that has slowly warmed over the gentler fires of my feast. You expected a consuming fire, but I have chosen a subtler method for you. Though it hasn't seemed much to you at times, my fire has been sufficient. Likewise, doing what is in your heart will not always feel enough, but trust me, it will be more than enough. I don't share this to burden you with the past, but to remind you for the future. Let it be a lesson, hard learned and never forgotten, to bite your tongue rather than allow it to bite another. Before, you spoke to Coil in ugly ignorance. Henceforth, you must speak to him in beautiful truth. Will you accept this task?"

Grit studied Coil, still sitting with his sword in his lap. "I fear a part of him is lost."

"He is not lost," Kinsmon said. "He is only just finding his way, and find it he will. You must know by now, I will not leave him to wander in the dark. Think of all whom you met in your travels. Have I ever left you without help?"

Grit was quiet a moment. Then she looked at Kinsmon. "On the mountain. When the man tried to steal my necklace."

"Did he succeed?"

"No, but . . ."

Kinsmon crossed his arms. "And how did you escape him?"

"The bridge, but that was only . . ."

"Only what, Grit? Only a fluke that you were able to cross with confidence a bridge in such disrepair as to repel a man intent on thievery, to make him believe you were either a fool or a demon? Oh, my dear Grit of Berth and Stone, you, too, are only just beginning to find your way."

He wrapped his arm around Grit's drooping shoulders and motioned for the others, who had been watching silently from a distance, to approach. Dagger, Sire Stone, and the twins joined Kinsmon and Grit beside Coil.

"Tend to Coil, Dagger," Kinsmon said. "Sing to him from Castle Concord's collection, perhaps. Your voice will soothe him now and the song may aid him in days to come."

Dagger eased himself onto the ground beside Coil. In a deep, gentle bass, he sang one of the songs Bard had played on his flute.

*"Do not fear, my child,*
*For I am by your side.*
*No darkness can come nigh,*
*That I will not dispel.*
*So rest awhile, my child.*
*I am by your side."*

Sire Stone buried his face in his hand. "Oh, my child, if only I'd been at your side, if only I'd insisted Berth and the girls join me in my hut . . . The boy was neither old enough, nor big enough for half of what he wanted. I tried so hard to teach him to restrain his ambition. But now, I've lost both Slate and Berth." He looked out over the Western Sea. "I should have watched her hut more closely. I'll never absolve myself of their blood."

Kinsmon held up his hand. "Do not to abuse yourself over what you cannot change. You must pour your energies into preparing the Threshan army. They are a fierce, but wholly unorganized lot at present."

Dagger, his arms wrapped around his bent knees, stopped singing and looked at Kinsmon. "My time of watching and waiting has come to an end, hasn't it?"

Kinsmon returned Dagger's searching gaze. "The coming war will involve great danger, but you, Dagger, may triumph where no one else imagines to battle. Eat first, and then go. Koradin is yours to claim."

"I'll go with him," Grit said. "He can't defeat Strike alone."

Kinsmon, with his unfathomable brown eyes, looked her in the eye and spoke in a calm, steady voice. "Grit of Berth and Stone, I have never doubted your courage. The day will soon come when Dagger will need your help, but for the present, you are needed in Thresh. But enough of this! You are all in need of nourishment. Come, feast with me before the new day dawns."

Dagger helped Coil to his feet, and they followed Kinsmon toward the woods. Just before reaching the tree line, Kinsmon turned around. Sire Stone remained on the beach, his head bowed low.

Kinsmon cocked his head to one side. "Stone, do you not desire my feast?"

A pained expression crossed the sire's face. "I tasted of your feast once before and rejected it. The sweetness of that one bite never left my tongue, though, and I have strived to allow its sweetness to flow into my interactions with others. In this, I've failed more often than I've succeeded. I have spent years seeking to find your table once more, Kinsmon, if only to look upon it. But surely . . ." He paused, the difficulty of his confession apparent on his strained features. "Surely you have not preserved a place for me."

"Surely, I have!" Kinsmon let out a laugh of hope and joy and other marvelous things Grit had yet to name. "Come, take your seat and feast to your heart's content!"

With a sweep of his outstretched arm, Kinsmon motioned for Sire Stone to join the group heading into forest. Just inside the woods, a table spread end to end with luscious dishes waited. Kinsmon stood at the head of his table as the others found their seats. To his left sat Coil, Grit, and Oath. On his right were Dagger, Stone, and Seal.

In the time while they feasted, no one spoke of Berth or Slate or impending war. There would be plenty of time for dark thoughts later. Now was a time to delight in the bounty of Kinsmon's feast. They ate to satiety and beyond, gentle laughter and pleasant chatter wafting across the table. Seal alone did not speak, though her face shone with joy as brightly as all the others.

Kinsmon, who finished eating first, rushed none of his guests. He allowed them to eat perhaps a little more than they should and to talk a little longer than they needed. Through it all, Grit felt light and happy, as she had never before thought possible to feel. It was like a strangely pleasant dream, only sweeter, for it was as real as life itself. She pressed a morsel of fruit to the roof of her mouth. As the tangy juice rolled over her tongue, she glanced at Coil. *I know what wound lies beneath his tunic, and yet I have never seen him look so well.*

While it was still dark, Dagger pushed his chair from the table. Rising, he addressed Kinsmon. "I do not wish to delay. Unless you object, I will go now."

Kinsmon nodded his assent, and Dagger departed with a farewell bow. The others sat silently. Kinsmon, alone in unruffled serenity, studied their troubled faces.

"Stone, the council has many matters to discuss this morning. They'll need your input. I'll accompany you to the Outer Ring. When I return, I will speak privately with the rest of you." Kinsmon pulled something from his pocket. "Before we go, though, I have one thing more. Catch!"

A small, white object sailed over Dagger's abandoned plate. Sire Stone snatched it out of the air. He turned his hand and opened his fist, his eyes widening as he beheld Kinsmon's gift.

"It is identical to the stone you first gave me," he whispered.

"My promises cannot be lost," Kinsmon said. "Even when they are given away, they always return. You may ask Grit if you doubt me."

Grit fingered the pearl at her neck and glanced at the bloodstained one Coil wore. "He speaks truthfully, sire, though it is a mystery to me how it happens."

Kinsmon rose, indicating for Sire Stone to follow him. As the two men left the clearing, Seal and Oath wandered to the shore to splash in the shallows.

Coil pushed his chair back and stood, his legs more steady than they had been before the meal. Grit rose also and followed Coil to stand between two trees. Together they looked out over the rocky shore and the grey sea.

"It seems a lifetime ago we stood on this beach and you asked if I'd come to mock you or to kill you," Coil said. "I might ask the same of you, but somehow, I suspect you'll do neither."

Grit shrugged. "I didn't know better than to ask how my closest ally would harm me."

"It seems there were many things we didn't know," Coil said.

They stood in silence for several minutes. As the waves fell upon the pebbled beach, Grit thought of the warm waters and white sand of the Southern Sea. Longing and belonging wrestled in her inner being.

With a soft laugh, Coil broke her reverie. "Your closest ally?"

Grit slipped her hand into Coil's and smiled upon the Western Sea. "My closest ally."

In the rising light of morning, Kinsmon ran to join Seal and Oath at the water's edge. At the place where gentle waves almost dare to kiss bare toes, he stooped face-to-face with Oath. He touched the first three fingers of his right hand to his lips and then to hers. Oath nodded slowly as he spoke to her. Grit could neither hear Kinsmon's words nor see Oath's face, but both smiled as he removed his fingers from her lips.

He bent before Seal as he had before Oath. He touched his fist to his chest, and then to hers. Putting an arm around her shoulder, he turned her body toward the forest. He swept his free arm from north to south. With a sudden shake of her head, Seal looked into Kinsmon's solemn face. As Kinsmon nodded, a reassuring smile crept over his face.

"What is he doing?" Coil asked.

Grit studied the trio at the shoreline. "I don't know what Kinsmon is doing, but I do know Kinsmon. At least, I know him enough to know he won't harm them. Is it me, Coil, or does it seem to you Kinsmon hears Seal's thoughts?"

"It does. It truly does."

Grit and Coil remained shoulder to shoulder while Kinsmon and the twins chased one another around the beach. After ten minutes, Kinsmon touched his lips to each girl's head, placed something around their necks, and sent them off to the village. Where pebbles gave way to soil, Seal and Oath glanced back at Kinsmon, as if they knew they would not see him for some time.

Kinsmon did not acknowledge the twins' forlorn gazes. His attention was on Grit and Coil. He crossed the beach and stood in front of them.

"You must report to the council, too, Coil of Dara," he said. "Meet me here when you are through. When you found the Amity berries I planted in your forest and when you paired them with various herbs, you began to uncover the secrets of the forest. There is much more for you to learn."

Coil squeezed Grit's hand and released it.

Kinsmon turned to Grit. "Your sire has agreed to host you as long as you need. I advise you to establish a home of your own as quickly as possible. It is crucial to your purpose in Thresh."

"My purpose in Thresh?" She glanced at Coil's retreating form, pained already by their separation. "I have done all I set out to do here."

Kinsmon's eyes sparkled with amusement. "Do you mean to tell me you are ready to return to the Southern Sea?"

Grit opened her mouth to speak, but found no words to answer Kinsmon's teasing question. *I don't know what holds me here, in this village I swore to forget, but I cannot leave now, not without Coil. Maybe not even with Coil. But why? Why am I here? What more must I do?*

Kinsmon put a hand on her shoulder. "You will discover your purpose in time. By now, though you may not know what I am doing, you know me. At least you know me enough to know I will do you no harm."

Grit narrowed her eyes at Kinsmon. Had he somehow heard her conversation with Coil just a few minutes earlier? He laughed softly and shook his head.

"You have much to learn, Grit of Berth and Stone, but today I ask one thing only. Establish your hut, by all means, but more importantly, remember who named you. Learn what it means to be Grit. You will face opposition, but hold fast to my assurance that something true and beautiful and good will come of all this."

He touched his lips to her head as he had to Seal's and Oath's. "Now, go to the village and figure out where to make your home."

Grit hesitated, reluctant to leave Kinsmon, afraid that without him, she would not have the strength to remain in Thresh when the Southern Sea beckoned. She knew, in the core of her being, Kinsmon would not stay long, and she feared what she might become without him or Ezekiel, Dagger, or Scarlett to speak sense to the madness in her head. At last, with shoulders drooping, she turned toward Thresh. She had only taken three steps when Kinsmon called her name.

"Grit, there is one thing more. I did not ask you to begin your task alone, nor will I leave you to complete it alone."

She resumed her walk to the village with a lighter step. She did not know what Kinsmon was doing; that was true. That she knew Kinsmon was also true. But the truth that astounded her most was that Kinsmon, who had just read her secret fear, knew her.

# FORTY-ONE

The first step for a dameling wishing to establish a hut was to inform the council of her intentions to build. Grit set out for the meetinghouse, hoping to find a gathered council. The streets of Thresh were full of warriors eager to fight and awaiting direction. Groups clustered together, discussing what ought to be done about Strike. Their conversations quieted as Grit passed. Some bowed their heads to show their respect for the only Threshan who had dared to follow Dame Berth into a suicide attack. Others eyed her suspiciously, wary of the exiled dameling who had returned to conquer their champion. Arrow was right. Going back was difficult.

"You have brought trouble upon us, Grit of Stone!" A familiar voice bellowed from behind her. Which was worse, the accusation of treachery or the absence of her dame's name? She couldn't tell.

The sireling continued, his rage silencing the crowd. "You struck down our champion. How do we know you did not lead Strike into our village?"

Grit wheeled to face the young warrior who strode after her. Shaggy brown hair hung to his shoulders, and his brown eyes accused her of all the wrong in the world.

Grit retraced her steps to meet him. "Talon of March and Swot, I'm surprised your sire didn't teach you better than to speak ignorantly. Your champion is better now than he was before my return, and I assure you I did not lead Strike into this village. I would rather die than betray my home." Unable to suppress her indignation, she spat on Talon's boot.

*My home. I called this place my home. Thresh. And yes, I'd rather die than see it destroyed.* She faced Talon with her hands on her hips, daring him to oppose her further. He pounded his fist into his palm.

"You stabbed Coil in the heart. He kept his vow to you, but still you planted your foul dagger in his heart."

Grit dropped her hands from her hips. She wanted Talon on her side. "And it nearly killed me to do so. After all those years of calling our matches, you must know Coil and I never sparred maliciously. It was all sport. Do not accuse me of treachery, especially against the one who has always been my closest ally. Believe me when I tell you it was for his survival as much as my own that I did what I did. As for the rest of your foolishness, I intend to establish a hut on the Outer Ring and fight against Strike beside you and Coil and the rest of the warriors. Let us be allies, Talon. We cannot afford unnecessary enemies."

Talon scrutinized Grit from head to toe. He sighed deeply and shook his hair out of his eyes again.

"You are right in saying we cannot afford unnecessary enemies, and I grant that you and Coil always seemed more like allies than adversaries. But I'll pledge no alliance with you until I see with my own eyes our champion restored and your word fulfilled."

"But you will speak no more foolish lies of me, either?" Grit's hand rested on her dagger.

Talon nodded. "I won't, but you must know others will."

"Let them." Grit's gaze rested on Merit of Shore and Brakken, who stood behind Talon. "I will shame them all if it comes to that."

She started toward the center of the village, but turned back to Talon. "I wasn't lying. Coil is well. He'll be with Kinsmon today. You should ask your sire what that name means. And for the record, my dame acknowledged me. You may stop calling me Grit of Stone."

She did not wait for Talon's response, but trotted toward the meetinghouse. She would establish herself on the Outer Ring and fight for Thresh, just as she had told Talon, but first she needed to settle a few things with the council.

The council was still in session as Grit strode through the meetinghouse door. She stopped short, confused by the sight of four empty seats at the council table. Coil sat in the chair that had belonged to Dame Berth, holding in his hands a small scroll much like those on which Talon used to record their sparring matches.

"Of the council, Sires Pierce, Hawk, Glade, and Palter." Coil unrolled the scroll as he read. "And in the first, Varlet of Dara and Turf of Elna and Bord. These last have been in Strike's service longest, but only now have any of them shown their true allegiance. They have left, cowards under the veil of night, and will not return to Thresh except to destroy us. Let them follow Strike to their shame, every one of them. They are vile men who shed the blood of those who do not oppose them."

Sage Brakken cleared his throat. "If I interpret rumors correctly, the same accusation might be leveled at you, Coil of Dara."

Lips pursed, Coil rolled up the scroll and tucked it into his pocket. He folded his hands on the table and looked at Sage Brakken.

"So may it be. But if a man is to hang for deeds he'd rather forget, neither warrior nor sage could spare his own neck. Cast judgment on me if you will, Sage Brakken, but there are men who know even the secrets of sages. I caution you, if the occasion arises, I will not hesitate to call them as witnesses against you, for I would hate to die alone."

Brakken narrowed his eyes at Coil. Grit stepped forward.

"I wish to address the council," she said. "Where are the rest of its members?"

The seven council members sitting around the table shifted their gazes from one to another.

Finally, Sire Stone spoke. "You heard Coil. They've left. This is the council."

"We're missing a third of our fighting force as well," said a broad shouldered, middle-aged man sitting beside Sire Stone. Sire Flex's voice, crisp and voluminous, matched his person perfectly. His body, tight, muscular, and neat, filled the chair in which he sat. "Coil's report leaves no doubt they betrayed us to Strike and joined his force last night."

Sire Stone watched Grit closely. "Turf of Elna and Bord, who stood guard behind Berth's hut is, as you heard, among the missing."

Grit clenched her jaw. Turf's confident boasting of future glory when she and Dagger entered Thresh made perfect sense.

"Turf of Elna and Bord." She turned her head to the side and spat on the floor. "He is a traitorous fool to barter with Strike. What actions will the council take?"

"As it stands now, our warriors, for all their fury, are fumbling babes before Strike's massive army. The battles ahead will demand more of them than they can give. With Coil's help, Sire Flex and I hope to build a force equal to recovering Koradin and the entire region from Strike and to ensure he is never again able to raise an army against us." Sire Stone looked around the council table.

"It can wait a day or so." Coil rose from his chair.

Sire Flex sat forward. "Where are you going? Whether or not you are yet fit to fight, you ought to be here."

"I have engagements elsewhere," Coil said, and he walked out of the meetinghouse without another word.

Together with the council, Grit watched him go. It was as useless to ask as to demand his remaining with them.

Sage Brakken pounded his fists on the table. "But where is he going?"

"Coil has gone to confer with our strongest ally." Grit looked directly at the diminutive sire seated next to Sage Brakken. "Kinsmon has arrived in Thresh. Perhaps that means something to you, Sire Swot."

"Kinsmon? Here in Thresh?" Sire Swot wrung his hands. "How intriguing! Surely it means something . . . Perhaps he . . . Explain . . . Could it really . . . Where is . . ." Sire Swot shook his head in wonderment, his lips moving rapidly but uttering only the occasional disjointed phrase.

"There he goes again. We won't get another sensible word out of him today." Sage Brakken squinted his cloudy eyes at Grit. "Why have you come before us, anyway?"

"I search for a site for my hut. I also wish to make it known that my dame acknowledged me before her demise."

Sage Brakken waved his hand dismissively. "Go ahead with the hut. As for the other matter, can anyone confirm your dame's acknowledgement?"

"Slate of Berth and Stone could, as could Strike of the Northern Mountains." Grit heard, but could not restrain, the indignation resounding in every syllable she uttered. "If you had bothered to get out of your bed last night, Sage Brakken, you would know no one else had courage enough to leave the Outer Ring."

Sage Brakken sat back, arms crossed. "It won't do. You may be bolder than all of Thresh, but without a witness, you remain Grit of Stone."

"That's it? Will there be no discussion?" She looked from one council member to the next, but none offered support.

Sire Stone shook his head. His lips pursed together in a grim line.

"Without a witness, it's your word against Dame Berth's. The council rests on her last official stance. Your renunciation stands." Sage Brakken seemed to be enjoying himself. "And allow me to remind you when a sage speaks as firmly as I have, it is not a matter for a mere dameling to debate. Do you understand, Grit of Stone?"

Grit swallowed hard. "I do. I also understand that though you deny me her name, you cannot extract her blood from my veins."

Grit spun around and marched out of the meetinghouse. She had nothing more to say and no desire to hear any more that Sage Brakken might say to her.

# FORTY-TWO

G rit set her heart on finding a site as close to Coil's and Sire Stone's huts as she could manage. With so many warriors departed to follow Strike, she was sure to find a suitable site in the southwest arc of the Outer Ring. She passed three empty huts between the main road and Coil's hut. She might tear one down and rebuild, but something was off. None of the locations satisfied her. She continued past Sire Stone's hut, mentally measuring the distance each step took her farther away from Coil's door.

Soon she found herself in front of Dame Berth's hut. In life, Dame Berth had been strong and powerful. Her hut, like its builder, rose proud and strong above its scraggly gardens. Berth had constructed it of exceptionally durable materials, and had done so with extraordinary skill. Grit wasn't sure she could tear it down, even if she desired to do so.

It was beautiful. Strong and certain and beautiful. Besides the Southern Sea, it was the only home she'd really known.

Hand on hip, she circled the hut, scrutinizing it from every angle.

It was hers by right of inheritance, should she choose it. She stood on the pathway, backing up to get a fuller picture of the hut. Let Brakken try to shame her. He hadn't the power to remove her from whatever hut she chose. Let him call into question her ability to construct a hut of her own. He who stayed in his bed while Dame Berth faced Thresh's greatest enemy, let him doubt her honor. Ezekiel was right. Honor was not found in constructing a sturdy hut, but in living well within one's hut.

Seal and Oath leaned against either side of the doorframe. They watched Grit as she walked up the path toward them, their stony faces revealing nothing of their inner thoughts. The small bundles they held were the only indication that they waited to be cast onto the mercy of their sire. Grit stopped before the dameless, black-haired girls. Around their necks, each wore a gem strung from a thin gold thread, on Oath's, blue and on Seal's, red.

"This hut and all it contains are mine." Grit studied the twins to catch their reactions.

Oath looked at Seal intently, listening carefully to her silent twin's thoughts. Her blue eyes widened as she received Seal's decision. After a moment, both nodded solemnly and took one step backward into the hut. Oath raised her eyes to Grit's, a calm, serious expression on her childish face.

"It contains two babes." Oath's voice, though high and clear, sounded much older than her eight years. She smiled mischievously. Seal and Oath invited Grit into a beautiful and intricate world. They alone possessed the map to this world, but perhaps they would guide her through it. *To waver is weakness . . .*

"Give me your packs, my babes. Seal, fetch water. Oath, potatoes. If you see Sire Stone, invite him to dine with your new guardian this evening."

The twins sprinted away to perform their first tasks for their new guardian. Grit picked their hastily packed bundles from the ground. She fingered the rough cloth. What had she done?

She crossed the threshold, soaking in all the familiar details of the hut in which she had been raised. There was the bed on which Dame Berth had lain, with two thin mats neatly rolled and pushed close together at its foot. There were the empty places where she and Slate had slept. There were the table and chairs, the fireplace with the iron pan hanging above its mantel, and the chairs flanking the hearth.

She sank into one of the chairs, cradling the twins' packs on her lap. She opened the first of the packs, uncertain to which twin it belonged. An odd assortment of items—wooden bowls, silver spoons, an embroidered cloth—fell out. The second pack held a similar collection of items surely not acquired through honest means.

*The little thieves.* She set the pilfered items on the table. They'd have to return everything to its proper home. *Sire Stone will approve, but I'm sure the rest of the village will think me mad to have claimed those babes.*

Was she mad? She wouldn't be the first madwoman in Thresh. Scarlett would have taken the girls in her arms, kissed their foreheads, and told them all would be well. Could she rear Seal and Oath with that kind of tenderness? She didn't have it in her, not really. It had been a fluke, claiming her siblings as her babes. How would she ever fulfill her duties to them?

She turned her efforts to sweeping, her mind ricocheting between past, present, and future difficulties and Kinsmon's instruction to do what was in her heart. He promised something beautiful would come of all of this, but when?

Bright light filled the room. Startled, she looked up to find a head of golden curls streaked with pink peering in at the doorway.

Coil whistled, his forearms resting against either side of the doorframe. He scanned the interior of Grit's newly claimed abode. "A pair of ravens told me you'd taken over their nest. May I enter?"

Grit studied Coil from his muddy boots to his halo of curls sticking out in every direction from his round, grinning face. Her gaze lingered on his chest, which rose and fell in a strong, steady rhythm. Over Coil's heart, a dark gray pearl strung on a silver cord stood in contrast to his clean, white shirt. The necklace was identical in all but color to the one Grit had placed around his neck. Somehow, she was sure of it, Kinsmon had touched her necklace and made it Coil's. She felt it in her chest first, but soon a pure, warm, unguarded smile spread across her face.

"Enter if you must." Stifling her laughter, she forced a disinterested expression. "Your hair is pink, and I'd have it no other way."

****

Sire Stone and Coil dined as guests in Grit's hut that evening. A quiet, pleasant meal, Grit knew it would be a memory she'd never wish to forget. Even as conversation turned to dark and weighty matters, cherished company lightened the burdens pressing upon her heart and mind.

When Oath rested her head on Seal's shoulder, and Seal struggled to restrain a silent yawn, Grit rose from the table and guided the twins to their mats. Sire Stone and Coil carried their chairs outside while Grit spread a blanket over the girls. Leaning over them, she pushed aside her long-standing reservations. She could try to be like Scarlett. She kissed the tops of their dark heads. Each girl raised a hand to the spot Grit kissed, as if unsure what had graced their heads. They were asleep before Grit reached the open door. She stepped into the yard, pulling the door closed behind her.

Sire Stone rose from his chair. "I'm off to bed. Tomorrow, training begins in earnest. Grit, will you join us on the training fields?"

"I will, but there are many who will not like it. Some people aren't particularly fond of me." Her palm rested on the hilt of her dagger

"They don't have to like you," Coil said. "They just have to know you're on their side."

"Humph," Grit said.

Sire Stone yawned. "Well, then, I'll see you both on the training fields tomorrow morning."

Sire Stone headed down the path, but stopped midway between the hut and the road. He stood with his head bowed and removed the leather cord from around his neck. After a moment, he turned and walked back to Grit.

"This is rightfully yours. It's the key to Berth's . . ." He pursed his lips, took a deep breath, and corrected himself. "It is the key to your hut."

He placed something hard into Grit's hand and gently wrapped her fingers over it. Grit opened her fist to study the long, gray key.

"She was not always as harsh as you have known her to be," Sire Stone said. "When I first came to Thresh, untested and distrusted, Berth was a tender girl of fifteen. Strong enough to spar any sireling, she still lived under her dame's roof. In all of Thresh, she alone welcomed me without reservation. When the council secured me, she snuck food to me. When they decided my fate, she secretly taught me the ways of the village, revealing to me the weakness of the man I would spar to gain admittance. I'm not sure I could have survived those days, let alone achieved the honor of a hut in the Outer Ring, without her devotion and advice. The food helped too, naturally."

"What was she like, Sire Stone?" Grit turned the key over in her hand.

"She was the sort of woman who would risk all for what she held sacred." Sire Stone brushed Grit's hair away from her eyes. "If you will study yourself, I think you will discover the best of your dame. Do not allow the fear of loss and the opinions of others to persuade you from your course."

He smiled sadly and turned to go. As Sire Stone headed to his hut, Grit took the seat he had vacated. She played with the key. Coil studied the front garden and glanced at Grit periodically. They sat in silence for several minutes, content to listen to their private thoughts and the soothing sounds of the village night. Occasionally, a dame's impatient command to a sleepless babe or a sireling's loud guffaw disrupted the quiet, but even these sounds did not disturb the peace Grit shared with Coil.

"So you met Kinsmon." She slid the key into her pocket.

Coil's face beamed in the dim light. "I did. And you were right—I like him very much. Among other things, he shared with me the secret to growing lush, plump berries, larger than any you've ever seen." He made a circle with his thumb and forefinger to represent the dimensions of an enormous berry.

Grit bit her lip to keep from telling Coil that she had seen such berries as he dreamt of growing.

He leaned forward in his seat, his eyes alight with joyful anticipation. *Something beautiful, that's what Kinsmon promised.*

"He said I could transplant my berry bushes closer to the village," Coil said. "He had other ideas, too. I'm eager to see what I can grow right here in Thresh. Or rather what we can grow, Grit, if you will help me."

"I will. In exchange, you must assist me in keeping my ravens out of nests into which they have not been invited. They must have stolen from every hut in Thresh."

Coil spit in his palm and held out his hand. "We have a deal, Grit of Berth and Stone, though I think my end of the agreement will be harder to uphold."

Just as Grit's hand touched Coil's, something fluttered at the edge of her line of vision. A dark mass descended upon the far end of the pathway. She and Coil rose together and prowled toward the creature. Grit was almost upon it before she clearly distinguished its form from the shrub beside which it had landed.

"It's an eagle," she whispered over her shoulder. She crouched down to speak to the bird. "What are you doing here?"

"He travels with me," a familiar voice said, "and is most thankful you chose not to shoo him away. You have learned much, my dear Grit of Berth and Stone."

Grit whirled about to find Kinsmon seated in the chair she had just left. His legs stretched out in front of him as he leaned back in the chair, his hands behind his head. How had he come to be there?

He smiled warmly at Grit. "Have you found your purpose, dear girl?"

Grit started to speak, but quickly clamped her mouth shut. She shook her head.

"I don't know," she said. She looked from Coil to her hut and imagined the training fields beyond the Outer Ring.

"What have I instructed you to do, Grit?" Kinsmon leaned forward and rested his elbows on his knees.

"Just what is in my heart to do."

"And have you done that so far?"

She nodded. "But I don't know that it will always work. Some of the villagers, Kinsmon, they look at me with hatred. I see it in their eyes and in every gesture they make toward me."

"Did I not tell you they would hate you? Did I not tell you they would spit on you and harass you?"

As Kinsmon rose from the chair, Coil interlaced his fingers with Grit's. His calluses scratched against hers.

"Seal and Oath are my gift to you," Kinsmon said. "They will love and honor you as no babes have ever loved and honored a dame. Let their admiration and my promise of something beautiful to come sustain you when others shun

311

both you and the aid you would give them. Whatever comes, remember you are my heart and hands. I will guide your heart; I expect you to follow with your hands."

"Why do you not tell me more?" She searched his kind face for an answer.

Kinsmon brushed his finger against her cheek. "Dear, dear Grit of Berth and Stone, if I revealed everything to you, I am certain you would cower in a most shameful manner. Do not compel me to embarrass you before your brave and beloved hunter. Instead, trust that I know what I am doing. I have not failed you yet, have I?"

"No."

"And I will not fail you ever. You will not always see me, but I have not left you to fulfill your purpose alone. Unless I am mistaken, you have already arranged for assistance with Seal and Oath."

Grit clenched Coil's hand. She was no Scarlett, but surely Kinsmon didn't mean to take Coil from her. "I don't suppose you approve our alliance?"

"Dearest Grit," Kinsmon said with a quiet laugh. "I approved of this alliance long before you developed an affinity for pink hair."

Coil unsheathed his broadsword and held it away from his body. "Are you sure you will not take this weapon from me, Kinsmon? I no longer wish to wield it. In fact, I despise it."

Kinsmon held up a hand and shook his head. "No, Coil. You must keep your sword. You will not use it as you have in the past, but use it you must. In time, it will cease to accuse you of the innocent blood it has spilled and will begin to remind you of the innocent blood it preserves. And it will preserve much innocent blood, Coil of Dara, before a new age dawns in Chasmaria. Let that promise strengthen you when your darkest regrets assault your peace."

Kinsmon gently pushed the sword toward Coil. Reluctantly, the sireling sheathed his sword, never taking his gaze from Kinsmon.

Grit edged closer to Coil so their shoulders touched. Kinsmon sighed and kissed first Grit, and then Coil, on the tops of their bowed heads. As quickly and quietly as the eagle had landed on the path, Kinsmon was gone.

Coil wrapped both arms around Grit and held her close for a long moment. Rosemary mixed with earth, sweat, and other herbs filled her with the sweet smell of Coil. She could stay forever, but he released her, kissed her softly on the forehead, and walked slowly to his hut without a backward glance. Just as Seal and Oath had done when Grit kissed them goodnight, Grit put her hand to the place where Coil's lips had touched her forehead.

When the light from Coil's window gave way to darkness, Grit turned to enter her own hut. By the moonlight shining through an open window, she made out the single form of Seal and Oath snuggled together on Seal's mat, their long, silky hair intertwining. It was right that they be together. Now where would she sleep?

In a corner against the rough wall, a lumpy bed called to her exhausted body. Grit crossed the room, pulled back the blankets, patted the straw mattress, and flopped into the bed. Whatever objections the council might raise, she was Grit of Berth and Stone, and this is where she would lay her weary head.

# ABOUT THE AUTHOR

Lisa lives in a small Southern town with her husband and four children. Having found school incredibly dull, she teaches her children at home, where backyard forts, imaginary worlds, and a Great Dane puppy make things like Latin and long division bearable. She works with middle school youth at her church and is actively involved in her local chapter of South Carolina Writers Workshop.

She blogs at <u>waitingforaname.wordpress.com</u> and can be found on Twitter <u>https://twitter.com/ScouterWife</u> and Facebook <u>https://www.facebook.com/authorlisadunn</u>.

CPSIA information can be obtained
at www.ICGtesting.com
Printed in the USA
FFOW03n0539260116
20707FF

9 780996 129756